5/6

CW00725778

Born in Derry in 1931, Sean McMahon was educated at St Columb's College, Derry, and Queen's University, Belfast. He teaches mathematics at St Columb's College and in his spare time writes articles and literary reviews. He has edited and compiled several anthologies, including *The Best of the Bell* (1978), *A Book of Irish Quotations* (1984), *Rich and Rare: A Book of Ireland* (1984), and *The Poolbeg Book of Children's Verse* (1987).

MY NATIVE LAND
·A CELEBRATION of BRITAIN·

EDITED BY SEAN MCMAHON

POOLBEG

A Paperback Original
First published 1987 by
Poolbeg Press Ltd.,
Knocksedan House,
Swords, Co. Dublin, Ireland

© Sean McMahon 1987

ISBN 0 905169 97 2

Cover illustration by John Short
Typeset by Busby Typesetting and Design, Exeter.
Printed by The Guernsey Press Ltd.,
Vale, Guernsey, Channel Islands.

Acknowledgements

The publishers wish to thank the following for their kind permission to reprint copyright material:

John Murray (Publishers) Limited for "A Subaltern's Love-Song" and "Pot-Pourri from a Surrey Garden" from *Collected Poems* by John Betjeman; Macmillan (London and Basingstoke) for "Stately as a Galleon" from *Stately as a Galleon* by Joyce Grenfell; International Music Publishers for "I Leave My Heart in an English Garden" by Christopher Hassall, "Old Sam" by Stanley Holloway, and "A Nightingale Sang in Berkeley Square" by Eric Maschwitz; Curtis Brown Group Limited on behalf of the Estate of Hugh Kingsmill for "Two Poems (After A.E. Housman)" by Hugh Kingsmill from *The Best of Kingsmill* edited by Michael Holroyd; Chappell Music Limited for "Keep the Home Fires Burning" by Ivor Novello and Lena Ford and "We'll Gather Lilacs" by Ivor Novello; David Higham Associates Limited for "Dear Gwalia" by Dylan Thomas from *Under Milkwood* published by Dent.

While every attempt has been made to contact all the copyright holders, Poolbeg Press apologises for any omissions or errors in the above list, and would be happy to be notified of any corrections to be incorporated in future editions.

Contents

Introduction 17

1

My Native Land

The British Grenadiers *Anon* 23
Rule Britannia *James Thomson* 24
Scots, Wha Hae *Robert Burns* 26
O Caledonia! *Sir Walter Scott* 28
The Homes of England *Felicia Dorothea Hemans* 29
The Armada *Lord Macaulay* 31
The Song of the Western Men *Robert Stephen Hawker* 35
The Private of the Buffs *Sir Francis Doyle* 37
The Land of My Fathers *Talhaiarn* 39
The Patriot *Robert Browning* 40
The Englishman *W.S. Gilbert* 42
The Old Brigade *Fred E. Weatherly* 43
England, My England *W.E. Henley* 44
Land of Hope and Glory *Arthur Christopher Benson* 46
Vitaî Lampada *Sir Henry Newbolt* 47
The Absent-Minded Beggar *Rudyard Kipling* 49
Mandalay *Rudyard Kipling* 51
After Dunkirk *Sir Winston Churchill* 54
The Battle of Britain *Sir Winston Churchill* 56
The Soldier *Rupert Brooke* 58
Keep the Home Fires Burning
   Ivor Novello and Lena Guilbert Ford 59

2

In Youth Is Pleasure

Ring a-Ring o' Roses *Anon*   63
A Madrigal *Anon*   64
Nursery Rhymes *Anon*   65
In Youth is Pleasure *Robert Wever*   67
Golden Slumbers *Thomas Dekker*   68
To the Virgins, to Make Much of Time *Robert Herrick*   69
Come Lasses and Lads *Anon*   70
The Blind Boy *Colley Cibber*   72
Against Idleness and Mischief *Isaac Watts*   73
Against Quarrelling and Fighting *Isaac Watts*   74
The Lamb *William Blake*   75
There Was a Naughty Boy *John Keats*   76
Young and Old *Charles Kingsley*   77
From Goblin Market *Christina Rossetti*   78
When I Was One-and-Twenty *A.E. Housman*   80

3

My Love and I

The Passionate Shepherd to His Love *Christopher Marlowe* 83
'Shall I compare thee?' *William Shakespeare* 85
'It was a lover and his lass' *William Shakespeare* 86
'Drink to me only' *Ben Jonson* 87
To Althea from Prison *Richard Lovelace* 88
A Red Red Rose *Robert Burns* 90
Sally in Our Alley *Henry Carey* 91
Early One Morning *Anon* 94
The Girl I Left Behind Me *Anon* 95
Ca' the Yowes to the Knowes *Anon* 97
The Lass of Richmond Hill *Leonard MacNally* 98
Jenny Kiss'd Me *James Henry Leigh Hunt* 100
Alice, Where Art Thou? *Alfred Bunn* 101
Dashing Away with the Smoothing Iron *Anon* 103
Polly Perkins *Anon* 104
All Through the Night *Talhaiarn* 106
'When I am dead' *Christina Rossetti* 107
Thora *Fred E. Weatherly* 108
When I Was a King in Babylon *W.E. Henley* 109
Bredon Hill *A.E. Housman* 110
My Old Dutch *Albert Chevalier* 112
Kashmiri Song *Laurence Hope* 114
Non Sum Qualis Eram *Ernest Dowson* 115
We'll Gather Lilacs *Ivor Novello* 116
A Subaltern's Love-Song *Sir John Betjeman* 117

4
Realms of Gold

I Saw a Peacock with a Fiery Tail *Anon*   121
On his Life-Work *Edward Gibbon*   122
The Tyger *William Blake*   123
The Reaper *William Wordsworth*   124
Kubla Khan *Samuel Taylor Coleridge*   126
Ozymandias *Percy Bysshe Shelley*   128
On First Looking into Chapman's Homer *John Keats*   129
Ode to a Nightingale *John Keats*   130
From the Rubàiyàt of Omar Khayyàm *Edward Fitzgerald* 133
The Splendour Falls *Alfred Tennyson*   135
Monna Lisa *Walter Pater*   136
The Fairy Chorus *Fiona Macleod*   137
'When I set out for Lyonesse' *Thomas Hardy*   138
'When 'omer smote 'is bloomin lyre' *Rudyard Kipling*   139
The Old Ships *James Elroy Flecker*   140

5
The Glory of the Garden

Sumer is Icumen in *Anon*   145
London Bells *Anon*   146
Winter and Spring *William Shakespeare*   148
The Fine Old English Gentleman *Anon*   150
The Derby Ram *Anon*   152
The Lincolnshire Poacher *Anon*   155
The Miller of Dee *Anon*   156
The Roast Beef of Old England
  Richard Leveridge and Henry Fielding   158
Hunting Song *Henry Fielding*   159
There's Nae Luck aboot the House *W.J. Mickle*   161
Caller Herrin' *Carolina Oliphant*   163
Jerusalem *William Blake*   165
John Peel *John Woodcock Graves*   166
Linden Lea *William Barnes*   167
Home-Thoughts from Abroad *Robert Browning*   169
Pied Beauty *Gerard Manley Hopkins*   170
Up from Somerset *Fred E. Weatherly*   171
Glorious Devon *Sir Harold Boulton*   173
Lovliest of trees *A.E. Housman*   175
Knocked 'em in the Old Kent Road *Albert Chevalier*   176
The Glory of the Garden *Rudyard Kipling*   178
The Rolling English Road *G.K. Chesterton*   180
Adlestrop *Edward Thomas*   182
Old Father Thames *Anon*   183
On Ilkley Moor Baht 'at *Anon*   184
Sussex by the Sea *Anon*   185
A Nightingale Sang in Berkeley Square *Eric Maschwitz*   187
Pot Pourri from a Surrey Garden *John Betjeman*   189
I Leave my Heart in an English Garden
  Christopher Hassall   191

6
The Humour of It

The Twa Corbies *Anon* 195

Letter to the Right Honourable,
  the Earl of Chesterfield *Samuel Johnson* 196

Elegy on the Death of a Mad Dog *Oliver Goldsmith* 198

To a Louse *Robert Burns* 200

An Austrian Army *Alaric A. Watts* 202

She was Poor but She was Honest *Anon* 203

The Owl and the Pussycat *Edward Lear* 205

Father William *Lewis Carroll* 207

The Modern Major-Gineral *W.S. Gilbert* 209

Tit Willow *W.S. Gilbert* 211

The Ruined Maid *Thomas Hardy* 212

Champagne Charlie *George Leybourne* 213

The Man on the Flying Trapeze *George Leybourne* 214

The Ladies *Rudyard Kipling* 216

Henry King *Hilaire Belloc* 218

Matilda *Hilaire Belloc* 219

Ruthless Rhymes *Harry Graham* 221

Clerihews *E.C. Bentley* 223

Two Poems (after A.E. Housman) *Hugh Kingsmill* 224

Old Sam *Stanley Holloway* 225

Mad Dogs and Englishmen *Noël Coward* 228

She Was One of the Early Birds *T.W. Connor* 231

Dahn the Plug'ole *Anon* 233

Stately as a Galleon *Joyce Grenfell* 234

Dear Gwalia *Dylan Thomas* 236

7

In Vacant or in Pensive Mood

Psalm 100   *William Kethe*   241
'All the world's a stage'   *William Shakespeare*   242
'The expense of spirit in a waste of shame'
    William Shakespeare   244
The Bell   *John Donne*   245
O God, Our Help   *Isaac Watts*   246
Elegy Written in a Country Churchyard   *Thomas Gray*   247
The Solitude of Alexander Selkirk   *William Cowper*   252
A Man's a Man for a' That   *Robert Burns*   254
Auld Lang Syne   *Robert Burns*   256
The Daffodils   *William Wordsworth*   258
Lead, Kindly Light   *John Henry, Cardinal Newman*   259
Nearer, My God   *Sarah Flower Adams*   260
Say Not the Struggle Naught Availeth   *A.H. Clough*   262
The Lost Chord   *Adelaide Ann Proctor*   363
Onward, Christian Soldiers   *Sabine Baring-Gould*   265
'No worst, there is none'   *Gerard Manley Hopkins*   267
Invictus   *W.E. Henley*   268
When Earth's Last Picture is Painted   *Rudyard Kipling*   269
'They are not long, the weeping and the laughter'
    Ernest Dowson   270
The Donkey   *G.K. Chesterton*   271

8

Tales of Land and Sea

Sir Patrick Spens   *Anon*   275

The Wife of Usher's Well   *Anon*   277

Heart of Oak   *David Garrick*   279

Johnnie Cope   *Adam Skirving*   280

Lochinvar   *Sir Walter Scott*   282

The Farmer's Boy   *Robert Bloomfield*   284

Ye Mariners of England   *Thomas Campbell*   286

Casabianca   *Felicia Dorothea Hemans*   288

Billy Boy   *Anon*   290

The Mermaid   *Anon*   292

What Shall We do with the Drunken Sailor   *Anon*   294

The Arab's Farewell to his Steed   *C.E.S. Norton*   295

The Charge of the Light Brigade   *Alfred, Lord Tennyson*   297

The Last Buccaneer   *Charles Kingsley*   299

Drake's Drum   *Sir Henry Newbolt*   301

The Trumpeter   *John Francis Barron*   302

The Green Eye of the Yellow God   *J. Milton Hayes*   304

Sunset and Evening Star

A Lyke-Wake Dirge   *Anon*   309
'That time of year thou may'st in me behold'
  William Shakespeare   311
'Fear no more the heat o' the sun'   *William Shakespeare*   312
'Adieu, farewell earth's bliss'   *Thomas Nashe*   313
'How many miles to Babylon?'   *Anon*   315
Mr Valiant-for-Truth Crosses the River   *John Bunyan*   316
The Flowers of the Forest   *Jean Eliot*   317
Proud Maisie   *Sir Walter Scott*   318
The Land of the Leal   *Carolina Oliphant*   319
We'll Go No More a-Roving   *Lord Byron*   321
Abide with Me   *Henry Francis Lyte*   322
Sunset and Evening Star   *Alfred, Lord Tennyson*   323
Tears, Idle Tears   *Alfred, Lord Tennyson*   324
The Darkling Thrush   *Thomas Hardy*   325
Love's Old Sweet Song   *J. Clifton Bingham*   327

Biographical Index   328
Index of Titles   355

FOR BRIAN

My Native Land

Breathes there the man, with soul so dead,
Who never to himself hath said,
   This is my own, my native land!
Whose heart hath ne'er within him burn'd,
As home his footsteps he hath turn'd,
   From wandering on a foreign strand!
If such there breathe, go, mark him well;
For him no minstrel raptures swell;
High though his titles, proud his name,
Boundless his wealth as wish can claim:
Despite those titles, power, and pelf,
The wretch, concentred all in self,
Living, shall forfeit fair renown,
And, doubly dying, shall go down
To the vile dust, from whence he sprung,
Unwept, unhonour'd, and unsung.

Sir Walter Scott

Introduction

For an Irishman, and one with a plangently Irish name, to compile an anthology of British verse, song and prose amounts to *hubris* of such a level as to leave Sophocles green with envy. In mitigation of this apparent arrogance and in the unlikely hope of warding off the coming *nemesis*, I can offer merely a few squeaks of explanation and the conviction that such surpassing richness as there is should continually be mined. Whatever extreme nationalists may say or think (and I include in that description all the Celtic nations that fringe England) a large part of their literary culture is British. The reasons for this may not reflect much glory on them and even less on the British but it is a historical fact and cannot be gainsaid. Acculturalisation may be part of conquest but in a world of mass media, mid-Atlanticism and the death of liberal education, treasures that are still available and freely given should be accepted as gladly and as critically as individual response suggests. I turned to this compilation after a comparable delving in Irish literary culture. The experience was enjoyable and the response gratifying. I looked for an equivalent anthology of Britain and finding there was none, decided with my publisher's blessing to invent one.

My Native Land is a rag-bag (what is called in Northern Ireland a 'gather-up') of the songs, poems and occasional bits of prose that are the property of ordinary people. It is not in any sense an exclusive collection: it is positively unacademic, a kind of people's anthology, that word being used without connotations of class. If my instincts are right and my culling wisely made the majority of readers should find nothing new in this book. They should recognise a line or two from each entry, be acquainted with the full text of most and even have some pieces off by heart. My task was made very difficult by the vast amount of suitable material. One could, for example, create a very fat book with nothing in it but bits from a collection of Nursery Rhymes, from Shakespeare, W.S. Gilbert, Kipling and John Betjeman and every piece would have deserved its place. All these are the property of people who would deny any personal literary interests or tastes. To use a rough measure, they are sources from which quotations might be made for use in, say, *Crossroads* or *Coronation Street*, or fodder for a pub-quiz. They are part of the experience of most people who have reached the age of forty, the 1944 Education Act generation. Since there are many more sources than the writers named and since all deserve their place, selection has proved essential and the compiler places his head thereby on the critical block. I have tried to make the choice as unpersonal as possible. Earlier decades produced anthologies with such titles as *Speak For England* and *A Book of Scotland*. One favourite of mine, though its contents were much grander than this one's, was called *The Knapsack*. This book is, I suppose, a kind of knapsack companion with memories of school, camp-fires, great-uncles at Christmas parties and fine-sounding songs sung in the bath.

If selection was difficult, categorisation presented problems too. Many pieces could have claimed entrance to several sections, as will be clear from the table of contents. The first section, which bears the title of the book, 'My Native Land', after Scott's apostrophe in *The Lay of the Last Minstrel*, is about patriotism and duty, two topics that need careful handling. Patriotism is only the last refuge of the scoundrel as a form of moral blackmail. The pieces in this section deal mainly with a simpler age when it really was 'dulce et decorum est pro patria mori' – or at least to fight for it abroad to preserve peace and prosperity at home. The section 'In Youth Is Pleasure' even in its ambivalence is self-explanatory. In general, the pieces seemed tinged with sadness, viewed from the deadly cosiness of late middle-age. 'My Love and I' seems sufficiently specific to make further comment superfluous. 'Realms of Gold' contains those pieces which partake of magic, mystery and high romance.

'The Glory of the Garden' is a celebration of Britain the habitat, its cities, towns, villages and shires. It holds the beauty and sense of a finer patriotism, perhaps, the not very specific Britain in each Briton's heart. Section 6 is about humour, the most defiantly British section and one not fully understood by the rest of the world. The section called 'In Vacant or in Pensive Mood' shows the British in what Lord Macaulay called one of their periodic fits of morality and even rarer of philosophising. Section 8 has stories of high adventure on land and, even more likely, on sea, as befits an island race. They show a confidence a cockiness even, that has faded with the coming of the global village but there is an exhilaration and an infectious excitement that can still be felt. Lastly, in 'Sunset and Evening Star' there is the relinquishing of life and the last setting forth from a country as much a demi-paradise as a vale of tears.

There are many anthologies in print, each the result of quarrying particular seams, from the most esoteric of poetry to the most pop of songs. The mines, as I have said, are vast. One thinks of the music-hall songs and monologues of five decades, the musical comedy tradition from Gilbert and Sullivan to Webber and Rice, the golden treasuries of poets old and new. From these I have garnered a kind of sampler that should come home to the reader without strain. The result *is* a rag-bag, inevitably selective and therefore more infuriating to every single reader because of inclusions than exclusions. There is very little here that is modern; who can tell what will stand the test of time? Anything that has been included seems certain to pass that test. Yet some subjectivity is inevitable. So be it! Each man is his own anthologist. This book will have served its purpose if it succeeds in throwing some dim light upon half-remembered pleasures.

My thanks are due to many friends for suggestions and advice. I would name in particular Anne Furneaux of the Law Department, Ealing College of Higher Education, William Morton of the Covent Garden Orchestra and David James of Gwent and Limavady. Thanks, too, to Philip MacDermott, Margaret Daly, and the ever-patient, resolutely firm Hilary O'Donoghue, whose editorial skills were needed as never before.

1

My Native Land

The British Grenadiers

Anon

Little is known about the origin of this song except that though the words were printed by 1690 the tune is older. Grenadiers were soldiers of foot specially trained to handle and use grenades.

Some talk of Alexander, and some of Hercules,
Of Hector and Lysander, and such great names as these;
But of all the world's brave heroes there's none that can
    compare,
With a tow row row row row row to the British Grenadier.

Whene'er we are commanded to storm the palisades
Our leaders march with fuses, and we with hand grenades;
We throw them from the glacis about the enemies' ears,
Sing tow row row row row row to the British Grenadiers.

Then let us fill a bumper and drink a health to those
Who carry caps and pouches and wear the louped clothes;
May they and their commanders live happy all their years,
With a tow row row row row row for the British Grenadiers.

Rule, Britannia

James Thomson

This stirring song with music by Thomas Arne was performed in the Masque, *Alfred*, in the grounds of the Prince of Wales' house on 1 August 1740. The first eight notes of Arne's tune were said by Wagner to exemplify the whole British character so perhaps it is as well to note that Thomson's words are admonitory ('Rule!') rather than triumphant.

When Britain first, at heaven's command,
   Arose from out the azure main;
This was the charter of the land,
   And guardian Angels sung this strain:
     'Rule, Britannia, rule the waves;
     Britons never will be slaves.'

The nations, not so blest as thee,
   Must, in their turns, to tyrants fall:
While thou shalt flourish great and free,
   The dread and envy of them all.
     'Rule, etc.

Still more majestic shalt thou rise,
   More dreadful, from each foreign stroke:
As the loud blast that tears the skies,
   Serves but to root thy native oak.
     'Rule, etc.

Thee haughty tyrants ne'er shall tame:
   All their attempts to bend thee down,
Will but arouse thy generous flame;
   But work their woe, and thy renown.
     'Rule, etc.

To thee belongs the rural reign;
   Thy cities shall with commerce shine:
All thine shall be the subject main,
   And every shore it circles thine.
       'Rule, etc.

The Muses, still with freedom found,
   Shall to thy happy coast repair:
Blest isle! with matchless beauty crowned,
   And manly hearts to guard the fair.
       'Rule, Britannia, rule the waves:
       Britons never will be slaves.'

Scots, Wha Hae

Robert Burns

A dramatic address supposedly given by King Robert Bruce
(1274 - 1329) on the eve of the great battle of Bannockburn
(24 June 1314) when he secured independence for Scotland after
the decisive defeat of Edward II. Wallace had been a hero of
the earlier war and had defeated Edward I at Stirling Bridge
in 1297 but was captured and executed in London in 1305.

Scots, wha hae wi' Wallace bled,
Scots wham Bruce has aften led,
Welcome to your gory bed
    Or to victorie!

Now's the day, and now's the hour:
See the front o' battle lour,
See approach proud Edward's power –
    Chains and slaverie!

Wha will be a traitor knave?
Wha can fill a coward's grave?
Wha sae base as be a slave? –
    Let him turn, and flee!

Wha for Scotland's King and Law
Freedom's sword will strongly draw,
Freeman stand, or freeman fa',
    Let him follow me!

By Oppression's woes and pains,
By your sons in servile chains,
We will drain our dearest veins
    But they shall be free!

Lay the proud usurpers low!
Tyrants fall in every foe!
Liberty's in every blow!
    Let us do, or die!

O Caledonia!

Sir Walter Scott

Scott's most famous lines from *The Lay of the Last Minstrel* (1805), better known even than those about Young Lochinvar. His own patriotism was not of the separatist kind. In fact he helped his Lowland compatriots acquiesce in the death of Gaelic Scotland by allowing their emotional feelings about their country free rein in English.

> O Caledonia! stern and wild,
> Meet nurse for a poetic child!
> Land of brown heath and shaggy wood,
> Land of the mountain and the flood,
> Land of my sires! what mortal hand
> Can e'er untie the filial band,
> That knits me to thy rugged strand!

The Homes of England

Felicia Dorothea Hemans

Mrs Hemans was in her time a much more popular poet than many of her more justly famous contemporaries. Now she is known for just a few lines: the first pair of this one and the opening line of the much-parodied 'Boy on the Burning Deck'. This poem served as the parodic base for one of Noël Coward's funnier songs.

The stately homes of England,
    How beautiful they stand
Amidst their tall ancestral trees,
    O'er all the pleasant land!
The deer across their greensward bound,
    Through shade and sunny gleam;
And the swan glides past them with the sound
    Of some rejoicing stream.

The merry homes of England!
    Around their hearths by night,
What gladsome looks of household love
    Meet in the ruddy light!
There woman's voice flows forth in song,
    Or childhood's tale is told,
Or lips move tunefully along
    Some glorious page of old.

The blessed homes of England!
    How softly on their bowers
Is laid the holy quietness
    That breathes from Sabbath hours!
Solemn, yet sweet, the church-bell's chime
    Floats through their woods at morn;
All other sounds, in that still time,
    Of breeze and leaf are born.

The cottage homes of England!
　By thousands on her plains,
They are smiling o'er the silvery brooks,
　And round the hamlet fanes.
Through glowing orchards forth they peep,
　Each from its nook of leaves;
And fearless there the lowly sleep,
　As the bird beneath their eaves.

The free fair homes of England!
　Long, long, in hut and hall,
May hearts of native proof be reared
　To guard each hallowed wall!
And green for ever be the groves,
　And bright the flowery sod,
Where first the child's glad spirit loves
　Its country and its God!

The Armada

Lord Macaulay

After 'Horatius', this is Macaulay's best-known verse. It makes a fine recitation and the last two-thirds give a fine romantic tour of Elizabethan England.

Attend, all ye who list to hear our noble England's praise;
I tell of the thrice famous deeds she wrought in ancient
      days,
When that great fleet invincible against her bore in vain
The richest spoils of Mexico, the stoutest hearts of Spain.

It was about the lovely close of a warm summer day,
There came a gallant merchant-ship full sail to Plymouth
      Bay;
Her crew hath seen Castile's black fleet, beyond Aurigny's
      isle,
At earliest twilight, on the waves lie heaving many a mile.
At sunrise she escaped their van, by God's especial grace;
And the tall Pinta, till the noon, had held her close in chase.
Forthwith a guard at every gun was placed along the wall;
The beacon blazed upon the roof of Edgecumbe's lofty hall;
Many a light fishing-bark put out to pry along the coast,
And with loose rein and bloody spur rode inland many a
      post.
With his white hair unbonneted, the stout old sheriff comes;
Behind him march the halberdiers; before him sound the
      drums;
His yeomen round the market cross make clear an ample
      space;
For there behoves him to set up the standard of Her Grace.
And haughtily the trumpets peal, and gaily dance the bells,
As slow upon the labouring wind the royal blazon swells.
Look how the Lion of the sea lifts up his ancient crown,
And underneath his deadly paw treads the gay lilies down.

So stalked he when he turned to flight, on that famed Picard
    field,
Bohemia's plume, and Genoa's bow, and Caesar's eagle
    shield.
So glared he when at Agincourt in wrath he turned to bay,
And crushed and torn beneath his claws the princely hunters
    lay.
Ho! strike the flagstaff deep, Sir Knight: ho! scatter flowers,
    fair maids:
Ho! gunners, fire a loud salute: ho! gallants, draw your
    blades:
Thou sun, shine on her joyously; ye breezes, waft her wide;
Our glorious SEMPER EADEM, the banner of our pride.
The freshening breeze of eve unfurled that banner's massy
    fold;
The parting gleam of sunshine kissed that haughty scroll of
    gold;
Night sank upon the dusky beach, and on the purple sea,
Such night in England ne'er had been, nor e'er again shall be.
From Eddystone to Berwick bounds, from Lynn to Milford
    Bay,
That time of slumber was as bright and busy as the day;
For swift to east and swift to west the ghastly war-flame
    spread,
High on St Michael's Mount it shone: it shone on Beachy
    Head.
Far on the deep the Spaniard saw, along each southern shire,
Cape beyond cape, in endless range those twinkling points
    of fire.
The fisher left his skiff to rock on Tamar's glittering waves:
The rugged miners poured to war from Mendip's sunless
    caves:
O'er Longleat's towers, o'er Cranbourne's oaks, the fiery
    herald flew:
He roused the shepherds of Stonehenge, the rangers of
    Beaulieu.
Right sharp and quick the bells all night rang out from
    Bristol town.

And ere the day three hundred horse had met on Clifton
      down;
The sentinel on Whitehall gate looked forth into the night,
And saw o'erhanging Richmond Hill the streak of blood-red
      light.
Then bugle's note and cannon's roar the deathlike silence
      broke,
And with one start, and with one cry, the royal city woke.
At once on all her stately gates arose the answering fires;
At once the wild alarum clashed from all her reeling spires;
From all the batteries of the Tower pealed loud the voice of
      fear;
And all the thousand masts of Thames sent back a louder
      cheer:
And from the furthest wards was heard the rush of hurrying
      feet,
And the broad streams of pikes and flags rushed down each
      roaring street;
And broader still became the blaze, and louder still the din,
As fast from every village round the horse came spurring in:
And eastward straight from wild Blackheath the warlike
      errand went,
And roused in many an ancient hall the gallant squires of
      Kent.
Southward from Surrey's pleasant hills flew those bright
      couriers forth;
High on bleak Hampstead's swarthy moor they started for
      the north;
And on, and on, without a pause, untired they bounded still:
All night from tower to tower they sprang; they sprang from
      hill to hill:
Till the proud peak unfurled the flag o'er Darwin's rocky dales,
Till like volcanoes flared to heaven the stormy hills of Wales,
Till twelve fair counties saw the blaze on Malvern's lonely
      height,
Till streamed in crimson on the wind the Wrekin's crest of
      light,
Till broad and fierce the star came forth on Ely's stately fane,
And tower and hamlet rose in arms o'er all the boundless plain;

Till Belvoir's lordly terraces the sign to Lincoln sent,
And Lincoln sped the message on o'er the wide vale of Trent;
Till Skiddaw saw the fire that burned on Gaunt's embattled
      pile,
And the red glare on Skiddaw roused the burghers of Carlisle.

The Song of the Western Men

Robert Stephen Hawker

Based upon an old Cornish rhyme, 'And Shall Trelawny Die?'
which celebrated the threatened execution of Sir John Trelawny
(1650 - 1721), Bishop of Bristol, who was one of seven bishops
imprisoned in the Tower by James II after the Monmouth
Rebellion in 1685. He survived to play an important part in the
High Church revival in the reign of Queen Anne.

A good sword and a trusty hand!
   A merry heart and true!
King James's men shall understand
   What Cornish lads can do.

And have they fixed the where and when?
   And shall Trelawny die?
Here's twenty thousand Cornish men
   Will know the reason why!

Out spake their captain brave and bold,
   A merry wight was he:
'If London Tower were Michael's hold,
   We'd set Trelawny free!

'We'll cross the Tamar, land to land,
   The Severn is no stay,
With "one and all," and hand in hand,
   And who shall bid us nay?

'And when we come to London Wall,
   A pleasant sight to view,
Come forth! come forth! ye cowards all,
   Here's men as good as you.

'Trelawny he's in keep and hold,
   Trelawny he may die;
But here's twenty thousand Cornish bold
   Will know the reason why!'

The Private of the Buffs

Sir Francis Doyle

An anticipatory piece of honest Kiplingism from a man who worshipped the army even though he never became a soldier.

Last night, among his fellow roughs
    He jested, quaffed, and swore;
A drunken private of the Buffs,
    Who never looked before.
Today, beneath the foeman's frown,
    He stands in Elgin's place,
Ambassador from Britain's crown,
    And type of all her race.

Poor, reckless, rude, low-born, untaught,
    Bewildered, and alone,
A heart, with English instinct fraught,
    He yet can call his own.
Ay, tear his body limb from limb,
    Bring cord, or axe, or flame,
He only knows, that not through *him*
    Shall England come to shame.

For Kentish hop-fields round him seem'd,
    Like dreams, to come and go;
Bright leagues of cherry-blossom gleam'd,
    One sheet of living snow;
The smoke, above his father's door,
    In gray soft eddyings hung;
Must he then watch it rise no more,
    Doom'd by himself, so young?

Yes, honour calls! with strength like steel
   He puts the vision by.
Let dusky Indians whine and kneel,
   An English lad must die.
And thus, with eyes that would not shrink,
   With knee to man unbent,
Unfaltering on its dreadful brink,
   To his red grave he went.

Vain, mightiest fleets of iron framed;
   Vain, those all-shattering guns;
Unless proud England keep, untamed,
   The strong heart of her sons.
So let his name through Europe ring –
   A man of mean estate,
Who died, as firm as Sparta's king,
   Because his soul was great.

The Land of my Fathers

(Hen wlad fy Nhadau)

Talhaiarn

English words by Thomas Oliphant

Poem written to an old Welsh air in the early nineteenth century which has become an unofficial Welsh National Anthem.

Mae hen wlad fy Nhadau yn anwyl i mi
Gwlad beirdd a chantorion, enwogion o fri
Ei gwrol ryfelwyr, gwladgarwyr tra mad
Tros rhyddid collasant eu gwaed.
Gwlad, Gwlad, pleidiol wyf i'm Gwlad
Tra mor yn fur, ir bur hoff bau
O, bydded i'r heniaith barhau!

The land of my fathers, the land of my choice
The land in which poets and minstrels rejoice;
The land where stern warriors were true to the core
While bleeding for freedom of yore.
Wales! Wales! favourite land of Wales!
While sea her wall, may nought befall
To mar the old language of Wales.

Mountainous old Cambria, the Eden of bards,
Each hill and each valley excite my regards:
To the ears of her patriots how charming still seems
The music that flows in her streams.

The Patriot

Robert Browning

One of the best examples of Browning's ability to tell a detailed story in a few lines. It is not clear who was the inspiration; the poet while being apolitical had a keen sense of betrayal.

It was roses, roses, all the way,
  With myrtle mixed in my path like mad:
The house-roofs seemed to heave and sway,
  The church-spires flamed, such flags they had,
A year ago on this very day.

The air broke into a mist with bells,
  The old walls rocked with the crowd and cries.
Had I said, 'Good folk, mere noise repels –
  But give me your sun from yonder skies!'
They had answered, 'And afterward, what else?'

Alack, it was I who leaped at the sun
  To give it my loving friends to keep!
Nought man could do, have I left undone:
  And you see my harvest, what I reap
This very day, now a year is run.

There's nobody on the house-tops now –
  Just a palsied few at the windows set;
For the best of the sight is, all allow,
  At the Shambles' Gate – or, better yet,
By the very scaffold's foot, I trow.

I go in the rain, and, more than needs,
  A rope cuts both my wrists behind;
And I think, by the feel, my forehead bleeds,
  For they fling, whoever has a mind,
Stones at me for my year's misdeeds.

Thus I entered, and thus I go!
   In triumphs, people have dropped down dead.
'Paid by the world, what dost thou owe
   Me?' – God might question; now instead,
'Tis God shall repay: I am safer so.

The Englishman

W.S. Gilbert

From Act 1 of *HMS Pinafore*, Gilbert & Sullivan's first popular full-length opera. The piece is largely satirical but there is unmistakable pride and earnestness shining through the drollery. The song was used to even greater ambivalent effect by Alan Bennett in his television play, *An Englishman Abroad*, which chronicled an episode from the Moscow life of Guy Burgess.

> He is an Englishman!
>> For he himself has said it,
>> And it's greatly to his credit,
> That he is an Englishman!
>> For he might have been a Roosian,
>> A French, or Turk, or Proosian,
> Or perhaps Itali-an!
>> But in spite of all temptations,
>> To belong to other nations,
> He remains an Englishman!
>> Hurrah!
> For the true-born Englishman!

The Old Brigade

Fred E. Weatherly

One of many music-hall and indeed concert tributes to the
conviction that the century of peace enjoyed by Georgians and
Victorians was paid for by Thin Red Lines, White Man's
Burdens and the maintenance of Pax Britannica abroad.

Where are the boys of the old Brigade,
    Who fought with us side by side?
Shoulder to shoulder, and blade by blade,
    Fought till they fell and died!
Who so ready and undismayed?
    Who so merry and true?
Where are the boys of the old Brigade?
    Where are the lads we knew?

Chorus
Then steadily shoulder to shoulder,
Steadily blade by blade!
Ready and strong, marching along
Like the boys of the old Brigade!

Over the sea far away they lie,
    Far from the land of their love;
Nations alter, the years go by,
    But Heav'n is still Heav'n above,
Not in the abbey proudly laid
    Find they a place or part;
The gallant boys of the old Brigade,
    They sleep in old England's heart.

Chorus

England, My England

W.E. Henley

The sort of jingoistic verse that sounds intolerable to most nowadays but was entirely heartfelt by its author and represented his concern that English youth should learn its destiny in good time.

What have I done for you,
England, my England?
What is there I would not do,
England, my own?
With your glorious eyes austere,
As the Lord were walking near,
Whisp'ring terrible things and dear
As the Song on your bugles blown,
England, England,
Round the world on your bugles blown!

Where shall the watchful Sun,
England, my England,
Match the masterwork you've done,
England, my own?
When shall he rejoice agen
Such a breed of mighty men
As come forward, one to ten,
To the Song on your bugles blown,
England, England,
Down the years on your bugles blown?

Ever the faith endures,
England, my England:
'Take and break us: we are yours,
England, my own!
Life is good, and joy runs high
Between English earth and sky;
Death is death; but we shall die
To the Song on your bugles blown,
England, England,
To the stars on your bugles blown!'

They call you proud and hard
England, my England:
You with worlds to watch and ward,
England, my own!
You whose mailed hand keeps the keys
Of such teeming destinies
You could know nor dread nor ease
Were the Song on your bugles blown,
England, England,
Round the Pit on your bugles blown!

Mother of Ships whose might,
England, my England,
Is the fierce old Sea's delight,
England, my own,
Chosen daughter of the Lord,
Spouse-in-Chief of the ancient sword,
There's the menace of the Word
In the Song on your bugles blown,
England, England,
Out of heaven on your bugles blown!

Land of Hope and Glory

Arthur Christopher Benson

Set to music by Elgar, this poem by one of three sons of the
Archbishop of Canterbury has become a regular feature of the
Last Night of the Proms where its triumphalism is mitigated by
cheerfulness.

Dear Land of Hope, thy hope is crowned,
God make thee mightier yet!
On Sov'ran brows, beloved, renowned,
Once more thy crown is set.
Thine equal laws, by Freedom gained,
Have ruled thee well and long;
By Freedom gained, by Truth maintained,
Thine Empire shall be strong.

Land of Hope and Glory,
Mother of the Free,
How shall we extol thee,
Who are born of thee?
Wider still and wider shall thy bounds be set;
God, who made thee mighty, make thee mightier yet;
God, who made thee mighty, make thee mightier yet.

Thy fame is ancient as the days,
As Ocean large and wide;
A pride that dares, and heeds not praise,
A stern and silent pride;
Not that false joy that dreams content
With what our sires have won;
The blood a hero sire hath spent
Still nerves a hero son.

Vitaï Lampada

Sir Henry Newbolt

Written with the author's own school, Clifton College, in mind, this piece has been guyed and deservedly so for its sub-Kipling jingoism. Yet for all its tunnel-vision view of a world centred in southern England, it expressed a genuine feeling and a confidence in the efficacy of personal sacrifice that has never been recovered. The title refers to the Greek torch-race, a relay-match in which a torch was kept burning and the flame passed on to the next runner.

There's a breathless hush in the Close to-night –
    Ten to make and the match to win –
A bumping pitch and a blinding light,
    An hour to play and the last man in.
And it's not for the sake of a ribboned coat,
    Or the selfish hope of a season's fame,
But his Captain's hand on his shoulder smote –
    'Play up! play up! and play the game!'

The sand of the desert is sodden red, –
    Red with the wreck of a square that broke; –
The Gatling's jammed and the Colonel dead,
    And the regiment blind with dust and smoke.
The river of death has brimmed his banks,
    And England's far, and Honour a name,
But the voice of a schoolboy rallies the ranks:
    'Play up! play up! and play the game!'

This is the word that year by year,
   While in her place the School is set,
Every one of her sons must hear,
   And none that hears it dare forget.
This they all with a joyful mind
   Bear through life like a torch in flame,
And falling fling to the host behind –
   'Play up! play up! and play the game!'

The Absent-Minded Beggar

Rudyard Kipling

Kipling's tribute to the Boer War privates. The 'Paul' is Oom ('uncle') Paul Kruger, one of the Boer leaders.

When you've shouted 'Rule Britannia,' when you've
    sung 'God save the Queen,'
  When you've finished killing Kruger with your mouth,
Will you kindly drop a shilling in my little tambourine
    For a gentleman in khaki ordered South?
He's an absent-minded beggar, and his weaknesses are
    great –
  But we and Paul must take him as we find him –
He is out on active service, wiping something off a slate –
    And he's left a lot of little things behind him!
Duke's son – cook's son – son of a hundred kings –
    (Fifty thousand horse and foot going to Table Bay!)
Each of 'em doing his country's work
    (and who's to look after their things?)
Pass the hat for your credit's sake,
              and pay – pay – pay!

There are girls he married secret, asking no permission to,
    For he knew he wouldn't get it if he did.
There is gas and coals and vittles, and the house-rent
    falling due,
  And it's more than rather likely there's a kid.
There are girls he walked with casual. They'll be sorry
    now he's gone,
  For an absent-minded beggar they will find him,
But it ain't the time for sermons with the winter coming on.
  We must help the girl that Tommy's left behind him!
Cook's son – Duke's son – son of a belted Earl –
    Son of a Lambeth publican – it's all the same to-day!

Each of 'em doing his country's work
  (and who's to look after the girl?)
Pass the hat for your credit's sake,
              and pay – pay – pay!

There are families by thousands, far too proud to beg or
    speak,
  And they'll put their sticks and bedding up the spout,
And they'll live on half o' nothing, paid 'em punctual
    once a week,
  'Cause the man that earns the wage is ordered out.
He's an absent-minded beggar, but he heard his country call,
  And his reg'ment didn't need to send to find him!
He chucked his job and joined it – so the job before us all
  Is to help the home that Tommy's left behind him!
Duke's job – cook's job – gardener, baronet, groom,
  Mews or palace or paper-shop, there's someone gone
    away!
Each of 'em doing his country's work
  (and who's to look after the room?)
Pass the hat for your credit's sake,
              and pay – pay – pay!

Let us manage so as, later, we can look him in the face,
  And tell him – what he'd very much prefer –
That, while he saved the Empire, his employer saved his
    place,
  And his mates (that's you and me) looked out for *her*.
He's an absent-minded beggar and he may forget it all,
  But we do not want his kiddies to remind him
That we sent 'em to the workhouse while their daddy
    hammered Paul,
  So we'll help the homes that Tommy left behind him!
Cook's home – Duke's home – home of a millionaire,
  (Fifty thousand horse and foot going to Table Bay!)
Each of 'em doing his country's work
  (and what have you got to spare?)
Pass the hat for your credit's sake,
              and pay – pay – pay!

Mandalay

Rudyard Kipling

A statement about the unmentioned subject, cohabitation with
the natives, sung with unblushing enthusiasm by elderly concert-
singers who never left England. Recent research has established
the story as part of Kipling's own experience.

By the old Moulmein Pagoda, lookin' lazy at the sea,
There's a Burma girl a-settin', and I know she thinks
    o' me;
For the wind is in the palm-trees, and the temple-bells
    they say:
'Come you back, you British soldier; come you back
    to Mandalay!'
        Come you back to Mandalay,
        Where the old Flotilla lay:
        Can't you 'ear their paddles chunkin' from
            Rangoon to Mandalay?
        On the road to Mandalay,
        Where the flyin'-fishes play,
        An' the dawn comes up like thunder outer
            China 'crost the Bay!

'Er petticoat was yaller an' 'er little cap was green,
An' 'er name was Supi-yaw-lat – jes' the same as Thee-
    baw's Queen,
An' I seed her first a-smokin' of a whackin' white cheroot,
An' a-wastin' Christian kisses on an 'eathen idol's foot:
        Bloomin' idol made o' mud –
        Wot they called the Great Gawd Budd –
        Plucky lot she cared for idols when I kissed
            'er where she stud!
        On the road to Mandalay . . .

When the mist was on the rice-fields an' the sun was
    droppin' slow,
She'd git 'er little banjo an' she'd sing '*Kulla-lo-lo!*'
With 'er arm upon my shoulder an' 'er cheek agin my
    cheek
We useter watch the steamers an' the *hathis* pilin' teak.
      Elephints a-pilin' teak
      In the sludgy, squdgy creek,
      Where the silence 'ung that 'eavy you was
        'arf afraid to speak!
      On the road to Mandalay . . .

But that's all shove be'ind me – long ago an' fur away,
An' there ain't no 'buses runnin' from the Bank to
    Mandalay;
An' I'm learnin' 'ere in London what the ten-year
    soldier tells:
'If you've 'eard the East a-callin', you won't never 'eed
    naught else.'
      No! you won't 'eed nothin' else
      But them spicy garlic smells,
      An' the sunshine an' the palm trees an' the
        tinkly temple-bells;
      On the road to Mandalay . . .

I am sick o' wastin' leather on these gritty pavin'-stones,
An' the blasted English drizzle wakes the fever in my bones;
Tho' I walks with fifty 'ousemaids outer Chelsea to the
    Strand,
An' they talks a lot o' lovin', but wot do they understand?
      Beefy face an' grubby 'and –
      Law! wot do they understand?
      I've a neater, sweeter maiden in a cleaner,
        greener land!
      On the road to Mandalay . . .

Ship me somewheres east of Suez, where the best is
    like the worst,
Where there aren't no Ten Commandments an' a man
    can raise a thirst;
For the temple-bells are callin', an' it's there that I
    would be –
By the old Moulmein Pagoda, looking lazy at the sea;
        On the road to Mandalay,
        Where the old Flotilla lay,
        With our sick beneath the awnings when we
            went to Mandalay!
        On the road to Mandalay,
        Where the flyin'-fishes play,
        An' the dawn comes up like thunder outer
            China 'crost the Bay!

After Dunkirk

From a Speech delivered on 18 June 1940

Sir Winston Churchill

Churchill's rasping voice, his lateral lisp and his Augustan periods were as much a part of the Finest Hours as the Black-Out and the All-Clear.

During the first four years of the last war the Allies experienced nothing but disaster and disappointment. That was our constant fear: one blow after another, terrible losses, frightful dangers. Everything miscarried. And yet at the end of those four years the morale of the Allies was higher than that of the Germans, who had moved from one aggressive triumph to another, and who stood everywhere triumphant invaders of the lands into which they had broken. During that war we repeatedly asked ourselves the question: How are we going to win? and no one was able ever to answer it with much precision, until at the end, quite suddenly, quite unexpectedly, our terrible foe collapsed before us, and we were so glutted with victory that in our folly we threw it away.

We do not yet know what will happen in France or whether the French resistance will be prolonged, both in France and in the French Empire overseas. The French Government will be throwing away great opportunities and casting adrift their future if they do not continue the war in accordance with their Treaty obligations, from which we have not felt able to release them. The House will have read the historic declaration in which, at the desire of many Frenchmen – and of our own hearts – we have proclaimed our willingness at the darkest hour in French history to conclude a union of common citizenship in this struggle. However matters may go in France or with the French Government, or other French Governments, we in this island and in the British Empire will never lose our sense of comradeship with the French people. If we are now called upon to endure what they have been suffering, we shall emulate their courage, and if final victory rewards our toils they shall share the gains, aye, and freedom shall be restored to all. We abate nothing of our just demands; not one jot or tittle do we recede. Czechs, Poles, Norwegians, Dutch, Belgians have joined their causes to our own. All these shall be restored.

What General Weygand called the Battle of France is over. I expect that the battle of Britain is about to begin. Upon this battle depends the survival of Christian civilization. Upon it depends our own British life, and the long continuity of our institutions and our Empire. The whole fury and might of the enemy must very soon be turned on us. Hitler knows that he will have to break us in this island or lose the war. If we can stand up to him, all Europe may be free and the life of the world may move forward into broad, sunlit uplands. But if we fail, then the whole world, including the United States, including all that we have known and cared for, will sink into the abyss of a new Dark Age made more sinister, and perhaps more protracted, by the lights of perverted science. Let us therefore brace ourselves to our duties, and so bear ourselves that, if the British Empire and its Commonwealth last for a thousand years, men will still say, 'This was their finest hour.'

The Battle of Britain

From a Speech delivered to the House of Commons on 20 August 1940

Sir Winston Churchill

Not all Churchill's speeches were broadcast by him. In some cases the House of Commons talks were recorded by the actor Norman Shelley (BBC Radio's Dr Watson) whose impersonation was masterly.

The great air battle which has been in progress over this island for the last few weeks has recently attained a high intensity. It is too soon to attempt to assign limits either to its scale or to its duration. We must certainly expect that greater efforts will be made by the enemy than any he has so far put forth. Hostile airfields are still being developed in France and the Low Countries, and the movement of squadrons and material for attacking us is still proceeding. It is quite plain that Herr Hitler could not admit defeat in his air attack on Great Britain without sustaining most serious injury. If, after all his boastings and blood-curdling threats and lurid accounts trumpeted round the world of the damage he has inflicted, of the vast numbers of our Air Force he has shot down, so he says, with so little loss to himself; if after tales of the panic-stricken British crushed in their holes cursing the plutocratic Parliament which has led them to such a plight; if after all this his whole air onslaught were forced after a while tamely to peter out, the Fuhrer's reputation for veracity of statement might be seriously impugned. We may be sure, therefore, that he will continue as long as he has the strength to do so, and as long as any preoccupations he may have in respect of the Russian Air Force allow him to do so.

The enemy is, of course, far more numerous than we are. But our new production already, as I am advised, largely exceeds his, and the American production is only just beginning to flow in. It is a fact, as I see from my daily returns, that our bomber and fighter strengths now, after all this fighting, are larger than they have ever been. We believe that we shall be able to continue the air struggle indefinitely and as long as the enemy pleases, and the longer it continues the more rapid will be our approach, first towards that parity, and then into that superiority in the air, upon which in a large measure the decision of the war depends.

The gratitude of every home in our island, in our Empire, and indeed throughout the world, except in the abodes of the guilty, goes out to the British airmen who, undaunted by odds, unwearied in their constant challenge and mortal danger, are turning the tide of the world war by their prowess and by their devotion. Never in the field of human conflict was so much owed by so many to so few.

The Soldier

Rupert Brooke

Brooke's most famous poem was written in 1914 in the fit of self-sacrifice that gripped the youth of Britain in the first few months of the Kaiser's war before the wretched reality of the trenches became known. It was in a sense prophetic but Brooke's own death of blood-poisoning was pedestrian – almost *civilian*.

If I should die, think only this of me:
   That there's some corner of a foreign field
That is for ever England. There shall be
   In that rich earth a richer dust concealed;
A dust whom England bore, shaped, made aware,
   Gave, once, her flowers to love, her ways to roam,
A body of England's, breathing English air,
   Washed by the rivers, blest by suns of home.

And think, this heart, all evil shed away,
   A pulse in the eternal mind, no less
     Gives somewhere back the thoughts by England given;
Her sights and sounds; dreams happy as her day;
   And laughter, learnt of friends; and gentleness,
     In hearts at peace, under an English heaven.

Keep the Home Fires Burning

Ivor Novello and Lena Guilbert Ford

This song was written at the request of Novello's mother, Dame
Clara Novello Davies, who felt that 'Tipperary' had become
tiresome after months of iteration. He supplied the first lines
and Miss Ford completed the verses and chorus in half an hour.
It made its composer £16000 and eventually suffered the same
iterative fate as 'Tipperary'. When it was published in 1915 it
was known as 'Till the Boys Come Home'.

They were summoned from the hillside,
They were called in from the glen
And the country found them ready
At the stirring call for men.
Let no tears add to their hardship
As the soldiers pass along
And although your heart is breaking,
Make it sing this cheery song.

Keep the Home fires burning,
While your hearts are yearning,
Though your lads are far away
They dream of Home;
There's a silver lining
Through the dark cloud shining.
Turn the dark cloud inside out
Till the boys come Home.

Over the seas there came a pleading,
'Help a Nation in distress!'
And we gave our glorious laddies
Honour bade us do no less.
For no gallant son of Britain
To a foreign yoke shall bend
And no Englishman is silent
To the sacred call of Friend.

2

In Youth Is Pleasure

Ring a-Ring o' Roses

Anon

Now a dance game for young children but historically a reminder
of the Black Death. The roses were the buboes, the posies the
fresh flowers carried for protection, 'atishu' the first active
symptom and 'we all fall down' speaks for itself.

Ring a ring of roses,
A pocket full of posies.
Atishu! Atishu!
We all fall down.

The cows are in the meadow,
Lying fast asleep.
Atishu! Atishu!
We all get up together again.

A Madrigal

Anon

From a miscellany published by William Jaggard in 1599 called *The Passionate Pilgrim*. Some of the poems in the collection are by Shakespeare so this pleasant if pedestrian piece is assigned to him.

Crabbéd Age and Youth
Cannot live together:
 Youth is full of pleasance,
Age is full of care;
 Youth like summer morn,
Age like winter weather,
 Youth like summer brave,
Age like winter bare:
 Youth is full of sport,
 Age's breath is short,
Youth is nimble, Age is lame:
 Youth is hot and bold,
 Age is weak and cold,
Youth is wild, and Age is tame:
 Age, I do abhor thee,
 Youth, I do adore thee;
O! my Love, my Love is young!
 Age, I do defy thee –
 O sweet shepherd, hie thee,
For methinks thou stay'st too long.

Nursery Rhymes

Anon

A short selection from a treasure-house of nursery rhymes, many of which, apart from their didactic and moralistic elements, had quite specific satirical references. Most of them are sixteenth and seventeenth century in origin.

Don't Care

Don't Care didn't care,
　Don't Care was wild,
Don't Care stole plum and pear
　Like any beggar's child.

Don't Care was made to care,
　Don't Care was hung.
Don't Care was put in a pot
　And boiled till he was done.

Come, let's to Bed

Come, let's to bed,
　Says Sleepy-head;
Sit up awhile, says Slow;
　Hang on the pot,
　Says Greedy-gut,
Let's sup before we go.

Crosspatch

Crosspatch,
　Draw the latch,
Sit by the fire and spin.
　Take a cup
　And drink it up,
And call your neighbours in.

Rub-a-dub-dub

Rub-a-dub-dub,
   Three men in a tub,
And how do you think they got there?
   The butcher, the baker,
   The candlestick-maker,
   They all jumped out of a rotten potato,
'Twas enough to make a man stare.

Tweedledum and Tweedledee

Tweedledum and Tweedledee
   Agreed to have a battle,
For Tweedledum said Tweedledee
   Had spoiled his nice new rattle.
Just then flew down a monstrous crow,
   As black as a tar-barrel,
Which frightened both those heroes so,
   They quite forgot their quarrel.

In Youth Is Pleasure

Robert Wever

The 'harbour' is an older version of 'arbour' and this poignant poem is Wever's only surviving piece. It became the motif for one of Louis MacNiece's 'quest' plays for the Third Programme and provided the title for the Irish author, Benedict Kiely's second novel, *In a Harbour Green* (1949).

In a harbour grene aslepe whereas I lay,
The byrdes sang swete in the middes of the day,
I dreamed fast of mirth and play:
   In youth is pleasure, in youth is pleasure.

Methought I walked still to and fro,
And from her comany I could not go –
But when I waked it was not so:
   In youth is pleasure, in youth is pleasure.

Therefore my heart is surely pyght
Of her alone to have a sight
Which is my joy and hartes delight:
   In youth is pleasure, in youth is pleasure.

Golden Slumbers

Thomas Dekker

One of the great lullabies written by the agreeable Thomas
Dekker for his play *Patient Grissil*.

Golden slumbers kiss your eyes,
Smiles awake you when you rise;
Sleep, pretty maiden, do not cry,
And I will sing a lullaby.

Care you know not, therefore sleep,
While I o'er you watch do keep;
Sleep, pretty darling, do not cry,
And I will sing a lullaby.

To the Virgins, to Make Much of Time

Robert Herrick

Herrick's admonition may have had some special pleading, for though he never married and claimed to have led the chaste life a clergyman should, he loved erotic imagery. The shortness of youth and beauty needed little advertising in an age of short life expectancy. Herrick, who survived to be eighty-three, was very much an exception.

Gather ye rosebuds while ye may,
   Old Time is still a-flying:
And this same flower that smiles today
   Tomorrow will be dying.

The glorious lamp of heaven, the sun,
   The higher he's a-getting,
The sooner will his race be run,
   And nearer he's to setting.

That age is best which is the first,
   When youth and blood are warmer;
But being spent, the worse, and worst
   Times still succeed the former.

Then be not coy, but use your time,
   And while ye may, go marry:
For having lost but once your prime,
   You may for ever tarry.

Come, Lasses and Lads

Anon

A song first printed in 1672 when it was called 'The Rural Dance
about the Maypole'. It is a reminder of the rarity and therapeutic
wildness of the holidays of the period.

Come lasses and lads, get leave of your dads,
And away to the Maypole hie!
There every He has got him a She,
And the minstrel's standing by;
For Willy has got his Jill,
And Johnny has his Joan,
To trip it, trip it, trip it, trip it,
Trip it up and down,
To trip it, trip it, trip it, trip it,
Trip it up and down.

'You're out,' says Dick, 'Not I,' says Nick,
''Twas the fiddler played it wrong;'
''Tis true,' says Hugh, and so says Sue,
And so says ev'ryone.
The fiddler then began
To play the tune again,
And every girl did trip it, trip it,
Trip it to the men,
And every girl did trip it, trip it,
Trip it to the men.

'Goodnight,' says Harry. 'Goodnight,' says Mary,
'Goodnight,' says Poll to John.
'Goodnight,' says Sue, to her sweetheart Hugh,
'Goodnight,' says everyone.
Some walk'd and some did run,
Some loitered on the way,
And bound themselves by kisses twelve,
To meet the next holiday,
And bound themselves, by kisses twelve,
To meet the next holiday.

The Blind Boy

Colley Cibber

An execrated Poet Laureate's one claim to fame. It is a poem much loved by children in spite of its lugubrious theme. For all Pope's laceration, Cibber was an excellent actor and play-doctor. Unfortunately one of his patients was Shakespeare who did not need his ministrations.

O say what is that thing call'd Light,
   Which I must ne'er enjoy;
What are the blessings of the sight,
   O tell your poor blind boy!

You talk of wondrous things you see,
   You say the sun shines bright;
I feel him warm, but how can he
   Or make it day or night?

My day or night myself I make
   Whene'er I sleep or play;
And could I ever keep awake
   With me 'twere always day.

With heavy sighs I often hear
   You mourn my hapless woe;
But sure with patience I can bear
   A loss I ne'er can know.

Then let not what I cannot have
   My cheer of mind destroy:
Whilst thus I sing, I am a king,
   Although a poor blind boy.

Against Idleness and Mischief

Isaac Watts

From *Divine Songs for Children* and made immortal by Lewis Carroll's parody in *Alice's Adventures in Wonderland*: 'How doth the little crocodile / Improve his shining tail.'

How doth the little busy bee
  Improve each shining hour,
And gather honey all the day
  From every opening flower!

How skilfully she builds her cell!
  How neat she spreads the wax!
And labours hard to store it well
  With the sweet food she makes.

In works of labour or of skill,
  I would be busy too;
For Satan finds some mischief still
  For idle hands to do.

In books, or work, or healthful play,
  Let my first years be passed,
That I may give for every day
  Some good account at last.

Against Quarrelling and Fighting

Isaac Watts

Further moral advice from Dr Watts. He seems to have been a poor ornithologist if he believed the first line of the second verse in the second piece.

I

Let dogs delight to bark and bite,
    For God has made them so;
Let bears and lions growl and fight,
    For 'tis their nature too.

But children, you should never let
    Such angry passions rise;
Your little hands were never made
    To tear each others' eyes.

II

Whatever brawls disturb the street,
    There should be peace at home;
Where sisters dwell and brothers meet,
    Quarrels should never come.

Birds in their little nests agree;
    And 'tis a shameful sight,
When children of one family
    Fall out, and chide and fight.

The Lamb

William Blake

To Blake in his mysticism the lamb and the tiger were part of
God's kingdom indivisible. His poems to each are very touching
and persuasive.

> Little lamb, who made thee?
> Dost thou know who made thee,
> Gave thee life, and bade thee feed
> By the stream and o'er the mead.
> Gave thee clothing of delight,
> Softest clothing, woolly, bright;
> Gave thee such a tender voice,
> Making all the vales rejoice?
> Little lamb, who made thee?
> Dost thou know who made thee?
>
> Little lamb, I'll tell thee;
> Little lamb, I'll tell thee;
> He is called by thy name,
> For He calls Himself a Lamb;
> He is meek, and He is mild,
> He became a little child.
> I a child, and thou a lamb,
> We are called by His name.
> Little lamb, God bless thee!
> Little lamb, God bless thee!

There Was a Naughty Boy

John Keats

Keats in a light-hearted mood writing to his sister, Fanny.

There was a naughty Boy,
And a naughty Boy was
he,
He ran away to Scotland
The people for to see –

Then he found
That the ground
Was as hard,
That a yard
Was as long,
That a song
Was as merry,
That a cherry
Was as red –
That lead
Was as weighty,
That fourscore
Was as eighty,
That a door
Was as wooden
As in England –

So he stood in his shoes
And he wonder'd,
He wonder'd,
He stood in his shoes
And he wonder'd.

Young and Old

Charles Kingsley

The old, old story in a very acceptable form in spite of the Rev
Charles' professional moralising.

When all the world is young, lad,
　And all the trees are green;
And every goose a swan, lad,
　And every lass a queen;
Then hey for boot and horse, lad,
　And round the world away;
Young blood must have its course, lad,
　And every dog his day.

When all the world is old, lad,
　And all the trees are brown;
And all the sport is stale, lad,
　And all the wheels run down;
Creep home, and take your place there,
　The spent and maimed among:
God grant you find one face there,
　You loved when all was young.

From Goblin Market

Christina Rossetta

The list of the goblins' wares in this strange poem about the
intricacies of Victorian family life.

Morning and evening
Maids heard the goblins cry:
'Come buy our orchard fruits,
Come buy, come buy:
Apples and quinces,
Lemons and oranges,
Plump unpecked cherries,
Melons and raspberries,
Bloom-down-cheeked peaches,
Swart-headed mulberries,
Wild free-born cranberries,
Crab-apples, dewberries,
Pine-apples, blackberries,
Apricots, strawberries; –
All ripe together
In summer weather –
Morns that pass by,
Fair eaves that fly;
Come buy, come buy:
Our grapes fresh from the vine,
Pomegranates full and fine,
Dates and sharp bullaces,
Rare peaches and greengages,
Damsons and bilberries,

Taste them and try:
Currants and gooseberries,
Bright fire-like barberries,
Figs to fill your mouth,
Citrons from the South,
Sweet to tongue and sound to eye;
Come buy, come buy.'

When I Was One-and-Twenty

A.E. Housman

From *The Shropshire Lad*, the sequence of poems that showed a much softer side to this acerbic academic and critic.

When I was one-and-twenty
  I heard a wise man say,
'Give crowns and pounds and guineas
  But not your heart away;
Give pearls away and rubies
  But keep your fancy free.'
But I was one-and-twenty,
  No use to talk to me.

When I was one-and-twenty
  I heard him say again,
'The heart out of the bosom
  Was never given in vain;
'Tis paid with sighs a plenty
  And sold for endless rue.'
And I am two-and-twenty,
  And oh, 'tis true, 'tis true.

3

My Love and I

The Passionate Shepherd to his Love

Christopher Marlowe

A song in the idyllic strain written with mild self-parody not long before Marlowe's death. It was this piece that caused Shakespeare to refer to him as the 'dead Shepherd' in *As You Like It* (III, v). Sir Walter Raleigh wrote 'The Nymph's Answer' in which the sensible lady said, 'If all the world and love were young / And truth in every shepherd's tongue / These pretty pleasures *might* me move / To live with thee and be thy love.'

Come live with me and be my Love,
And we will all the pleasures prove
That hills and valleys, dale and field,
And all the craggy mountains yield.

There will we sit upon the rocks
And see the shepherds feed their flocks,
By shallow rivers, to whose falls
Melodious birds sing madrigals.

There will I make thee beds of roses
And a thousand fragrant posies,
A cap of flowers, with a kirtle
Embroider'd all with leaves of myrtle.

A gown made of the finest wool,
Which from our pretty lambs we pull,
Fair linéd slippers for the cold,
With buckles of the purest gold.

A belt of straw and ivy buds
With coral clasps and amber studs:
And if these pleasures may thee move,
Come live with me and be my Love.

Thy silver dishes for thy meat
As precious as the gods do eat,
Shall on an ivory table be
Prepared each day for thee and me.

The shepherd swains shall dance and sing
For thy delight each May-morning:
If these delights thy mind may move,
Then live with me and be my Love.

'Shall I compare thee?'

William Shakespeare

A love poem so perfect that one can forgive the slightly smug
f quite accurate prophecy of immortality. It is sonnet XVIII.

Shall I compare thee to a summer's day?
    Thou art more lovely and more temperate:
Rough winds do shake the darling buds of May,
    And summer's lease hath all too short a date:
Sometime too hot the eye of heaven shines,
    And often is his gold complexion dimmed;
And every fair from fair sometime declines,
    By chance, or nature's changing course untrimmed;
But thy eternal summer shall not fade,
    Nor lose possession of that fair thou owest,
Nor shall death brag thou wanderest in his shade,
    When in eternal lines to time thou growest;
        So long as men can breathe, or eyes can see,
        So long lives this, and this gives life to thee.

'It was a lover and his lass'

William Shakespeare

A song from *As You Like It*, which is neatly ironic when one considers it was sung for Touchstone and Audrey whose marriage was in Jacques' cynical words, 'but for two months victuall'd'.

It was a lover and his lass
   With a hey and a ho, and a hey-nonino!
That o'er the green cornfield did pass
In the spring time, the only pretty ring time,
When birds do sing hey ding a ding ding:
   Sweet lovers love the Spring.

Between the acres of the rye
These pretty country folks would lie:

This carol they began that hour,
How that a life was but a flower:

And therefore take the present time
   With a hey and a ho, and a hey-nonino!
For love is crownéd with the prime
In spring time, the only pretty ring time,
When birds do sing hey ding a ding ding:
   Sweet lovers love the Spring.

'Drink to me only'

Ben Jonson

Jonson's poem, also known as 'To Celia' comes from a collection
called *The Forest* (1616). Jonson who was a prodigious Greek
scholar used the prose of the fourth century writer, Philostratus,
to make this tribute.

> Drink to me only with thine eyes,
>   And I will pledge with mine;
> Or leave a kiss but in the cup
>   And I'll not look for wine.
> The thirst that from the soul doth rise
>   Doth ask a drink divine;
> But might I of Jove's nectar sup,
>   I would not change for thine.
>
> I sent thee late a rosy wreath,
>   Not so much honouring thee
> As giving it a hope that there
>   It could not wither'd be;
> But thou thereon didst only breathe
>   And sent'st it back to me;
> Since when it grows, and smells, I swear,
>   Not of itself but thee!

To Althea from Prison

Richard Lovelace

'Althea' was one of two inspirations of Lovelace's love poetry, the other being 'Lucasta', his betrothed, Lucy Sacheverell, who on report of his death in France married another man. His imprisonment was suffered in 1642 when he presented a public declaration in favour of the King.

When Love with unconfinéd wings
   Hovers within my gates,
And my divine Althea brings
   To whisper at the grates;
When I lie tangled in her hair
   And fetter'd to her eye,
The Gods that wanton in the air
   Know no such liberty.

When flowing cups run swiftly round
   With no allaying Thames,
Our careless heads with roses crown'd,
   Our hearts with loyal flames;
When thirsty grief in wine we steep,
   When healths and draughts go free –
Fishes that tipple in the deep
   Know no such liberty.

When, like committed linnets, I
   With shriller throat shall sing
The sweetest, mercy, majesty
   And glories of my King;
When I shall voice aloud how good
   He is, how great should be,
Enlargéd winds, that curl the flood,
   Know no such liberty.

Stone walls do not a prison make,
    Nor iron bars a cage;
Minds innocent and quiet take
    That for an hermitage:
If I have freedom in my love
    And in my soul am free,
Angels alone, that soar above,
    Enjoy such liberty.

A Red, Red Rose

Robert Burns

Nobody wrote love songs with such passion, sweetness and such universal application as Burns but then his detractors said he had much need of and much practice in the art.

O, my luve's like a red, red rose,
    That's newly sprung in June.
O, my luve's like the melodie,
    That's sweetly play'd in tune.

As fair art thou, my bonnie lass,
    So deep in luve am I,
And I will luve thee still, my dear,
    Till a' the seas gang dry.

Till a' the seas gang dry, my dear,
    And the rocks melt wi' the sun!
And I will luve thee still, my dear,
    While the sands o' life shall run.

And fare thee weel, my only luve,
    And fare thee weel a while!
And I will come again, my luve,
    Tho, it were ten thousand mile!

Sally in Our Alley

Henry Carey

The author gave this account of the origin of this song: 'A shoemaker's apprentice making a holiday with his sweetheart, treated her with a sight of Bedlam, the puppet shows, the flying chairs, and all the elegancies of Moorfields, whence, proceeding to the Farthing Pie House, he gave her a collation of buns, cheese-cakes, gammon of bacon, stuffed beer and bottled ale, through all which scenes the author dodged them.'

Of all the girls that are so smart
   There's none like pretty Sally;
She is the darling of my heart,
   And she lives in our alley.
There is no lady in the land
   Is half so sweet as Sally;
She is the darling of my heart,
   And she lives in our alley.

Her father he makes cabbage-nets
   And through the streets does cry 'em;
Her mother she sells laces long
   To such as please to buy 'em:
But sure such folks could ne'er beget
   So sweet a girl as Sally!
She is the darling of my heart,
   And she lives in our alley.

When she is by, I leave my work,
   I love her so sincerely;
My master comes like any Turk,
   And bangs me most severely –
But let him bang his bellyful,
   I'll bear it all for Sally;
She is the darling of my heart,
   And she lives in our alley.

Of all the days that's in the week
   I dearly love but one day –
And that's the day that comes betwixt
   A Saturday and Monday;
For then I'm drest all in my best
   To walk abroad with Sally;
She is the darling of my heart,
   And she lives in our alley.

My master carries me to church,
   And often am I blamed
Because I leave him in the lurch
   As soon as text is named;
I leave the church in sermon-time
   And slink away to Sally;
She is the darling of my heart,
   And she lives in our alley.

When Christmas comes about again
   O then I shall have money;
I'll hoard it up, and box and all,
   I'll give it to my honey:
I would it were ten thousand pound,
   I'd give it all to Sally;
She is the darling of my heart,
   And she lives in our alley.

My master and the neighbours all
   Make game of me and Sally,
And, but for her, I'd better be
   A slave and row a galley;
But when my seven long years are out
   O then I'll marry Sally, –
O then we'll wed, and then we'll bed,
   But not in our alley!

Early One Morning

Anon

A seventeenth century tune much sung and detested by school-children. It can be quite moving when sung properly by an English tenor.

Early one morning, just as the sun was rising,
I heard a maid sing in the valley below:
'O don't deceive me, O never leave me!
How could you use a poor maiden so?'

'Remember the vows that you made to your Mary,
Remember the bower where you vowed to be true;
O don't deceive me, O never leave me!
How could you use a poor maiden so?'

'O gay is the garland and fresh are the roses,
I've culled from the garden to bind on thy brow.
O don't deceive me, O never leave me!
How could you use a poor maiden so?'

Thus sung the poor maiden, her sorrows bewailing,
Thus sung the poor maid in the valley below.
'O don't deceive me, O never leave me;
How could you use a poor maiden so?'

The Girl I Left Behind Me

Anon

The traditional march-away song of the British Army. The Brighton Camp reference dates it as c.1794. The names of other camps could easily be substituted without doing too much violence to the metre.

I'm lonesome since I crossed the hill,
And o'er the moor and valley
Such heavy thoughts my heart do fill,
Since parting with my Sally.
I seek no more the fine or gay,
For each does but remind me
How swiftly pass'd the hours away
With the girl I left behind me.

Oh, ne'er shall I forget the night,
The stars were bright above me,
And gently lent their silv'ry light,
When first she vow'd to love me.
But now I'm bound to Brighton camp,
Kind heaven, then pray, guide me,
And send me safely back again
To the girl I've left behind me.

Her golden hair in ringlets fair,
Her eyes like diamonds shining,
Her slender waist, with carriage chaste,
May leave the swan repining.
Ye gods above, O hear my prayer,
To my beauteous fair to bind me,
And send me safely back again
To the girl I've left behind me.

The bee shall honey taste no more,
The dove become a ranger,
The falling waters cease to roar,
Ere I shall seek to change her.
The vows we register'd above
Shall ever cheer and bind me
In constancy to her I love,
The girl I've left behind me.

Ca' the Yowes to the Knowes

Anon

Eighteenth-century Scots version of pastoral. 'Row'ng in a plaid'
is a nice pun on the old merrymaking and the taking by the bride
of her husband's surname in marriage.

Ca' the yowes to the knowes,
Ca' them where the heather grows,
Ca' them where the burnie rowes,
My bonnie dearie.

'Will ye gang down yon water side,
That thro' the glen does saftly glide,
And I shall rowe thee in my plaid,
My bonnie dearie?'

'Ye sall hae rings and ribbons meet,
Calf-leather shoon upon your feet,
And in my bosom ye sall sleep,
My bonnie dearie.'

'I was brought up at nae sic school,
My shepherd lad, to play the fool,
Nor sit the livelong day in dool,
Lanely and eerie.'

'Yon yowes and lammies on the plain,
Wi' a' the gear my dad did hain,
I'se gie thee, if thoul't be mine ain,
My bonnie dearie.'

'Come weel, come wae, whate'er betide,
Gin ye'll prove true, I'se be your bride,
And ye sall rowe me in your plaid,
My winsome dearie.'

The Lass of Richmond Hill

Leonard MacNally

A song written by one of several 'moles' in our collection for though it is quintessentially English it was written by an Irishman. McNally is a mole in a double sense, an Irishman in a purely English collection and a Crown agent admitted to the conclaves of the United Irishmen. The Richmond is the Yorkshire one and the lass, Miss L'Anson, the daughter of William L'Anson of Hill House who afterwards became the poet's wife.

On Richmond Hill there lives a lass,
More bright than Mayday morn,
Whose charms all other maids surpass,
A rose without a thorn.
This lass so neat, with smiles so sweet,
Has won my right goodwill
I'd crowns resign to call thee mine,
Sweet lass of Richmond Hill;
Sweet lass of Richmond Hill,
Sweet lass of Richmond Hill,
I'd crowns resign to call thee mine,
Sweet lass of Richmond Hill.

Ye zephyrs gay that fan the air,
And wanton thro' the grove,
O whisper to my charming fair,
'I die for her I love.'
This lass so neat, with smiles so sweet,
Has won my right goodwill,
I'd crowns resign to call thee mine,
Sweet lass of Richmond Hill;

Sweet lass of Richmond Hill,
Sweet lass of Richmond Hill,
I'd crowns resign to call thee mine,
Sweet lass of Richmond Hill.

Jenny Kiss'd Me

James Henry Leigh Hunt

A neat compliment to Jane Welsh about whose marriage to
Thomas Carlyle Samuel Butler said, 'It was very good of God
to let Carlyle and Mrs Carlyle marry one another and so make
two people miserable instead of four.' The poem formed the basis
of a popular song of the 1950s.

> Jenny kiss'd me when we met,
>   Jumping from the chair she sat in;
> Time, you thief, who love to get
>   Sweets into your list, put that in!
> Say I'm weary, say I'm sad,
>   Say that health and wealth have miss'd me,
> Say I'm growing old, but add,
>   Jenny kiss'd me.

Alice, Where Art Thou?

Alfred Bunn

A grand old after-dinner song by the librettist of Balfe's *Bohemian Girl*. He was known mockingly as 'the Poet Bunn'.

The birds sleeping gently,
Sweet Lyra gleameth bright;
Her rays tinge the forest,
And all seems glad to-night
The winds sighing by me,
Cooling my fevered brow;
The stream flows as ever,
Yet, Alice, where art thou?
One year back this even,
And thou wert by my side,
And thou wert by my side
Vowing to love me!
One year past this even
And thou wert by my side,
Vowing to love me, Alice, whate'er might betide.

The silver rain falling,
Just as it falleth now;
And all things slept gently!
Ah! Alice, where art thou!
I've sought thee by lakelet,
I've sought thee on the hill,
And in the pleasant wild-wood,
When winds blew cold and chill!
I've sought thee in forest,
I'm looking heav'nward now;

I'm looking heav'nward now,
Oh! there mid the starshine!
I've sought thee in forest
I'm looking heav'nward now;
Oh! there amid starshine, Alice, I know art thou!

Dashing Away with the Smoothing Iron

Anon

Folk-song about the prolonged cleaning preparation for Sabbath finery as practised in darkest Somerset.

'Twas on a Monday morning,
When I beheld my darling,
She looked so neat and charming
In every high-degree;
She looked so neat and nimble, O,
A-washing of her linen, O,
Dashing away with the smoothing iron,
Dashing away with the smoothing iron,
She stole my heart away.

'Twas on a Tuesday morning, etc.
A-hanging out her linen, O, etc.

'Twas on a Wednesday morning, etc.
A-starching of her linen, O, etc.

'Twas on a Thursday morning, etc.
A-ironing of her linen, O, etc.

'Twas on a Friday morning, etc.
A-folding of her linen, O, etc.

'Twas on a Saturday morning, etc.
A-airing of her linen, O, etc.

'Twas on a Sunday morning, etc.
A-wearing of her linen, O, etc.

Polly Perkins

Anon

Anonymous nineteenth century London song with some authentic Victorian cockney pronunciations. A version is sung in Tyneside where the girl is called 'Cushey Butterfield'.

I am a broken-hearted milkman, in grief I'm arrayed,
Through keeping of the company of a young servant maid,
Who lived on board and wages the house to keep clean
In a gentleman's family near Paddington Green.

Chorus
She was as beautiful as a butterfly
   And as proud as a Queen
Was pretty little Polly Perkins of
   Paddington Green.

She'd an ankle like an antelope and a step like a deer,
A voice like a blackbird, so mellow and clear,
Her hair hung in ringlets so beautiful and long,
I thought that she loved me but I found I was wrong.

When I'd rattle in a morning and cry 'milk below',
At the sound of my milk-cans her face she would show
With a smile upon her countenance and a laugh in her eye,
If I thought she'd have loved me, I'd have laid down to die.

When I asked her to marry me she said 'Oh! what stuff',
And told me to 'drop it, for she had quite enough
Of my nonsense' – at the same time I'd been very kind,
But to marry a milkman she didn't feel inclined.

'Oh, the man that has me must have silver and gold,
A chariot to ride in and be handsome and bold,
His hair must be curly as any watch spring,
And his whiskers as big as a brush for clothing.'

The words that she uttered went straight through my heart,
I sobbed and I sighed, and straight did depart;
With a tear on my eyelid as big as a bean,
Bidding good-bye to Polly and Paddington Green.

In six months she married, – this hard-hearted girl,
But it was not a Wi-count, and it was not a Nearl,
It was not a 'Baronite', but a shade or two wuss,
It was a bow-legged conductor of a twopenny bus.

All Through the Night

(Ar hyd y nos)

Talhaiarn

English words by Thomas Oliphant

The most famous Welsh song of all, here rendered as a lovesong.

Yn fy nghwsg fy hoff ddymuniad
 Ar hyd y nos.
Yw breuddwydio am fy ngharaid
 Ar hyd y nos.

While the moon her watch is keeping
 All through the night;
While the weary world is sleeping
 All through the night
O'er my bosom gently stealing,
Visions of delight revealing
Breathes a pure and holy feeling
 All through the night.

Fondly then I dream of thee, love
 All through the night.
Waking, still thy form I see, love,
 All through the night.
When this mortal coil is over,
Will this gentle spirit hover
O'er the bed where sleeps thy lover
 All through the night.

'When I am dead'

Christina Rossetti

A poem of technical perfection, strong feeling and dry irony, entirely typical of its passionate, reserved author.

When I am dead, my dearest,
  Sing no sad songs for me;
Plant thou no roses at my head,
  Nor shady cypress tree:
Be the green grass above me
  With showers and dewdrops wet:
And if thou wilt, remember,
  And if thou wilt, forget.

I shall not see the shadows,
  I shall not feel the rain;
I shall not hear the nightingale
  Sing on as if in pain:
And dreaming through the twilight
  That doth not rise nor set,
Haply I may remember,
  And haply may forget.

Thora

Fred E. Weatherly

Strong, throbbing drawing-room ballad, very popular with strong, throbbing baritones.

I stand in a land of roses,
But I dream of a land of snow,
Where you and I were happy,
In the years of long ago.
Nightingales in the branches,
Stars in the magic skies,
But I only hear you singing,
I only see your eyes.

Come! come! come to me, Thora,
Come once again and be
Child of my dream, light of my life,
Angel of love to me!

I stand again in the North land,
But in silence and in shame;
Your grave is my only landmark,
And men have forgotten my name.
'Tis a tale that is truer and older
Than any the sagas tell,
I lov'd you in life too little,
I love you in death too well.

Speak! speak! speak to me, Thora,
Speak from your Heav'n to me;
Child of my dream, love of my life,
Hope of my world to be!

When I Was a King in Babylon

W.E. Henley

Can the Victorians have been quite so unaware of their own psychology as this poem popular with both sexes seems to suggest? Or are we the silly ones to find it a can of worms?

Or ever the knightly years were gone
    With the old world to the grave,
I was a King in Babylon
    And you were a Christian Slave.

I saw, I took, I cast you by,
    I bent and broke your pride.
You loved me well, or I heard them lie,
    But your longing was denied.
Surely I knew that by and by
    You cursed your gods and died.

And a myriad suns have set and shone
    Since then upon the grave
Decreed by the King in Babylon
    To her that had been his Slave.

The pride I trampled is now my scathe,
    For it tramples me again.
The old resentment lasts like death,
    For you love, yet you refrain.
I break my heart on your hard unfaith,
    And I break my heart in vain.

Yet not for an hour do I wish undone
    The deed beyond the grave,
When I was a King in Babylon
    And you were a Virgin Slave.

Bredon Hill

A. E. Housman

Bredon Hill is in Hereford, two and a half miles from Cheltenham but near enough for the Shropshire Lad to make the Sabbath journey.

In summertime on Bredon
  The bells they sound so clear;
Round both the shires they ring them
  In steeples far and near,
  A happy noise to hear.

Here of a Sunday morning
  My love and I would lie,
And see the coloured counties,
  And hear the larks so high
  About us in the sky.

The bells would ring to call her
  In valleys miles away:
'Come all to church, good people;
  Good people, come and pray.'
  But here my love would stay.

And I would turn and answer
  Among the springing thyme,
'Oh, peal upon our wedding,
  And we will hear the chime,
  And come to church in time.'

But when the snows at Christmas
  On Bredon top were strown,
My love rose up so early
  And stole out unbeknown
  And went to church alone.

They tolled the one bell only,
   Groom there was none to see,
The mourners followed after,
   And so to church went she,
   And would not wait for me.

The bells they sound on Bredon,
   And still the steeples hum.
'Come all to church, good people,'
   Oh, noisy bells, be dumb;
   I hear you, I will come.

My Old Dutch

Albert Chevalier

The cream of cockney humour and pathos by one of its finest
exponents.

I've got a pal,
  A reg'lar out an' outer,
She's a dear good old gal.
  I'll tell yer all about 'er.
It's many years since fust we met,
  'Er 'air was then as black as jet,
It's whiter now, but she don't fret,
  Not my old gal!

Chorus
We've been together now for forty years,
  An' it don't seem a day too much,
There ain't a lady livin' in the land
  As I'd 'swop' for my dear old Dutch.

I calls 'er Sal,
  'Er proper name is Sairer,
An' yer may find a gal
  As you'd consider fairer.
She ain't a angel – she can start
  A-jawin' till it makes yer smart,
She's just a *woman*, bless 'er 'eart,
  Is my old gal!

Sweet fine old gal,
   For worlds I wouldn't lose 'er,
She's a dear good old gal,
   An' that's what made me choose 'er.
She's stuck to me through thick and thin,
   When luck was out, when luck was in,
Ah! wot a wife to me she's been,
   An' wot a *pal*!

I sees yer Sal –
   Yer pretty ribbons sportin'!
Many years now, old gal,
   Since them young days of courtin'
I ain't a coward, still I trust
   When we've to part, as part we must,
That Death may come and take me fust
   To wait . . . my pal!

Kashmiri Song

Laurence Hope

Also known by its first four words, this poem tells the story, believed true, of a love affair between a Kashmiri Rajah and a married English lady. The author's *nom-de-plume* concealed the identity of a passionate Gloucestershire lady, Adela Florence Cory, whose poems were written out of actual experience of India and who committed suicide on her husband's death.

Pale hands I loved beside the Shalimar,
Where are you now? Who lies beneath your spell?
Whom do you lead on Rapture's roadway, far,
Before you agonize them in farewell?
Pale hands I loved beside the Shalimar,
Where are you now? Where are you now?

Pale hands, pinked tipped, like Lotus buds that float
On those cool waters where we used to dwell,
I would have rather felt you round my throat
Crushing out life, than waving me farewell!
Pale hands I loved beside the Shalimar,
Where are you now? Where are you now?

Non Sum Qualis Eram

Ernest Dowson

Poem by the most *fin-de-siècle* poet of all, the type of all incense-laden roisterers. The poem provided such contrasting artists as Margaret Mitchell and Cole Porter with titles. In spite of a relatively small output, Dowson has enjoyed a remarkable popularity.

Last night, ah, yesternight, betwixt her lips and mine
There fell thy shadow, Cynara! thy breath was shed
Upon my soul between the kisses and the wine;
And I was desolate and sick of an old passion,
   Yea, I was desolate and bow'd my head:
I have been faithful to thee, Cynara! in my fashion.

All night upon mine heart I felt her warm heart beat,
Night-long within mine arms in love and sleep she lay;
Surely the kisses of her bought red mouth were sweet;
But I was desolate and sick of an old passion,
   When I awoke and found the dawn was gray:
I have been faithful to thee, Cynara! in my fashion.

I have forgot much, Cynara! gone with the wind,
Flung roses, roses, riotously with the throng,
Dancing, to put thy pale lost lilies out of mind;
But I was desolate and sick of an old passion,
   Yea, all the time, because the dance was long:
I have been faithful to thee, Cynara! in my fashion.

I cried for madder music and for stronger wine,
But when the feast is finish'd and the lamps expire,
Then falls thy shadow, Cynara! the night is thine;
And I am desolate and sick of an old passion,
   Yea, hungry for the lips of my desire:
I have been faithful to thee, Cynara! in my fashion.

We'll Gather Lilacs

Ivor Novello

It is remarkable that David Davies (stage name Novello) should have written the great civilian songs for two world wars, at least in retrospect. This heavily nostalgic but irresistible piece was written for *Perchance To Dream* which opened in April 1945 in the Hippodrome and ran for 1030 performances. The song could be sung with some confidence that the dream would come true.

Although you're far away
And life is sad and grey
I have a scheme, a dream to try.
I'm thinking, dear, of you
And all I meant to do.
When we're together, you and I
We'll soon forget our care and pain
And find such lovely things to share again.

We'll gather lilacs in the spring again
And walk together down an English lane
Until our hearts have learned to sing again
When you come home once more.
And in the evening by the firelight's glow
You'll hold me close and never let me go
Your eyes will tell me all I want to know
When you come home once more

We'll learn to love anew
The simple joys we knew
And shared together night and day.
We'll watch without a sigh
The moments speeding by
When life is free and hearts are gay
My dream is here for you to share
And in my heart my dream becomes a prayer.

A Subaltern's Love-Song

Sir John Betjeman

The lady whose euphonious name so stirred Betjeman to write
a modern classic was the canteen supervisor at the Ministry of
Information where the poet worked at the beginning of the War.
The name and the lady were introduced to him by Sir Kenneth
Clark, who had an instinct for such things. The piece conjures
up a middle-class golden age whose decent serenity seems quite
incredible in our rawer age.

Miss J. Hunter Dunn, Miss J. Hunter Dunn,
Furnish'd and burnish'd by Aldershot sun,
What strenuous singles we played after tea,
We in the tournament – you against me!

Love-thirty, love-forty, oh! weakness of joy,
The speed of a swallow, the grace of a boy,
With carefullest carelessness, gaily you won,
I am weak from your loveliness, Joan Hunter Dunn.

Miss Joan Hunter Dunn, Miss Joan Hunter Dunn,
How mad I am, sad I am, glad that you won.
The warm-handled racket is back in its press,
But my shock-headed victor, she loves me no less.

Her father's euonymus shines as we walk,
And swing past the summer-house, buried in talk,
And cool the verandah that welcomes us in
To the six-o'clock news and a lime-juice and gin.

The scent of the conifers, sound of the bath,
The view from my bedroom of moss-dappled path,
As I struggle with double-end evening tie,
For we dance at the Golf Club, my victor and I.

On the floor of her bedroom lie blazer and shorts
And the cream-coloured walls are be-trophied with sports,
And westering, questioning settles the sun
On your low-leaded window, Miss Joan Hunter Dunn.

The Hillman is waiting, the light's in the hall,
The pictures of Egypt are bright on the wall,
My sweet, I am standing beside the oak stair
And there on the landing's the light on your hair.

By roads 'not adopted', by woodlanded ways,
She drove to the club in the late summer haze,
Into nine-o'clock Camberley, heavy with bells
And mushroomy, pine-woody, evergreen smells.

Miss Joan Hunter Dunn, Miss Joan Hunter Dunn,
I can hear from the car-park the dance has begun.
Oh! full Surrey twilight! importunate band!
Oh! strongly adorable tennis-girl's hand!

Around us are Rovers and Austins afar,
Above us, the intimate roof of the car,
And here on my right is the girl of my choice,
With the tilt of her nose and the chime of her voice,

And the scent of her wrap, and the words never said,
And the ominous, ominous dancing ahead.
We sat in the car park till twenty to one
And now I'm engaged to Miss Joan Hunter Dunn.

4

Realms of Gold

I saw a Peacock with a Fiery Tail

Anon

A typical riddle verse used in children's chapbooks and a neat way of emphasising the importance of punctuation. The comma in each line is moved back to mid-line.

I saw a Peacock with a fiery tail,
I saw a blazing Comet drop down hail,
I saw a Cloud with ivy circled round,
I saw a sturdy Oak creep on the ground,
I saw a Pismire swallow up a whale,
I saw a raging Sea brim full of ale,
I saw a Venice Glass sixteen foot deep,
I saw a Well full of men's tears that weep,
I saw their Eyes all in a flame of fire,
I saw a House as big as the moon and higher,
I saw the Sun even in the midst of night,
I saw the Man that saw this wondrous sight.

On His Life-Work

Edward Gibbon

Gibbon's own acount of the beginnings and completion of his great life's work. The work was not only splendid history but it was splendidly written in the prose of English Literature's most elegant period. And if nothing else it provided Latin teachers with the useful phrase, 'Best left in the decent obscurity of a classical language'.

(i)

It was at Rome, on the 15th of October 1764, as I sat musing amidst the ruins of the Capitol, while the bare-footed fryars were singing vespers in the Temple of Jupiter, that the idea of writing the decline and fall of the city first started to my mind. But my original plan was circumscribed to the decay of the city rather than of the empire: and, though my reading and reflections began to point towards that object, some years elapsed, and several avocations intervened, before I was seriously engaged in the execution of that laborious work.

(ii)

I have presumed to mark the moment of conception: I shall now commemorate the hour of my final deliverance. It was on the day, or rather night, of the 27th of June 1787, between the hours of eleven and twelve, that I wrote the last lines of the last page, in a summer-house in my garden. After laying down my pen, I took several turns in a *berceau*, or covered walk of acacias, which commands a prospect of the country, the lake, and the mountains. The air was temperate, the sky was serene, the silver orb of the moon was reflected from the waters, and all nature was silent. I will not dissemble the first emotions of joy on the recovery of my freedom, and, perhaps, the establishment of my fame. But my pride was soon humbled, and a sober melancholy was spread over my mind, by the idea that I had taken an everlasting leave of an old and agreeable companion, and that whatsoever might be the future date of my History, the life of the historian must be short and precarious.

The Tyger

William Blake

Blake's mystic view of reality was based upon the unity of creation, man, animal, earth and God. The tiger was as true a manifestation of this divine unity as the lamb.

Tyger! Tyger! burning bright
In the forests of the night,
What immortal hand or eye
Could frame thy fearful symmetry?

In what distant deeps or skies
Burnt the fire of thine eyes?
On what wings dare he aspire?
What the hand dare seize the fire?

And what shoulder, and what art,
Could twist the sinews of thy heart?
And when thy heart began to beat,
What dread hand? and what dread feet?

What the hammer? what the chain?
In what furnace was thy brain?
What the anvil? what dread grasp
Dare its deadly terrors clasp?

When the stars threw down their spears,
And water'd heaven with their tears,
Did he smile his work to see?
Did He who made the Lamb make thee?

Tyger! Tyger! burning bright
In the forests of the night,
What immortal hand or eye,
Dare frame thy fearful symmetry?

The Reaper

William Wordsworth

A poem written in 1805 owing something to Dorothy Wordsworth's journal of their Scottish tour of 1803 and also to a book called *Tour in Scotland* by Thomas Wilkinson, a friend of Wordsworth's, which contains the sentence: 'Passed by a female who was reaping alone, she sang in Erse as she bended over her sickle, the sweetest human voice I ever heard. Her strains were tenderly melancholy, and felt delicious long after they were heard no more.'

Behold her, single in the field,
    Yon solitary Highland Lass!
Reaping and singing by herself;
    Stop here, or gently pass!
Alone she cuts and binds the grain,
And sings a melancholy strain;
O listen! for the vale profound
Is overflowing with the sound.

No nightingale did ever chaunt
    More welcome notes to weary bands
Of travellers in some shady haunt,
    Among Arabian sands:
A voice so thrilling ne'er was heard
In spring-time from the cuckoo-bird,
Breaking the silence of the seas
Among the farthest Hebrides.

Will no one tell me what she sings?
   Perhaps the plaintive numbers flow
For old, unhappy, far-off things,
   And battles long ago:
Or is it some more humble lay,
Familiar matter of to-day?
Some natural sorrow, loss, or pain,
That has been, and may be again?

Whate'er the theme, the maiden sang
   As if her song could have no ending;
I saw her singing at her work,
   And o'er the sickle bending;
I listen'd, motionless and still;
And, as I mounted up the hill,
The music in my heart I bore,
Long after it was heard no more.

Kubla Khan

Samuel Taylor Coleridge

A poem as famous in the story of its truncation as in its residual
text. Coleridge was living in the country on the Somerset-Devon
border. One day he fell asleep while reading an account of the
travels of Marco Polo and his meeting with the Khan Kubla of
Tartary. On awaking he was conscious of having composed two
or three hundred lines on this theme and immediately set down
this fragment. He was interrupted by 'a person from Porlock'
and on returning to his task found that he could not remember
the rest.

In Xanadu did Kubla Khan
A stately pleasure-dome decree:
Where Alph, the sacred river, ran
Through caverns measureless to man
   Down to a sunless sea.
So twice five miles of fertile ground
With walls and towers were girdled round:
And there were gardens bright with sinuous rills,
Where blossomed many an incense-bearing tree;
And here were forests ancient as the hills,
Enfolding sunny spots of greenery.

But oh! that deep romantic chasm which slanted
Down the green hill athwart a cedarn cover!
A savage place! as holy and enchanted
As e'er beneath a waning moon was haunted
By woman wailing for her demon-lover!
And from this chasm, with ceaseless turmoil seething,
As if this earth in fast thick pants were breathing,
A mighty foundation momently was forced:
Amid whose swift half-intermitted burst
Huge fragments vaulted like rebounding hail,
Or chaffy grain beneath the thresher's flail:

And 'mid these dancing rocks at once and ever
It flung up momently the sacred river.
Five miles meandering with a mazy motion
Through wood and dale the sacred river ran,
Then reached the caverns measureless to man,
And sank in tumult to a lifeless ocean:
And 'mid this tumult Kubla heard from far
Ancestral voices prophesying war!

   The shadow of the dome of pleasure
   Floated midway on the waves;
   Where was heard the mingled measure
   From the foundation and the caves.
It was a miracle of rare device,
A sunny pleasure-dome with caves of ice!

   A damsel with a dulcimer
   In a vision once I saw:
   It was an Abyssinian maid,
   And on her dulcimer she played,
   Singing of Mount Abora.
   Could I revive within me
   Her symphony and song,
   To such a deep delight 'twould win me,
That with music loud and long,
I would build that dome in air,
That sunny dome! those caves of ice!
And all who heard should see them there,
And all should cry, Beware! Beware!
His flashing eyes, his floating hair!
Weave a circle round him thrice,
And close your eyes with holy dread,
For he on honey-dew hath fed,
And drunk the milk of Paradise.

Ozymandias

Percy Bysshe Shelley

The Ozymandias of this sonnet is Rameses II whose tomb at
Thebes in Upper Egypt was a noted wonder of the East.

I met a traveller from an antique land
  Who said: Two vast and trunkless legs of stone
Stand in the desert. Near them on the sand,
  Half sunk, a shatter'd visage lies, whose frown
And wrinkled lip and sneer of cold command
  Tell that its sculptor well those passions read
Which yet survive, stamp'd on these lifeless things,
  The hand that mock'd them and the heart that fed;

  And on the pedestal these words appear:
'My name is Ozymandias, king of kings:
  Look on my works, ye Mighty, and despair!'
Nothing beside remains. Round the decay
  Of that colossal wreck, boundless and bare,
The lone and level sands stretch far away.

On First Looking into Chapman's Homer

John Keats

Geoffrey Chapman was a poet, playwright and contemporary and rival of Shakespeare. He is now best known through this sonnet as a verse translator of Homer. Keats derived a lot of inspiration from Chapman and other Elizabethan and Jacobean writers, and the sonnet itself is what Romantic poetry is all about. As if it matters, it was not 'stout Cortez' who first saw the Pacific but one of his companions, Vasco Nunez de Balboa, nor was *he* silent. In fact he said, 'Hombre!'

Much have I travell'd in the realms of gold,
    And many goodly states and kingdoms seen;
    Round many western islands have I been
Which bards in fealty to Apollo hold.
Oft of one wide expanse had I been told
    That deep-brow'd Homer ruled as his demesne;
    Yet did I never breathe its pure serene
Till I heard Chapman speak out loud and bold:
Then felt I like some watcher of the skies
    When a new planet swims into his ken;
Or like stout Cortez when with eagle eyes
    He star'd at the Pacific – and all his men
Look'd at each other with a wild surmise –
    Silent, upon a peak in Darien.

Ode to a Nightingale

John Keats

Keats at his most narcotic and phthisic. Pulmonary physicians can read in this poem an accurate syndrome of tuberculosis symptoms observed by an exact diagnostician.

My heart aches, and a drowsy numbness pains
 My sense, as though of hemlock I had drunk,
Or emptied some dull opiate to the drains
 One minute past, and Lethe-wards had sunk:
'Tis not through envy of thy happy lot,
 But being too happy in thine happiness,
  That thou, light-wingéd Dryad of the trees,
   In some melodious plot
 Of beechen green, and shadows numberless,
  Singest of summer in full-throated ease.

O for a draught of vintage! that hath been
 Cool'd a long age in the deep-delvéd earth,
Tasting of Flora and the country green,
 Dance, and Provencal song, and sunburnt mirth!
O for a beaker full of the warm South,
 Full of the true, the blushful Hippocrene,
  With beaded bubbles winking at the brim,
   And purple-stainéd mouth;
 That I might drink, and leave the world unseen,
  And with thee fade away into the forest dim:

Fade far away, dissolve, and quite forget
   What thou among the leaves hast never known,
The weariness, the fever, and the fret
   Here, where men sit and hear each other groan;
Where palsy shakes a few, sad, last grey hairs,
    Where youth grows pale, and spectre-thin, and dies;
      Where but to think is to be full of sorrow
         And leaden-eyed despairs;
    Where Beauty cannot keep her lustrous eyes,
      Or new Love pine at them beyond to-morrow.

Away! away! for I will fly to thee,
   Not charioted by Bacchus and his pards,
But on the viewless wings of Poesy,
   Though the dull brain perplexes and retards:
Already with thee! tender is the night,
    And haply the Queen-Moon is on her throne,
    Cluster'd around by all her starry Fays;
        But here there is no light,
    Save what from heaven is with the breezes blown
      Through verdurous glooms and winding mossy ways.

I cannot see what flowers are at my feet,
   Nor what soft incense hangs upon the boughs,
But, in embalmèd darkness, guess each sweet
   Wherewith the seasonable month endows
The grass, the thicket, and the fruit-tree wild;
    White hawthorn, and the pastoral eglantine;
      Fast-fading violets cover'd up in leaves;
        And mid-May's eldest child
    The coming musk-rose, full of dewy wine,
      The murmurous haunt of flies on summer eves.

Darkling I listen; and, for many a time
  I have been half in love with easeful Death,
Call'd him soft names in many a muséd rhyme,
  To take into the air my quiet breath;
Now more than ever seems it rich to die,
  To cease upon the midnight with no pain,
    While thou art pouring forth thy soul abroad
      In such an ecstasy!
  Still wouldst thou sing, and I have ears in vain –
    To thy high requiem become a sod.

Thou wast not born for death, immortal Bird!
  No hungry generations tread thee down;
The voice I hear this passing night was heard
  In ancient days by emperor and clown:
Perhaps the self-same song that found a path
  Through the sad heart of Ruth, when, sick for home,
    She stood in tears amid the alien corn;
      The same that oft-times hath
  Charm'd magic casements, opening on the foam
    Of perilous seas, in faery lands forlorn.

Forlorn! the very word is like a bell
  To toll me back from thee to my sole self!
Adieu! the fancy cannot cheat so well
  As she is famed to do, deceiving elf.
Adieu! Adieu! thy plaintive anthem fades
  Past the near meadows, over the still stream,
    Up the hill-side; and now 'tis buried deep
      In the next valleyglades;
  Was it a vision, or a waking dream?
    Fled is that music: do I wake or sleep?

From The Rubàiyàt of Omar Khayyàm

Edward Fitzgerald

Fitzgerald's translation of the quatrains (*rubais*) of the Persian poet, Omar the Tentmaker, may not be exact but it does, scholars say, reflect the spirit of the original. Much more to the point it was very acceptable to the romantic Victorians who remained unaware that the beloved in Omar's case, whatever about Fitzgerald's, was a boy.

Awake! for Morning in the Bowl of Night
Has flung the Stone that puts the Stars to Flight:
   And Lo! the Hunter of the East has caught
The Sultán's Turret in a Noose of Light.

Dreaming when Dawn's Left Hand was in the Sky,
I heard a Voice within the Tavern cry,
   'Awake, my Little ones, and fill the Cup
Before Life's Liquor in its Cup be dry.'

And as the Cock crew, those who stood before
The Tavern shouted – 'Open then the Door!
   You know how little while we have to stay,
And, once departed, may return no more.'

Now the New Year reviving old Desires,
The thoughtful Soul to Solitude retires,
   Where the WHITE HAND OF MOSES on the Bough
Puts out, and Jesus from the Ground suspires . . .

.   .   .

Think, in this batter'd Caravanserai
Whose Doorways are alternate Night and Day,
   How Sultán after Sultán with his Pomp
Abode his Hour or two, and went his way.

They say the Lion and the Lizard keep
The Courts where Jamshýd gloried and drank deep:
    And Bahrám, that great Hunter – the Wild Ass
Stamps o'er his Head, and he lies fast asleep.

I sometimes think that never blows so red
The Rose as where some buried Caesar bled;
    That every Hyacinth the Garden wears
Dropt in its Lap from some once lovely Head.

And this delightful Herb whose tender Green
Fledges the River's Lip on which we lean –
    Ah, lean upon it lightly! for who knows
From what once Lovely Lip it springs unseen!

                    .   .   .

Alas, that Spring should vanish with the Rose!
That Youth's sweet-scented Manuscript should close!
    The Nightingale that in the Branches sang,
Ah, whence, and whither flown again, who knows!

Ah, Love! could thou and I with Fate conspire
To grasp this sorry Scheme of Things entire,
    Would not we shatter it to bits – and then
Re-mould it nearer to the Heart's Desire!

Ah, Moon of my Delight who know'st no wane,
The Moon of Heaven is rising once again:
    How oft hereafter rising shall she look
Through this same Garden after me – in vain!

And when Thyself with shining Foot shall pass
Among the Guests Star-scatter'd on the Grass,
    And in thy joyous Errand reach the Spot
Where I made one – turn down an empty Glass!

The Splendour Falls

Alfred Tennyson

A song from Tennyson's narrative poem, *The Princess*, but certainly suggested by the Lakes of Killarney, seen on an Irish tour. The castle was Muckross Abbey.

The splendour falls on castle walls
   ' And snowy summits old in story:
The long light shakes across the lakes,
    And the wild cataract leaps in glory.
Blow, bugle, blow, set the wild echoes flying,
Blow, bugle; answer, echoes, dying, dying, dying.

O hark, O hark! how thin and clear,
    And thinner, clearer, farther going!
O sweet and far from cliff and scar
    The horns of Elfland faintly blowing!
Blow, let us hear the purple glens replying:
Blow, bugle; answer, echoes, dying, dying, dying.

O love, they die in yon rich sky,
    They faint on hill or field or river:
Our echoes roll from soul to soul,
    And grow for ever and for ever.
Blow, bugle, blow, set the wild echoes flying,
And answer, echoes, answer, dying, dying, dying.

Monna Lisa

Walter Pater

Art criticism as art form. Pater's description of Leonardo da
Vinci's great, enigmatic portrait of the wife of Francesco del
Giocondo is famous in its own right. Written in the 1870s its
reference to vampirism struck a contemporary chord: Sheridan
Le Fanu's great pre-Dracula tale, 'Carmilla', belongs to the
same period.

The presence that thus rose so strangely beside the waters, is expressive
of what in the ways of a thousand years men had come to desire. Hers
is the head upon which all 'the ends of the world are come,' and the
eyelids are a little weary. It is a beauty wrought out from within upon
the flesh, the deposit, little cell by cell, of strange thoughts and fantastic
reveries and exquisite passions. Set it for a moment beside one of those
white Greek goddesses or beautiful women of antiquity, and how would
they be troubled by this beauty, into which the soul with all its maladies
has passed? All the thoughts and experience of the world have etched
and moulded there, in that which they have of power to refine and
make expressive the outward form, the animalism of Greece, the lust
of Rome, the reverie of the middle age with its spiritual ambition and
imginative loves, the return of the Pagan world, the sins of the Borgias.
She is older than the rocks among which she sits; like the vampire,
she has been dead many times, and learned the secrets of the grave;
and has been a diver in deep seas, and keeps their fallen day about
her; and trafficked for strange webs with Eastern merchants: and, as
Leda, was the mother of Helen of Troy, and, as Saint Anne, the mother
of Mary; and all this has been to her but as the sound of lyres and
flutes, and lives only in the delicacy with which it has moulded the
changing lineaments, and tinged the eyelids and the hands. The fancy
of a perpetual life, sweeping together ten thousand experiences, is an
old one; and modern thought has conceived the idea of humanity as
wrought upon by, and summing up in itself, all modes of thought and
life. Certainly Lady Lisa might stand as the embodiment of the old
fancy, the symbol of the modern idea.

The Fairy Chorus

Fiona Macleod

Typical of the return to fantasy that affected the art and literature
of the end of the nineteenth century. Macleod (William Sharp)
was one of the Art Nouveau writers who reassured Yeats that
he was right to rediscover the *sidhe* and invent the Celtic Twilight.

How beautiful they are,
The lordly ones
Who dwell in the hills,
In the hollow hills.

They have faces like flowers,
And their breath is a wind
That blows over summer meadows,
Filled with dewy clover.

Their limbs are more white
Than shafts of moonshine:
They are more fleet
Than the March wind.

They laugh and are glad,
And are terrible:
When their lances shake and glitter
Every green reed quivers.

How beautiful they are,
How beautiful
The lordly ones
In the hollow hills.

'When I set out for Lyonnesse'

Thomas Hardy

The poem is one of several written about Hardy's visit to St Juliot, Cornwall, in March 1870 to make professional drawings for the restoration of the church there. He met and fell in love with Emma Gifford, the rector's sister-in-law who became his wife in 1874. Strictly speaking, Lyonnesse is the lost land lying between Land's End and the Isles of Scilly, birthplace of Tristan and the scene of Arthur's last battle.

When I set out for Lyonnesse,
  A hundred miles away,
  The rime was on the spray,
And starlight lit my lonesomeness
When I set out for Lyonnesse
  A hundred miles away.

What would bechance at Lyonnesse
  While I should sojourn there
  No prophet durst declare,
Nor did the wisest wizard guess
What would bechance at Lyonnesse
  While I should sojourn there.

When I came back from Lyonnesse
  With magic in my eyes,
  All marked with mute surmise
My radiance rare and fathomless,
When I came back from Lyonnesse
  With magic in my eyes!

'When 'Omer smote 'is bloomin' lyre'

Rudyard Kipling

One practical aspect of the poet's art revealed by a highly effective practitioner.

When 'Omer smote 'is bloomin' lyre,
   He'd 'eard men sing by land an' sea;
An' what he thought 'e might require,
   'E went an' took – the same as me!

The market-girls an' fishermen,
   The shepherds an' the sailors, too,
They 'eard old songs turn up again,
   But kep' it quiet – same as you!

They knew 'e stole; 'e knew they knowed.
   They didn't tell, nor make a fuss,
But winked at 'Omer down the road,
   An' 'e winked back – the same as us!

The Old Ships

James Elroy Flecker

A piece of Near Eastern magic written by the British Consul
in Beirut.

I have seen old ships sail like swans asleep
Beyond the village which men still call Tyre,
With leaden age o'ercargoed, dipping deep
For Famagusta and the hidden sun
That rings black Cyprus with a lake of fire;
And all those ships were certainly so old
Who knows how oft with squat and noisy gun,
Questing brown slaves or Syrian oranges,
The pirate Genoese
Hell-raked them till they rolled
Blood, water, fruit and corpses up the hold.
But now through friendly seas they softly run,
Painted the mid-sea blue or shore-sea green,
Still patterned with the vine and grapes in gold.

But I have seen,
Pointing her shapely shadows from the dawn
And image tumbled on a rose-swept bay,
A drowsy ship of some yet older day;
And, wonder's breath indrawn,
Thought I – who knows – who knows – but in that same
(Fished up beyond Æǽa, patched up new
 – Stern painted brighter blue –)
That talkative, bald-headed seaman came
(Twelve patient comrades sweating at the oar)
From Troy's doom-crimson shore,
And with great lies about his wooden horse
Set the crew laughing, and forgot his course.

It was so old a ship – who knows, who knows?
– And yet so beautiful, I watched in vain
To see the mast burst open with a rose,
And the whole deck put on its leaves again.

5

The Glory of the Garden

Sumer is Icumen in

Anon

The earliest extant English song-lyric dating from the thirteenth
century. It was set as a *rota* or round for four tenors and two
basses by a monk of Reading Abbey and the tune is still known
today.

Sumer is icumen in,
Lhude sing cuccu!
Groweth sed and bloweth med
And springeth the wode nu.
Sing cuccu!

Awe bleteth after lomb,
Lhouth after calve cu,
Bulluc sterteth, bucke verteth.
Murie sing cuccu!
Cuccu, cuccu,
Wel singes thu cuccu.
Ne swik thu naver nu!

Sing cuccu nu, Sing cuccu!
Sing cuccu,
Sing cuccu nu!

London Bells

Anon

A song for a street-game incorporating the voices of the bells of pre-1666 London churches. Many were destroyed in the Great Fire in May of that year. Its use has spread far beyond the city and the chiming tune was used for years as the call-signal for the BBC Home Service.

Gay go up, and gay go down,
To ring the bells of London town.

Bull's eyes and targets,
Say the bells of St Marg'ret's.

Brickbats and tiles,
Say the bells of St Giles'.

Halfpence and farthings
Say the bells of St Martin's.

Oranges and lemons,
Say the bells of St Clement's.

Pancakes and fritters,
Say the bells of St Peter's.

Two sticks and an apple,
Say the bells at Whitechapel.

Old Father Baldpate,
Say the slow bells at Aldgate.

Maids in white aprons,
Say the bells of St Cath'rine's.

Pokers and tongs,
Say the bells at St John's.

Kettles and pans,
Say the bells at St Ann's.

You owe me ten shillings,
Say the bells at St Helen's.

When will you pay me?
Say the bells at Old Bailey.

When I grow rich,
Say the bells at Fleetditch.

When will that be?
Say the bells at Stepney.

I am sure I don't know,
Says the great bell at Bow.

When I am old,
Say the bells at St Paul's.

Here comes a candle to light you
    to bed,
And here comes a chopper to chop
    off your head.

Winter and Spring

William Shakespeare

Two songs from the end of *Love's Labour Lost*, Shakespeare's most trendy play, in which he shows that he could torture a conceit with the best of the university wits. His townsman's knowledge of the country, generally accurate but not precise, is shown here. The turtles in *Spring* as in the *Song of Songs* are doves and not chelonians.

Winter

When icicles hang by the wall,
   And Dick the shepherd blows his nail,
And Tom bears logs into the hall,
   And milk comes frozen home in pail,
When blood is nipp'd, and ways be foul,
Then nightly sings the staring owl,
      To-whit!
To-who! – a merry note,
While greasy Joan doth keel the pot.
When all aloud the wind doth blow,
   And coughing drowns the parson's saw,
And birds sit brooding in the snow,
   And Marian's nose looks red and raw,
When roasted crabs hiss in the bowl,
Then nightly sings the staring owl,
      To-whit!
To-who! – a merry note,
While greasy Joan doth keel the pot.

Spring

When daisies pied and violets blue,
  And lady-smocks all silver-white,
And cuckoo-buds of yellow hue
  Do paint the meadows with delight,
The cuckoo then, on every tree,
Mocks married men; for thus sings he,
          Cuckoo!
Cuckoo, cuckoo! – O word of fear
Unpleasing to a married ear!
When shepherds pipe on oaten straws,
  And merry larks are ploughmen's clocks,
When turtles tread, and rooks, and daws,
  And maidens bleach their summer smocks
The cuckoo then, on every tree,
Mocks married men; for thus sings he,
          Cuckoo!
Cuckoo, cuckoo! – O word of fear,
Unpleasing to a married ear!

The Fine Old English Gentleman

Anon

A musical tribute to the belief that 'old and true' is always better than the observances of the current age. Pepys liked the song so much when he heard it in 1670 that he had his host write it down for him.

I'll sing you a good old song,
　That was made by a good old pate,
Of a fine old English gentleman
　Who had an old estate:
And who kept up his old mansion
　At a bountiful old rate
With a good old porter to relieve
　The old poor at his gate
Like a fine old English gentleman,
　All of the olden time.
Like a fine old English gentleman
　All of the olden time.

His hall so old was hung about
　With pikes and guns and bows
And swords and good old bucklers which
　Had stood against old foes.
'Twas there His Worship sat in state,
　In doublet and trunk hose
And quaffed his cup of good old sack
　To warm his good old nose –
Like a fine old English gentleman
　All of the olden time.

His Custom was, when Christmas came,
    To bid his friends repair
To his old hall, where feast and ball
    For them he did prepare:
And though the rich he entertained,
    He ne'er forgot the poor,
Nor were there any destitute
    E'er driven from the door
Of this good old English gentleman,
    All of the olden time.

Yet all at length must bend to fate,
    So, like the ebbing tide,
Declining gently to the last,
    This fine old man he died.
The widows' and the orphans' tears
    Bedewed his cold grave's side;
And where's the 'scutcheon that can show
    So much the worth and pride
Of the fine old English gentleman,
    One of the olden time?

But times and seasons though they change,
    And customs pass away,
Yet English hands and English hearts
    Will prove Old England's sway:
And though our coffers mayn't be filled
    As they were wont of yore,
We still have hands to fight, if need,
    And hearts to help the poor,
Like the good old English gentleman,
    All of the olden time.

The Derby Ram

Anon

A tall tale of a type very common in America in the nineteenth century. This one is a native product.

As I was going to Derby,
　'Twas on a market day,
I saw the finest ram, sir,
　That ever was fed on hay.
This ram was fat behind, sir,
　This ram was fat before,
This ram was ten yards high, sir,
　If he wasn't a little more.
　　That's a lie, that's a lie,
　　That's a tid i fa la lie.

Now the inside of this ram, sir,
　Would hold ten sacks of corn,
And you could turn a coach and six
　On the inside of his horn.
Now the wool upon his back, sir,
　It reached up to the sky,
And in it was a crow's nest,
　For I heard the young ones cry.
　　That's a lie, that's a lie,
　　That's a tid i fa la lie.

Now the wool upon his belly, sir,
   Went dragging on the ground,
And that was took to Derby, sir,
   And sold for ten thousand pound.
Now the wool upon his tail, sir,
   Was ten inches and an ell,
And that was took to Derby, sir,
   To toll the old market-bell.
     That's a lie, that's a lie,
     That's a tid i fa la lie.

Now the man that fed this ram, sir,
   He fed him twice a day,
And each time that he fed him, sir,
   He ate a rick of hay.
Now the man that watered this ram, sir,
   He watered him twice a day,
And each time that he watered him
   He drank the river dry.
     That's a lie, that's a lie,
     That's a tid i fa la lie.

Now the butcher that killed the ram, sir,
   Was up to his knees in blood,
And the boy that held the bowl, sir,
   Got washed away in the flood.
Now all the boys in Derby, sir,
   Went begging for his eyes,
They kicked them up and down the street,
   For they were a good football size.
     That's a lie, that's a lie,
     That's a tid i fa la lie.

Now all the women of Derby, sir,
   Went begging for his ears,
To make their leather aprons of
   That lasted them forty years.
And the man that fatted the ram, sir,
   He must be very rich,
And the man that sung this song, sir,
   Is a lying son of a bitch.
      That's the truth, that's the truth,
      That's the tid i fa la truth.

The Lincolnshire Poacher

Anon

A fine song which has survived educational mistreatment and
leaves one in no doubt as to the pronunciation of the word 'shire'.

When I was bound apprentice, in famous Lincolnsheer,
Full well I served my master for more than seven year,
Till I took up with poaching, as you shall quickly hear.
  Oh, 'tis my delight of a shiny night, in the season of the year.

As me and my comrades were setting of a snare,
'Twas then we seed the gamekeeper – for him we did not care,
For we can wrestle and fight, my boys, and jump o'er
     everywhere.
  Oh, 'tis my delight of a shiny night, in the season of the year.

As me and my comrades were setting four or five,
And taking on 'em up again, we caught the hare alive;
We caught the hare alive, my boys, and through the woods
     did steer.
  Oh, 'tis my delight of a shiny night, in the season of the year.

I threw him on my shoulder, and then we trudged home,
We took him to a neighbour's house and sold him for a crown,
We sold him for a crown, my boys, but I did not tell you where.
  Oh, 'tis my delight of a shiny night, in the season of the year.

Bad luck to every magistrate that lives in Lincolnsheer;
Success to every poacher that wants to sell a hare;
Bad luck to every gamekeeper that will not sell his deer.
  Oh, 'tis my delight of a shiny night, in the season of the year.

The Miller of Dee

Anon

The miller is the archetypal self-sufficient Englishman. The song
is rather older than its first stage appearance in Dr Arne's opera,
Love in a Village, in 1762.

There dwelt a miller hale and bold
   Down by the River Dee,
He worked and sang from morn till night,
   No lark more blithe than he,
And this the burden of his song
   For ever used to be –
I envy nobody, no, not I,
   Nor nobody envies me.

Thou'rt wrong, my friend, cried old King Hal
   Thou'rt wrong as wrong can be,
For had I half such health as thine
   I would gladly change with thee.
Then tell me now what makes thee sing,
   With heart so light and free,
While I am sad although I am king,
   Down by the River Dee?

The miller smiled and doffed his cap –
   I love my wife, said he,
I love my friends, I love my mill,
   I love my children three.
I owe no penny I cannot pay,
   I thank the River Dee,
That turns the mill to grind the corn,
   That feeds my babes and me.

Farewell, my friend! cried old King Hal,
  And happy may you be!
And had I half such health as thine
  I would gladly change with thee.
Thy mealy cap is worth my crown,
  Thy mill my kingdoms three,
Such men as thou are England's boast,
  Oh, miller of the Dee.

The Roast Beef of Old England

Richard Leveridge

Henry Fielding

The original song was composed and written by Richard
Leveridge who was a well-known performer at Drury Lane and
who used the talents of the bright young poor university men
who were trying to establish themselves in the city. Fielding,
already showing some of the talent with words that was to mark
his great novels, contributed lyrics to many songs and certainly
improved this one.

When mighty roast beef was the Englishman's food,
It ennobled our hearts, and enriched our blood;
Our soldiers were brave, and our courtiers were good.
Oh! the roast beef of old England!
And oh! for old England's roast beef!

Our fathers of old were robust, stout and strong,
And kept open house, with good cheer, all day long,
Which made their plump tenants rejoice in this song:
Oh! the roast beef of old England!
And oh! for old England's roast beef!

In those days, if fleets did presume on the main,
They seldom or never returned back again,
As witness the vaunting Armada of Spain.
Oh! the roast beef of old England!
And oh! for old England's roast beef!

Hunting Song

Henry Fielding

One of many spirited songs written by Fielding for his own and
other hacks' plays as he struggled to support himself as a young
lawyer in London. The nursery rhyme belongs to roughly the
same period.

The dusky night rides down the sky,
   And ushers in the morn;
The hounds all join in glorious cry,
   The huntsman winds his horn:
     And a-hunting we will go.

The wife around her husband throws
   Her arms, and begs his stay;
My dear, it rains, and hails, and snows,
   You will not hunt to-day.
     But a-hunting we will go.

A brushing fox in yonder wood,
   Secure to find we seek;
For why, I carried sound and good
   A cartload there last week.
     And a-hunting we will go.

Away he goes, he flies the rout,
   Their steeds all spur and switch;
Some are thrown in, and some thrown out,
   And some thrown in the ditch:
     But a-hunting we will go.

At length his strength to faintness worn,
   Poor Renard ceases flight;
Then hungry, homeward we return,
   To feast away the night:
     Then a-drinking we will go.

There's Nae Luck aboot the Hoose

W.J. Mickle

Mickle's only claim to modern fame though one of his poem's did suggest the theme of *Kenilworth* (1821). 'Gudeman' is the equivalent of the Irish 'Himself', the head of the household in pre-feminist days.

And are ye sure the news is true?
   And are ye sure he's weel?
Is this a time to think o' wark?
   Ye jades, fling by your wheel!
Is this a time to think o' wark
   When Colin's at the door?
Rax me my cloak – I'll to the quay,
   And see him come ashore.

   For there's nae luck aboot the hoose,
     Ther's nae luck ava',
   There's little pleasure in the hoose,
     When oor gudeman's awa'.

Rise up, and mak' a clean fireside,
   Put on the muckle pat;
Gie little Kate her cotton gown,
   And Jock his Sunday coat.
And mak' their shoon as black as slaes,
   Their stockings white as snaw;
It's a' to please my own gudeman,
   He likes to see them braw.

There are two hens into the crib,
    Have fed this month and mair,
Mak' haste and thraw their necks aboot
    That Colin weel may fare.
And spread the table neat and clean,
    Gar ilka thing look braw;
For wha can tell how Colin fared,
    When he was far awa'?

Bring down to me my bigonet,
    My bishop-satin gown,
For I maun tell the Bailie's wife,
    That Colin's come to town.
My Turkey slippers I'll put on,
    My stockings pearly blue,
And a' to pleasure our gudeman
    For he's baith leal and true.

Sae sweet his voice, sae smooth his tongue,
    His breath's like caller air,
His very fit has music in't
    As he comes up the stair.
And will I see his face again,
    And will I hear him speak?
I'm downright dizzy wi' the thought
    In troth I'm like to greet!

Caller Herrin'

Carolina Oliphant

'Caller' is 'fresh' and the song has been popular since its writing.
The concern for the fishermen ('Caller herrin's no got lightlie')
is entirely characteristic of the author who though of good family
knew poverty in her time.

Wha'll buy my caller herrin'?
　They're bonnie fish and halesome farin';
Wha'll buy my caller herrin',
　New drawn frae the Forth.

When ye were sleepin' on your pillows,
　Dream'd ye aught o' our puir fellows,
Darkling as they fac'd the billows,
　A' to fill the woven willows?
　　Buy my caller herrin',
　　New drawn frae the Forth.

Wha'll buy my caller herrin'?
　They're no brought here without brave darin';
Buy my caller herrin',
　Haul'd through wind and rain.
　　Wha'll buy my caller herrin'? etc.

Wha'll buy my caller herrin'?
　Oh, ye may ca' them vulgar farin' –
Wives and mithers, maist despairin',
　Ca' them lives o' men.
　　Wha'll buy my caller herrin'? etc.

When the creel o' herrin' passes,
  Ladies glad in silks and laces,
Gather in their braw pelisses,
  Cast their heads and screw their faces,
    Wha'll buy my caller herrin'? etc.

Caller herrin's no got lightlie: –
  Ye can trip the spring fu' tightlie;
Spite o' tauntin', flauntin', flingin',
  Gow had set you a' a-singing
    Wha'll buy my caller herrin'? etc.

Neebour wives, now tent my tellin';
  When the bonnie fish ye're sellin',
At ae word be in yere dealin' –
  Truth will stand when a' thin's failin',
  Wha'll buy my caller herrin'?
    They're bonnie fish and halesome farin',
  Wha'll buy my caller herrin',
    New drawn frae the Forth?

Jerusalem

William Blake

A song, almost a hymn, which has suffered a strange change
in its century and a half of life. In Blake's hands it was apocalyptic
and terrifying and his Jerusalem, far from the celestial city of
the Women's Institute carollers, was to be an earthly thing with
freedom (including free love) for all.

And did those feet in ancient time
Walk upon England's mountains green?
And was the holy Lamb of God
On England's pleasant pastures seen?

And did the Countenance Divine
Shine forth upon our clouded hills?
And was Jerusalem builded here
Among these dark Satanic Mills?

Bring me my Bow of burning gold!
Bring me my Arrows of desire!
Bring me my Spear! O clouds, unfold!
Bring me my Chariot of fire!

I will not cease from Mental Fight,
Nor shall my Sword sleep in my hand,
Till we have built Jerusalem
In England's green and pleasant land.

John Peel

John Woodcock Graves

The most famous hunting song written about the Camberland hunter who died in 1854 at the age of seventy-eight. It was composed by John Woodcock Graves who knew Peel and who often went hunting with him, in the local fashion, on foot. Graves said of Peel: 'He was of a very limited education beyond hunting. But no wile of fox or hare could evade his scrutiny.'

D'ye ken John Peel with his coat so grey,
D'ye ken John Peel at the break of the day,
D'ye ken John Peel when he's far, far away
With his hounds and his horn in the morning?

Chorus
For the sound of his horn brought me from my bed,
And the cry of his hounds, which he oft-times led,
Peel's 'View halloo' would awaken the dead,
Or the fox from his lair in the morning.

Yes, I ken John Peel, and Ruby too,
Ranter and Ringwood, Bellman and true;
From a find to a check, from a check to a view,
From a view to a death in the morning.

Then here's to John Peel, from my heart and soul,
Let's drink to his health, let's finish the bowl;
We'll follow John Peel, through fair and through foul,
If we want a good hunt in the morning.

D'ye ken John Peel with his coat so grey?
He lived at Troutbeck once on a day;
Now he has gone far, far away,
We shall ne'er hear his voice in the morning.

Linden Lea

William Barnes

An authentic poem by a native Dorsetshire man which in
Vaughan Williams' setting has become one of England's finest
songs. It was originally written in Dorset dialect by its author
who was a clergyman and an authority on local speech. The first
line of the third verse used to read, 'Let other vo'k mëake money
vaster'. The use of the word 'moot' ('debate') to describe the
gathering of oak-trees shows your true poet.

Within the woodlands, flow'ry gladed,
By the oak trees' mossy moot,
The shining grass blades, timber shaded,
Now do quiver under foot:
And birds do whistle overhead,
And water's bubbling in its bed;
And there for me.
The apple tree
Do lean down low in Linden Lea.

When leaves, that lately were a-springing,
Now do fade within the copse,
And painted birds do hush their singing,
Up upon the timber tops:
And brown leaved fruit's a-turning red,
In cloudless sunshine overhead,
With fruit for me,
The apple tree
Do lean down low in Linden Lea.

Let other folk make money faster,
In the air of dark-room'd towns:
I don't dread a peevish master,
Though no man may heed my frowns.
I be free to go abroad,
Or take again my homeward road.
To where, for me,
The apple tree
Do lean down low in Linden Lea.

Home-Thoughts from Abroad

Robert Browning

Browning lived in Italy for fifteen years until his wife's death
in 1861. The nostalgia won in the end: he spent the last thirty
years of his life in England. Did he ever long then for the gaudy
melon-flower?

Oh, to be in England
Now that April's there,
And whoever wakes in England
Sees, some morning, unaware,
That the lowest boughs and the brush-wood sheaf
Round the elm-tree bole are in tiny leaf,
While the chaffinch sings on the orchard bough
In England – now!

And after April, when May follows,
And the whitethroat builds, and all the swallows!
Hark, where my blossomed pear-tree in the hedge
Leans to the field and scatters on the clover
Blossoms and dewdrops – at the bent spray's edge –
That's the wise thrush; he sings each song twice over,
Lest you should think he never could recapture
The first fine careless rapture!
And though the fields look rough with hoary dew,
All will be gay when noontide wakes anew
The buttercups, the little children's dower,
 – Far brighter than this gaudy melon-flower!

Pied Beauty

Gerard Manley Hopkins

Hopkins' best-known poem, celebrating the mosaic and motley world he sadly inhabited.

> Glory be to God for dappled things –
>   For skies of couple-colour as a brinded cow;
>   For rose-moles all in stipple upon trout that swim;
> Fresh-firecoal chestnut-falls; finches' wings;
> Landscape plotted and pieced – fold, fallow, and plough
>   And áll trádes, their gear and tackle and trim.
>
> All things counter, original, spare, strange;
>   Whatever is fickle, freckled (who knows how?)
>   With swift, slow; sweet, sour; adazzle, dim;
> He fathers-forth whose beauty is past change:
>   Praise him.

Up from Somerset

Fred E. Weatherly

It was inevitable that the most prodigious lyricist of all should jump on the topographical band-wagon. Fred Weatherly was, after all, born in the county. The little bit of dialect here and there did not go amiss.

Oh, we came up from Somerset,
To see the Great Review;
There was Mary drest in her Sunday best,
And our boy Billee too.
The drums were rolling rub-a-dub,
The trumpets tootled too,
When right up rode His Majesty,
An' says 'An who be you?'

'Oh, we'm come up from Somerset,
Where the cider apples grow,
We'm come to see your Majesty,
An' how the world do go,
And when you're wanting anyone,
If you'll kindly let us know,
We'll all come up from Somerset,
Because we loves you so!'

Then the Queen she look'd at Mary,
'An' what's your name?' she said,
But Mary blush'd like any rose,
'An' hung her pretty head.
So I ups and nudges Mary,
'Speak up and tell her, do!'
So she said 'If it please, your Majesty,
My name is Mary too!

An' we'm come up from Somerset,
Where the cider apples grow,
Where the gals can hem an' sew an' stitch,
And also reap and hoe,
An' if you're wanting any gals,
An' will kindly let us know,
We'll all come from Somerset,
Because we loves you so!'

Then the King look'd down at Billee-boy,
Before they rode away,
'An' what is he going for to be?'
His Majesty did say.
So Billee pull'd his forelock,
And stood up trim and true,
'Oh, I'm going to be a soldier, Sir,
For I wants to fight for you!

For we'm come up from Somerset,
Where the cider apples grow,
For we're all King's men in Somerset,
As they were long, long ago,
An' when you're wanting soldier boys,
An' there's fighting for to do,
You just send word to Somerset,
An' we'll all be up for you!'

Glorious Devon

Sir Harold Boulton

The wisdom of writing topographical songs has long been understood by songsmiths: there is a certain local market. Yet Devon has a special place in the hearts of all Englishmen and all share in its glory.

Coombe and Tor, green meadow and lane,
Birds on the waving bough,
Beetling cliffs by the surging main,
Rich red loam for the plough;
Devon's the fount of the bravest blood
That braces England's breed,
Her maidens fair as the apple bud,
And her men are men indeed.

When Adam and Eve were dispossess'd
Of the Garden hard by Heaven,
They planted another one down in the West,
'Twas Devon, 'twas Devon, glorious Devon.

Spirits to old-world heroes wake,
By river and cove and hoe,
Grenville, Hawkins, Raleigh and Drake
And a thousand more we know;
To ev'ry land the wide world o'er
Some slips of the old stock roam,
Leal friends in peace, dread foes in war,
With hearts still true to home.

Old England's counties by the sea
From East to West are seven,
But the gem of that fair galaxy
Is Devon, is Devon, glorious Devon.

Dorset, Somerset, Cornwall, Wales,
May envy the likes of we,
For the flow'r of the West, the first, the best,
The pick of the bunch us be;
Squab pie, junket, and cyder brew,
Richest of cream from the cow,
What 'ud Old England without 'em do?
And where 'ud 'un be to now?

As crumpy as a lump of lead
Be a loaf without good leaven,
And the yeast Mother England do use for her bread
Be Devon, be Devon, glorious Devon.

Loveliest of Trees

A.E. Housman

In spite of his association with it, Housman did not know Shropshire all that well. Spring comes later in the west of England than in the south and east he really knew. One assumes a late Easter that year.

Loveliest of trees, the cherry now
Is hung with bloom along the bough,
And stands about the woodland ride
Wearing white for Eastertide.

Now, of my threescore years and ten,
Twenty will not come again,
And take from seventy springs a score,
It only leaves me fifty more.

And since to look at things in bloom
Fifty springs are little room,
About the woodlands I will go
To see the cherry hung with snow.

Knocked 'em in the Old Kent Road

Albert Chevalier

Chevalier's second most famous song. He was a very reluctant music-hall artiste, who needed strong persuasion to sing his own songs on stage.

Last week down our alley come a toff,
Nice old geezer with a nasty cough,
Sees my Missus, takes 's topper off,
In a very gentlemanly way!
'Ma'am,' says he, 'I have some news to tell,
Your rich uncle Tom of Camberwell,
Popped off recent which it ain't a sell
Leaving you 'is little donkey shay.'

Chorus
'Wot cher!' all the neighbours cried,
'Who're yer goin' to meet, Bill?
Have you bought the street, Bill?'
Laugh! I thought I should 'ave died,
Knocked 'em in the Old Kent Road!

Some say nasty things about the moke.
One cove thinks 'is leg is really broke.
That's 'is envy, 'cos we're carriage folk,
Like the toffs as ride in Rotten Row!
Straight it woke the alley up a bit,
Thought our lodger would 'ave 'ad a fit.
When my Missus who's a real wit
Says 'I 'ates a Bus because it's low!'

Chorus

When we starts the blessed donkey stops.
He won't move so out I quickly 'ops
Pals start whackin' 'im when down he drops,
Someone says 'e wasn't made to go.
Lor' it might 'ave been a four-in-'and
My old Dutch knows 'ow to do the grand.
First she bows and then she waves 'er 'and
Calling out 'Were goin' for a blow!'
Chorus

Ev'ry evenin' on the stroke of five
Me and Missus take a little drive.
You'd say, 'Wonderful they're still alive,'
Straight you saw that little donkey go.
I soon showed him that 'ed 'ave to do
Just whatever 'e wanted to;
Still I shan't forget that rowdy crew
'Ollerin', 'Woa! steady! Neddy Woa!'

Chorus

The Glory of the Garden

Rudyard Kipling

Patriotic and ecological reminder about the need to care for the *real* English wealth. It was the appropriate if somewhat presumptuous title of the British Arts Council report for 1984.

Our England is a garden that is full of stately views,
Of borders, beds and shrubberies and lawns and avenues,
With statues on the terraces and peacocks strutting by;
But the Glory of the Garden lies in more than meets
the eye.

For where the old thick laurels grow, along the thin
red wall,
You'll find the tool- and potting-sheds which are the
heart of all,
The cold-frames and the hot-houses, the dung-pits and
the tanks,
The rollers, carts, and drain-pipes, with the barrows
and the planks.

And there you'll see the gardeners, the men and
'prentice boys
Told off to do as they are bid and do it without noise;
For, except when seeds are planted and we shout to
scare the birds,
The Glory of the Garden it abideth not in words.

And some can pot begonias and some can bud a rose,
And some are hardly fit to trust with anything that grows;
But they can roll and trim the lawns and sift the sand
and loam,
For the Glory of the Garden occupieth all who come.

Our England is a garden, and such gardens are not made
By singing: – 'Oh, how beautiful,' and sitting in the shade
While better men than we go out and start their
        working lives
At grubbing weeds from gravel-paths with broken
        dinner-knives.

There's not a pair of legs so thin, there's not a head
        so thick,
There's not a hand so weak and white, nor yet a heart
        so sick,
But it can find some needful job that's crying to be done,
For the Glory of the Garden glorifieth every one.

Then seek your job with thankfulness and work till
        further orders,
If it's only netting strawberries or killing slugs on borders;
And when your back stops aching and your hands begin
        to harden,
You will find yourself a partner in the Glory of the Garden.

Oh, Adam was a gardener, and God who made him sees
That half a proper gardener's work is done upon his knees
So when your work is finished, you can wash your
        hands and pray
For the Glory of the Garden that it may not pass away!
And the Glory of the Garden it shall never pass away!

The Rolling English Road

G.K. Chesterton

Chesterton at his most English, verging on the jolliness that made
a later age distrust him, but contriving a poem of the heart of
the country that will outlive its critics.

Before the Roman came to Rye or out of Severn strode,
The rolling English drunkard made the rolling English road.
A reeling road, a rolling road, that rambles round the shire,
And after him the parson ran, the sexton and the squire;
A merry road, a mazy road, and such as we did tread
The night we went to Birmingham by way of Beachy Head.

I know no harm of Bonaparte and plenty of the Squire,
And for to fight the Frenchman I did not much desire;
But I did bash their baggonets because they came arrayed
To straighten out the crooked road an English drunkard
    made,
Where you and I went down the lane with ale-mugs in our
    hands,
The night we went to Glastonbury by way of Goodwin Sands.

His sins they were forgiven him; or why do flowers run
Behind him; and the hedges all strengthening in the sun?
The wild thing went from left to right and knew not which
    was which,
But the wild rose was above him when they found him in
    the ditch.
God pardon us, nor harden us; we did not see so clear
The night we went to Bannockburn by way of Brighton Pier.

My friends, we will not go again or ape an ancient rage,
Or stretch the folly of our youth to be the shame of age,
But walk with clearer eyes and ears this path that wandereth,
And see undrugged in evening light the decent inn of death;
For there is good news yet to hear and fine things to be seen
Before we go to Paradise by way of Kensal Green.

Adlestrop

Edward Thomas

There is no longer a station at Adlestrop but local people conscious of the village's claim to fame have affixed the name-plate to the bus-station. Cotswold people care about such things.

Yes, I remember Adlestrop –
The name, because one afternoon
Of heat the express-train drew up there
Unwontedly. It was late June.

The steam hissed. Someone cleared his throat.
No one left and no one came
On the bare platform. What I saw
Was Adlestrop – only the name

And willows, willow-herb, and grass,
And meadowsweet, and haycocks dry,
No whit less still and lonely fair
Than the high cloudlets in the sky.

And for that minute a blackbird sang
Close by, and round him, mistier,
Farther and farther, all the birds
Of Oxfordshire and Gloucestershire.

Old Father Thames

Anon

A song like 'Glorious Devon' and 'The Floral Dance' which owes
its fame not so much to intrinsic merit but to the marvellous
recordings made of it by the Australian bass-baritone, Peter
Dawson.

There's some folks who always worry,
And some folks who never care.
But in this world of rush and hurry
It matters neither here nor there.
Be steady and realistic,
Don't hanker for gold or gems.
Be carefree and optimistic,
Like old Father Thames.

Chorus
High in the hills, down in the dales,
Happy and fancy free,
Old Father Thames keeps rolling along
Down to the mighty sea.
What does he know, what does he care,
Nothing for you or me.
Old Father Thames keeps rolling along
Down to the mighty sea.
He never seems to worry,
Doesn't care for fortune's fame,
He never seems to hurry,
But he gets there just the same.
Kingdoms may come, kingdoms may go,
Whatever the end may be,
Old Father Thames keeps rolling along,
Down to the mighty sea.

On Ilkley Moor Baht 'at

Anon

The Yorkshire National Anthem, as its people insist, ignoring the implicit threat of secession that their chauvinism contains.

Wheear 'as tha been sin' ah saw thee?
On Ilk - ley Moor baht 'at.
Wheear 'as tha been sin' ah saw thee?
Wheear 'as tha been sin' ah saw thee?
Wheear 'as tha been sin' ah saw thee?
    sin' ah saw thee?
On Ilk - ley Moor baht 'at,
On Ilk - ley Moor baht 'at,
On Ilk - ley Moor baht 'at.

2. Tha's been a coortin', Mary Jane.

3. Tha'll go and get thi deeath o' cowld.

4. Then we shall ha' to bury thee.

5. Then t'worms'll come an' ate thee oop.

6. Then t'ducks'll come an' ate t'worms.

7. Then we shall go an' ate t'ducks.

8. Then we shall all 'ave eaten thee.

Sussex by the Sea

Anon

Another local song yet without a specifically local flavour. It has a jolly tune especially when played by a brass band but the only thing Sussexy is the title. Any other place-name (by the sea, of course) would have done, even Vladivostok.

Now is the time for marching,
Now let your hearts be gay,
Hark to the merry bugles
Sounding along our way.
So let your voices ring, my boys,
And take the time from me,
And I'll sing you a song
As we march along
Of Sussex by the sea.

Chorus:
For we're the men from Sussex,
Sussex by the sea,
We plough and sow and reap and mow
And useful men are we.
And when you go to Sussex,
Whoever you may be
You may tell them all
That we stand or fall
For Sussex by the sea.
Oh Sussex, Sussex by the sea,
Good old Sussex by the sea,
You may tell them all
That we stand or fall,
For Sussex by the sea.

Far o'er the seas we wander,
Wide thro' the world we roam,
Far from the kind hearts yonder,
Far from our dear old home.
But ne'er shall we forget, my boys,
And true we'll ever be,
To the girls so kind
That we left behind
In Sussex by the sea.

A Nightingale Sang in Berkeley Square

Eric Maschwitz

One of the great modern songs about London appreciated even
more by non-Londoners than by its natives. It was written in
1940 when the protective magic seemed to have ceased to work.

When true lovers meet in Mayfair,
So the legends tell,
Song-birds sing,
Winter turns to Spring,
Ev'ry winding street in Mayfair
Falls beneath the spell.
I know such enchantment can be,
'Cause it happened to me.

That certain night, the night we met,
There was magic abroad in the air.
There were angels dining at the Ritz,
And a nightingale sang in Berk'ley Square.
I may be right, I may be wrong
But I'm perfectly willing to swear,
That when you turned and smiled at me
A nightingale sang in Berk'ley Square.

The moon that lingered over London Town,
Poor puzzled moon, he wore a frown.
How could he know that we were so in love?
The whole darn' world seemed upside down.
The streets of town were paved with stars;
It was such a romantic affair,
And as we kissed and said 'goodnight'
A nightingale sang in Berk'ley Square.

Strange it was, how sweet and strange!
There was never a dream to compare
With that hazy, crazy night we met,
When a nightingale sang in Berk'ley Square.
This heart of mine beat loud and fast,
Like a merry-go-round in a fair,
For we were dancing cheek to cheek
And a nightingale sang in Berk'ley Square.

When dawn came stealing up, all gold and blue
To interrupt our rendezvous,
I still remember how you smiled and said,
'Was that a dream or was it true?'
Our homeward step was just as light
As the tap-dancing feet of Astaire,
And like an echo far away
A nightingale sang in Berk'ley Square.

I know 'cause I was there
That night in Berk'ley Square.

Pot Pourri from a Surrey Garden

John Betjeman

The title was derived from a book of quiet thoughts written by a lady who might be of a different species from Betjeman's 'Pam' but *she* is a great creation and many have loved her besides the poet.

Miles of pram in the wind and Pam in the gorse track,
   Coco-nut smell of the broom and a packet of Weights
Press'd in the sand. The thud of a hoof on a horse track –
       A horse-riding horse for a horse-track –
       Conifer country of Surrey approached
Through remarkable wrought-iron gates.

Over your boundary now, I wash my face in a bird-bath,
   Then which path shall I take? That over there by the pram?
Down by the pond? or else, shall I take the slippery third path,
       Trodden away with gymn. shoes,
       Beautiful fir-dry alley that leads
To the bountiful body of Pam?

Pam, I adore you, Pam, you great big mountainous sports girl,
   Whizzing them over the net, full of the strength of five;
That old Malvernian brother, you zephyr and khaki shorts girl,
       Although he's playing for Woking,
       Can't stand up
To your wonderful backhand drive.

See the strength of her arm, as firm and hairy as Hendren's;
   See the size of her thighs, the pout of her lips as, cross,
And full of a pent-up strength, she swipes at the rhododendrons,
       Lucky the rhododendrons,
       And flings her arrogant love-lock
Back with a petulant toss.

Over the redolent pinewoods, in at the bathroom casement,
 One fine Saturday, Windlesham bells shall call
Up the Butterfield aisle rich with Gothic enlacement,
   Licensed now for embracement,
   Pam and I, as the organ
Thunders over you all.

I Leave My Heart in an English Garden

Christopher Hassall

This song from *Dear Miss Phoebe* which opened at the Phoenix Theatre in 1950 seems at first sight no more than the animation of the chocolate box figures that come from the same source, J.M. Barrie's *Quality Street*. Yet in context the song has a remarkable effect. The combination of Hassall's deceptively simple lyrics and Harry Parr Davies' music changes what should be intolerably artificial into something very moving.

Breezes in the long grass ruffling my hair,
Hollyhock and bluebell, scenting the air.
Nothing in the world can ever be
Such a sweet memory;
Nothing in the world was ever so fair.

I leave my heart in an English garden
Safe where the elm and the oak stand by.
Tho' the years rise and roll away,
Still shall those watchmen stay
Bold in the blue of an English sky.
I leave my dreams in an English garden,
Safe where the breezes of England blow.
When the high ways are dark and drear,
I'll know there's sunshine here,
Bright where the roses of England grow.

Dawn on the Aegean redd'ning the foam,
Sunset over Cyprus, Springtime in Rome.
Lovely are the lands where, I dare say,
I could stay for a day;
None of them are quite as lovely as home.

6

The Humour of It

The Twa Corbies

Anon

Corbies are crows, and the poem in its compression and bleak
humour is a fine example of the Border ballad.

As I was walking all alane,
I heard twa corbies making a mane;
The tane unto the t'other say,
'Where sall we gang and dine to-day?'

'In behint yon auld fail dyke,
I wot there lies a new slain knight;
And naebody kens that he lies there,
But his hawk, his hound, and lady fair.

'His hound is to the hunting gane,
His hawk to fetch the wild-fowl hame,
His lady's ta'en another mate,
So we may mak our dinner sweet.

'Ye'll sit on his white hause-bane,
And I'll pike out his bonny blue een;
Wi ae lock o his gowden hair
We'll theek our nest when it grows bare.

'Mony a one for him makes mane,
But nane sall ken where he is gane;
Oer his white banes, when they are bare,
The wind sall blaw for evermair.'

Letter to the Right Honourable, The Earl of Chesterfield

Samuel Johnson

Philip Dormer Stanhope, 4th Earl of Chesterfield (1694 - 1773) is famous as a statesman and diplomat, and for the letters he wrote to his illegitimate son, Philip Stanhope, which represent a full, if slightly cynical, education for any young aristocrat. He had not responded to Johnson's original 'Plan' for the Dictionary in 1747 but eight years later, on its publication, wrote two articles in the *World* recommending it. Johnson's letter is a splendid example of the retort courteous.

February 7, 1755.

My Lord,

I have been lately informed, by the proprietor of the World, that two papers, in which my Dictionary is recommended to the public, were written by your Lordship. To be so distinguished is an honour, which, being very little accustomed to favours from the great, I know not well how to recieve, or in what terms to acknowledge.

When, upon some slight encouragement, I first visited your Lordship, I was overpowered, like the rest of mankind, by the enchantment of your address, and could not forebear to wish that I might boast myself *Le vainqueur du vainqueur de la terre*; - that I might obtain that regard for which I saw the world contending; but I found my attendance so little encouraged that neither pride nor modesty would suffer me to continue it. When I had once addressed your Lordship in public I had exhausted all the art or pleasing which a retired and uncourtly scholar can possess. I had done all that I could; and no man is well pleased to have his all neglected, be it ever so little.

Seven years, my Lord, have now passed since I waited in your outward rooms, or was repulsed from your door; during which time I have been pushing on my work through difficulties, of which it is useless to complain, and have brought it at last to the verge of publication, without one act of assistance, one word of encouragement, or one smile of favour. Such treatment I did not expect, for I never had a Patron before.

The shepherd in Virgil grew at last acquainted with Love, and found him a native of the rocks.

Is not a Patron, my Lord, one who looks with unconcern on a man struggling for life in the water, and, when he has reached ground, encumbers him with help? The notice which you have been pleased to take of my labours, had it been early, had been kind; but it has been delayed till I am indifferent, and cannot enjoy it; till I am solitary, and cannot impart it; till I am known, and do not want it. I hope it is no very cynical asperity not to confess obligations where no benefit has been received, or to be unwilling that the public should consider me as owing that to a Patron, which Providence has enabled me to do for myself.

Having carried on my work thus far with so little obligation to any favourer of learning, I shall not be disappointed though I should conclude it, if less be possible, with less; for I have been long awakened from that dream of hope, in which I once boasted myself with so much exultation, my Lord,

Your Lordship's most humble, most obedient servant,
Sam Johnson.

Elegy on the Death of a Mad Dog

Oliver Goldsmith

One of the jewels of the *Vicar of Wakefield* containing the famous
last line, typical of Goldsmith's gentle, topsy-turvy humour.

Good people all, of every sort,
  Give ear unto my song;
And if you find it wond'rous short,
  It cannot hold you long.

In Islington there was a man,
  Of whom the world might say,
That still a godly race he ran,
  Whene'er he went to pray.

A kind and gentle heart he had,
  To comfort friends and foes;
The naked every day he clad,
  When he put on his clothes.

And in that town a dog was found,
  As many dogs there be,
Both mongrel, puppy, whelp, and hound,
  And curs of low degree.

This dog and man at first were friends;
  But when a pique began,
The dog, to gain some private ends,
  Went mad and bit the man.

Around from all the neighbouring streets
  The wond'ring neighbours ran,
And swore the dog had lost its wits,
  To bite so good a man.

The wound it seem'd both sore and sad
   To every Christian eye;
And while they swore the dog was mad,
   They swore the man would die.

But soon a wonder came to light,
   That showed the rogues they lied:
The man recover'd of the bite,
   The dog it was that died.

To a Louse

Robert Burns

Famous poem originally subtitled 'On seeing one on a lady's bonnet at church' by the author who also wrote about a field-mouse, which is sharply satirical and mildly bromidic and contains his most quoted couplet.

Ha! whare ye gaun, ye crowlan ferlie,
Your impudence protects you fairly:
I canna say but ye strunt rarely,
   Owre gawze and lace;
Tho' faith, I fear ye dine but sparely
   On sic a place.

Ye ugly, creepan, blastet wonner,
Detestet, shunn'd, by saunt an' sinner,
How daur ye set your fit upon her,
   Sae fine a Lady!
Gae somewhere else and seek your dinner,
   On some poor body.

Swith, in some beggar's haffet squattle;
There ye may creep, and sprawl, and sprattle,
Wi'ither kindred, jumping cattle,
   In shoals and nations;
Whare horn nor bane ne'er daur unsettle
   Your thick plantations.

Now haud you there, ye're out o' sight,
Below the fatt'rels, snug and tight,
Na faith ye yet! ye'll no be right,
   Till ye've got on it,
The vera tapmost, towrin height
   O' Miss's bonnet.

My sooth! right bauld ye set your nose out,
As plump an' gray as onie grozet:
O for some rank, mercurial rozet,
  Or fell, red smeddum,
I'd gie you sic a hearty dose o't,
  Wad dress your droddum!

I wad na been surpriz'd to spy
You on an auld wife's flainen toy;
Or aiblins some bit duddie boy,
  On's wylecoat;
But Miss's fine Lunardi, fye!
  Haw daur ye do't?

O Jenny dinna toss your head,
An' set your beauties a' abread!
Ye little ken what cursed speed
  The blastie's makin!
Thae winks and finger-ends, I dread,
  Are notice takin!

O wad some Pow'r the giftie gie us
To see oursels as others see us!
It wad frae monie a blunder free us
  An' foolish notion:
What airs in dress an' gait wad lea'e us,
  And ev'n Devotion!

An Austrian Army

Alaric A. Watts

This famous alphabetic, alliterative poem about one of Austria's many attempts (1687) to wrest Belgrade from the Turks was published in *The Trifler,* the Westminster School magazine, in 1817.

An Austrian army awfully array'd,
Boldly by battery besieged Belgrade.
Cossack commanders cannonading come
Dealing destruction's devastating doom:
Every endeavour engineers essay,
For fame, for fortune fighting-furious fray!
Generals 'gainst generals grapple, gracious God!
How Heaven honours heroic hardihood!
Infuriate – indiscriminate in ill –
Kinsmen kill kindred – kindred kinsmen kill:
Labour low levels loftiest, longest lines,
Men march 'mid mounds, 'mid moles, 'mid murd'rous
        mines:
Now noisy noxious numbers notice nought
Of outward obstacles, opposing ought –
Poor patriots – partly purchased – partly press'd
Quite quaking, quickly 'Quarter! quarter!' quest:
Reasons returns, religious right redounds,
Suwarrow stops such sanguinary sounds.
Truce to thee, Turkey, triumph to thy train,
Unwise, unjust, unmerciful Ukraine!
Vanish, vain victory! Vanish, victory vain!
Why wish we welfare? Wherefore welcome were
Xerxes, Ximenes, Xanthus, Xavier?
Yield, yield, ye youths, ye yeomen, yield your yell:
Zeno's, Zimmermann's, Zoroaster's zeal,
Again attract; arts against arms appeal!

She was Poor but She was Honest

Anon

The stuff of the Penny-Gaff melodrama sung with some tongue-in-cheek reservation but now entirely guyed in spite of a general conviction about the truth of the last stanza.

She was poor but she was honest,
  Victim of a rich man's game;
First he loved her, then he left her,
  And she lost her maiden name.

Then she hastened up to London,
  For to hide her grief and shame;
There she met another rich man,
  And she lost her name again.

See her riding in her carriage,
  In the Park and all so gay;
All the nibs and nobby persons
  Come to pass the time of day.

See them at the gay theáter
  Sitting in the costly stalls;
With one hand she holds the programme,
  With the other strokes his hand.

See him have her dance in Paris
  In her frilly underclothes;
All those Frenchies there applauding
  When she strikes a striking pose.

See the little country village
  Where her aged parents live;
Though they drink champagne she sends them,
  Still they never can forgive.

In the rich man's arms she flutters
    Like a bird with a broken wing;
First he loved her, then he left her,
    And she hasn't got a ring.

See him in his splendid mansion
    Entertaining with the best,
While the girl as he has ruined
    Entertains a sordid guest.

See him riding in his carriage
    Past the gutter where she stands;
He has made a stylish marriage
    While she wrings her ringless hands.

See him in the House of Commons
    Passing laws to put down crime,
While the victim of his passions
    Slinks away to hide her shame.

See her on the bridge at midnight
    Crying, 'Farewell, faithless love!'
There's a scream, a splash – Good Heavens!
    What is she a-doing of?

Then they dragged her from the river,
    Water from her clothes they wrung;
They all thought that she was drownded,
    But the corpse got up and sung:

'It's the same the whole world over;
    It's the poor as gets the blame,
It's the rich that gets the pleasure –
    Ain't it all a bleeding shame!'

The Owl and the Pussy-Cat

Edward Lear

From *The Book of Nonsense* which Lear wrote in 1860 to amuse the grandchildren of his patron, the Earl of Derby, the catalogue of whose zoological garden he was illustrating.

The Owl and the Pussy-Cat went to sea
   In a beautiful pea-green boat,
They took some honey, and plenty of money,
   Wrapped up in a five-pound note.
The Owl looked up to the stars above,
   And sang to a small guitar,
'O lovely Pussy! O Pussy, my love,
   What a beautiful Pussy you are,
     You are,
     You are!
   What a beautiful Pussy you are!'

Pussy said to the Owl, 'You elegant fowl!
   How charmingly sweet you sing!
O let us be married! too long we have tarried
   But what shall we do for a ring?'
They sailed away for a year and a day,
   To the land where the Bong-tree grows,
And there in a wood a Piggy-wig stood,
   With a ring at the end of his nose,
     His nose,
     His nose,
   With a ring at the end of his nose.

'Dear Pig, are you willing to sell for one shilling
   Your ring?' Said the Piggy, 'I will.'
So they took it away, and were married next day
   By the Turkey who lives on the hill.
They dined on mince, and slices of quince,
   Which they ate with a runcible spoon;
And hand in hand, on the edge of the sand,
   They danced by the light of the moon,
     The moon,
     The moon,
   They danced by the light of the moon.

'You are old, Father William'

Lewis Carroll

A parody of a moral verse tract by Robert Southey (by far the
least of the Lake Poets) called 'The Old Man's Comforts and
How He Gained Them' which Alice Liddell would certainly have
known by heart.

'You are old, Father William,' the young man said,
　　'And your hair has become very white;
And yet you incessantly stand on your head –
　　Do you think, at your age, it is right?'

'In my youth,' Father William replied to his son,
　　'I feared it might injure the brain;
But, now that I'm perfectly sure I have none,
　　Why, I do it again and again.'

'You are old,' said the youth, 'as I mentioned before,
　　And have grown most uncommonly fat;
Yet you turned a back-somersault in at the door –
　　Pray, what is the reason of that?'

'In my youth,' said the sage, as he shook his grey locks,
　　I kept all my limbs very supple
By the use of this ointment – one shilling the box –
　　Allow me to sell you a couple?'

'You are old,' said the youth, 'and your jaws are too weak
　　For anything tougher than suet;
Yet you finished the goose, with the bones and the beak –
　　Pray, how did you manage to do it?'

'In my youth,' said his father, 'I took to the law,
  And argued each case with my wife;
And the muscular strength, which it gave to my jaw,
  Has lasted the rest of my life.'

'You are old,' said the youth, 'one would hardly suppose
  That your eye was as steady as ever;
Yet you balance an eel on the end of your nose –
  What made you so awfully clever?'

'I have answered three questions, and that is enough,'
  Said his father. 'Don't give yourself airs!
Do you think I can listen all day to such stuff?
  Be off, or I'll kick you down-stairs!'

The Modern Major-General

W.S. Gilbert

Gilbert's fastest patter-song from Act I of *The Pirates of Penzance* (1879). The model for General Stanley was Sir Garnet Wolseley (1833 - 1913) who was the general sent to relieve Khartoum and later given the task of reorganising the Army. He was not displeased with the characterisation and used to sing the song himself.

I am the very pattern of a modern Major-Gineral,
I've information vegetable, animal, and mineral;
I know the kings of England, and I quote the fights historical,
From Marathon to Waterloo, in order categorical;
I'm very well acquainted, too, with matters mathematical,
I understand equations, both the simple and quadratical;
About binomial theorem I'm teeming with a lot o' news,
With interesting facts about the square of the hypotenuse.
I'm very good at integral and differential calculus,
I know the scientific names of beings animalculous.
In short, in matters vegetable, animal, and mineral,
I am the very model of a modern Major-Gineral.

I know our mythic history – KING ARTHUR'S and SIR
    CARADOC'S,
I answer hard acrostics, I've a pretty taste for paradox;
I quote in elegiacs all the crimes of HELIOGABALUS,
In conics I can floor peculiarities parabolous.
I tell undoubted RAPHAELS from GERARD DOWS and
    ZOFFANIES,
I know the croaking chorus from the 'Frogs' of ARISTOPHANES;
Then I can hum a fugue, of which I've heard the music's
    din afore,
And whistle all the airs from that confounded nonsense 'Pinafore.'
Then I can write a washing-bill in Babylonic cuneiform,
And tell you every detail of CARACTACUS'S uniform.

In short, in matters vegetable, animal, and mineral,
I am the very model of a modern Major-Gineral.

In fact, when I know what is meant by 'mamelon' and 'ravelin,'
When I can tell at sight a Chassepôt rifle from a javelin,
When such affairs as *sorties* and surprises I'm more wary at,
And when I know precisely what is meant by Commissariat,
When I have learnt what progress has been made in modern
    gunnery,
When I know more of tactics than a novice in a nunnery,
In short, when I've a smattering of elementary strategy,
You'll say a better Major-Giner*al* has never *sat* a gee –
For my military knowledge, though I'm plucky and adventury,
Has only been brought down to the beginning of the century.
But still in learning vegetable, animal, and mineral,
I am the very model of a modern Major-Gineral!

Tit Willow

W.S. Gilbert

Gilbert in a gentle mood in *The Mikado* (1884).

On a tree by a river a little tom-tit
    Sang 'Willow, titwillow, titwillow!'
And I said to him, 'Dicky-bird, why do you sit
    Singing "Willow, titwillow, titwillow"?
Is it weakness of intellect, birdie?' I cried,
'Or a rather tough worm in your little inside?'
With a shake of his poor little head he replied,
    'Oh, willow, titwillow, titwillow!'

He slapped at his chest, as he sat on that bough,
    Singing 'Willow, titwillow, titwillow!'
And a cold perspiration bespangled his brow,
    'Oh, willow, titwillow, titwillow!'
He sobbed and he sighed, and a gurgle he gave,
Then he threw himself into the billowy wave,
And an echo arose from the suicide's grave –
    'Oh, willow, titwillow, titwillow!'

Now, I feel just as sure as I'm sure that my name
    Isn't Willow, titwillow, titwillow,
That 'twas blighted affection that made him exclaim,
    'Oh, willow, titwillow, titwillow!'
And if you remain callous and obdurate, I
Shall perish as he did, and you will know why,
Though I probably shall not exclaim as I die,
    'Oh, willow, titwillow, titwillow!'

The Ruined Maid

Thomas Hardy

Hardy in an uncharacteristically light mood but with an edge.

'O Melia, my dear, this does everything crown!
Who could have supposed I should meet you in Town?
And whence such fair garments, such prosperi-ty?'
'O didn't you know I'd been ruined?' said she.

 – 'You left us in tatters, without shoes or socks,
Tired of digging potatoes, and spudding up docks;
And now you've gay bracelets and bright feathers three!'
'Yes: that's how we dress when we're ruined,' said she.

 – 'At home in the barton you said "thee" and "thou,"
And "thik oon," and "theäs oon," and "t'other"; but now
Your talking quite fits 'ee for high compa-ny!'
'Some polish is gained with one's ruin,' said she.

 – 'Your hands were like paws then, your face blue and
      bleak
But now I'm bewitched by your delicate cheek,
And your little gloves fit as on any la-dy!'
'We never do work when we're ruined,' said she.

 – 'You used to call home-life a hag-ridden dream,
And you'd sigh, and you'd sock; but at present you seem
To know not of megrims or melancho-ly!'
'True. One's pretty lively when ruined,' said she.

 – 'I wish I had feathers, a fine sweeping gown,
And a delicate face, and could strut about Town!'
'My dear – a raw country girl, such as you be,
Cannot quite expect that. You ain't ruined,' said she.

Champagne Charlie

George Leybourne

The most famous song by George Leybourne (real name Joe Saunders) the self-styled Lion Comique. He dressed in imitation of the mid-Victorian swell with cigar, monocle and Dundreary whiskers and sang about the delights of dissipation. His private life was not free from practice of what he preached and he died at forty-two.

Some people go for funny drinks and down 'em by the pail,
Like coffee, cocoa, tea, and milk and even Adam's ale;
For my part they can keep the lot I never would complain,
I wouldn't touch the bloomin' stuff
I only drink champagne.

Chorus
For Champagne Charlie is my name,
Champagne drinking is my game,
There's no drink as good as fizz! fizz! fizz!
I'll drink ev'ry drop there is, is, is!
All round town it is the same,
By pop! pop! pop! I rose to fame,
I'm the Idol of the barmaids,
And Champagne Charlie is my name.

The Man on the Flying Trapeze

George Leybourne

Another of the songs made famous by Joe Saunders. It was
written in honour of Jules Leotard, the trapeze artist who gave
his name to the practice ballet costume.

Oh, the girl that I loved she was handsome,
I tried all I knew her to please.
But I couldn't please her a quarter as well
As the man on the flying trapeze.

Chorus
Oh, he flies through the air with the greatest of ease,
This daring young man on the flying trapeze.
His figure is handsome, all girls he can please,
And my love he purloined her away.

Last night as usual I went to her home.
There sat her old father and mother alone.
I asked for my love and they soon made it known
That she-e had flown away.

She packed up her box and eloped in the night,
To go-o with him at his ease.
He lowered her down from a four-story flight,
By means of his flying trapeze.

He took her to town and he dressed her in tights,
That he-e might live at his ease.
He ordered her up to the tent's awful height,
To appear on the flying trapeze.

Now she flies through the air with the greatest of ease,
This daring young girl on the flying trapeze.
Her figure is handsome, all men she can please,
And my love is purloinèd away.

Once I was happy, but now I'm forlorn,
Like an old coat that is tattered and torn,
Left to the wide world to fret and to mourn;
Betrayed by a maid in her teens.

The Ladies

Rudyard Kipling

More evidence of Kipling's tolerance of 'takin' yer fun where
ye find it' provided you were a soldier and stationed east of Suez
– self-exculpatory, too, amid the nuggets of commonsense.

I've taken my fun where I've found it;
  I've rogued an' I've ranged in my time
I've 'ad my pickin' o' sweethearts,
  An' four o' the lot was prime.
One was an 'arf-caste widow,
  One was a woman at Prome,
One was the wife of a *jemadar-sais*,
  An' one is a girl at 'ome.

Now I aren't no 'and with the ladies,
  For, takin' 'em all along,
You never can say till you've tried 'em,
  An' then you are like to be wrong.
There's times when you'll think that you mightn't,
  There's times when you'll know that you might;
But the things you will learn from the Yellow an' Brown,
  They'll 'elp you a lot with the White!

I was a young un at 'Oogli,
  Shy as a girl to begin;
Aggie de Castrer she made me,
  An' Aggie was clever as sin;
Older than me, but my first un –
  More like a mother she were –
Showed me the way to promotion an' pay,
  An' I learned about women from 'er!

Then I was ordered to Burma,
  Actin' in charge o' Bazar,

An' I got me a tiddy live 'eathen
　Through buying' supplies off 'er pa.
Funny an' yellow an' faithful –
　Doll in a teacup she were –
But we lived on the square, like a true-married pair,
　An' I learned about women from 'er!

Then we was shifted to Neemuch
　(Or I might ha' been keepin' 'er now),
An' I took with a shiny she-devil,
　The wife of a nigger at Mhow;
'Taught me the gipsy-folks' *bolee*;
　Kind o' volcano she were,
For she knifed me one night 'cause I wished she was white,
　And I learned about women from 'er!

Then I come 'ome in a trooper,
　'Long of a kid o' sixteen –
'Girl from a convent at Meerut,
　The straightest I ever 'ave seen.
Love at first sight was 'er trouble,
　She didn't know what it were;
An' I wouldn't do such, 'cause I liked 'er too much,
　But – I learned about women from 'er!

I've taken my fun where I've found it,
　An' now I must pay for my fun,
For the more you 'ave known o' the others
　The less will you settle to one;
An' the end of it's sittin' and thinkin',
　An' dreamin' Hell-fires to see;
So be warned by my lot (which I know you will not),
　An' learn about women from me!

Henry King

WHO CHEWED BITS OF STRING, AND WAS EARLY CUT OFF IN DREADFUL AGONIES

Hilaire Belloc

The pathological effects of playing internal cats-cradle.

The Chief Defect of Henry King
Was chewing little bits of String.
At last he swallowed some which tied
Itself in ugly Knots inside.
Physicians of the Utmost Fame
Were called at once; but when they came
They answered, as they took their Fees,
'There is no Cure for this Disease.
Henry will very soon be dead.'
His Parents stood about his Bed
Lamenting his Untimely Death,
When Henry, with his Latest Breath,
Cried 'Oh, my Friends, be warned by me,
That Breakfast, Dinner, Lunch, and Tea
Are all the Human Frame requires . . .'
With that, the Wretched Child expires.

Matilda

WHO TOLD LIES, AND WAS BURNED TO DEATH

Hilaire Belloc

Cautionary Tales and several books of *Beasts for Bad Children* from which this piece and the last are taken (along with *The Path to Rome* and some essays) are the bits of Belloc most likely to survive. But then, they are a splendid legacy. *The Second Mrs Tanqueray* was a mildly scandalous play by Sir Arthur Wing Pinero.

Matilda told such Dreadful Lies,
It made one Gasp and Stretch one's Eyes;
Her Aunt, who, from her Earliest Youth,
Had kept a Strict Regard for Truth,
Attempted to Believe Matilda:
The effort very nearly killed her,
And would have done so, had not She
Discovered this Infirmity.
For once, towards the Close of Day,
Matilda, growing tired of play,
And finding she was left alone,
Went tiptoe to the Telephone
And summoned the Immediate Aid
Of London's Noble Fire-Brigade.
Within an hour the Gallant Band
Were pouring in on every hand,
From Putney, Hackney Downs, and Bow.
With Courage high and Hearts a-glow,
They galloped, roaring through the Town,
'Matilda's House is Burning Down!'
Inspired by British Cheers and Loud
Proceeding from the Frenzied Crowd,
They ran their ladders through a score
Of windows on the Ball Room Floor;

And took Peculiar Pains to Souse
The Pictures up and down the House,
Until Matilda's Aunt succeeded
In showing them they were not needed;
And even then she had to pay
To get the Men to go away!

It happened that a few Weeks later
Her Aunt was off to the Theatre
To see that Interesting Play
The Second Mrs Tanqueray.
She had refused to take her Niece
To hear this Entertaining Piece:
A Deprivation Just and Wise
To Punish her for Telling Lies.
That Night a Fire *did* break out –
You should have heard Matilda Shout!
You should have heard her Scream and Bawl,
And throw the window up and call
To People passing in the Street –
(The rapidly increasing Heat
Encouraging her to obtain
Their confidence) – but all in vain!
For every time She shouted 'Fire!'
They only answered 'Little Liar!'
And therefore when her Aunt returned,
Matilda, and the House, were Burned.

Ruthless Rhymes

Harry Graham

Graham was writing splendid rhymes like these long before the Americans named black humour and supposed they invented it.

The Stern Parent

Father heard his Children scream,
So he threw them in the stream,
Saying, as he drowned the third,
'Children should be seen, *not* heard!'

Tender-Heartedness

Billy, in one of his nice new sashes,
Fell in the fire and was burnt to ashes;
Now, although the room grows chilly,
I haven't the heart to poke poor Billy.

The Englishman's Home

I was playing golf the day
    That the Germans landed;
All our troops had run away,
    All our ships were stranded;
And the thought of England's shame
Altogether spoilt my game.

Calculating Clara

O'er the rugged mountain's brow
    Clara threw the twins she nursed,
And remarked, 'I wonder now
    Which will reach the bottom first?'

Mr Jones

'There's been an accident!' they said,
'Your servant's cut in half; he's dead!'
'Indeed!' said Mr Jones, 'and please
Send me the half that's got my keys.'

Necessity

Late last night I slew my wife,
    Stretched her on the parquet flooring;
I was loth to take her life,
    But I *had* to stop her snoring!

Clerihews

E. C. Bentley

It is not given to many to invent a new literary form but Bentley managed to create this four-line, two-coupleted, succinct form of biography. He called it after his second name.

(i)

The Art of Biography
Is different from Geography.
Geography is about Maps,
But Biography is about Chaps.

(ii)

What I like about Clive
Is that he is no longer alive.
There is a great deal to be said
For being dead.

(iii)

I am *not* Mahomet.
– Far from it.
That is the mistake
All of you seem to make.

(iv)

George the Third
Ought never to have occurred.
One can only wonder
At so grotesque a blunder.

Two Poems
(after A.E. Housman)

Hugh Kingsmill

Two neat send-ups of Housman's *Shropshire Lad* by a master parodist.

(i)

What, still alive at twenty-two,
A clean upstanding chap like you?
Sure, if your throat 'tis hard to slit,
Slit your girl's, and swing for it.

Like enough, you won't be glad,
When they come to hang you, lad:
But bacon's not the only thing
That's cured by hanging from a string.

So, when the spilt ink of the night
Spreads o'er the blotting pad of light,
Lads whose job is still to do
Shall whet their knives, and think of you.

(ii)

'Tis Summer Time on Bredon,
    And now the farmers swear;
The cattle rise and listen
    In valleys far and near,
    And blush at what they hear.

But when the mists in autumn
    On Bredon tops are thick,
The happy hymns of farmers
    Go up from fold and rick,
    The cattle then are sick.

Old Sam

Stanley Holloway

One of many monologues made famous by Holloway who though
born in the East End of London could imitate northern English
accents so well that people from Yorkshire and Tyneside claimed
him as their own.

It occurred on the evening before Waterloo
    And troops were lined up on Parade,
And Sergeant inspecting 'em, he was a terror
    Of whom every man was afraid –

All excepting one man who was in the front rank,
    A man by the name of Sam Small,
And 'im and the Sergeant were both 'daggers drawn',
    They thought 'nowt' of each other at all.

As Sergeant walked past he was swinging his arm,
    And he happened to brush against Sam.
And knocking his musket clean out of his hand
    It fell to the ground with a slam.

'Pick it oop,' sais Sergeant, abrupt like but cool,
    But Sam with a shake of his head
Said, 'Seeing as tha' knocked it out of me hand,
    P'raps tha'll pick the thing oop instead.'

'Sam, Sam, pick oop tha' musket,'
    The Sergeant exclaimed with a roar.
Sam said 'Tha' knocked it doon, Reet!
    Then tha'll pick it oop, or it stays where it is, on't
      floor.'

The sound of high words very soon reached the ears
    Of an Officer, Lieutenant Bird,
Who says to the Sergeant, 'Now what's all this 'ere?'
    And the Sergeant told what had occurred.

'Sam, Sam, pick oop tha' musket,'
    Lieutenant exclaimed with some heat.
Sam said 'He knocked it doon. Reet!
    Then he'll pick it oop, or it stays where it is, at
        me feet.'

It caused quite a stir when the Captain arrived
    To find out the cause of the trouble;
And every man there, all excepting Old Sam,
    Was full of excitement and bubble.

'Sam, Sam, pick oop tha' musket,'
    Said Captain for strictness renowned.
Sam said 'He knocked it down. Reet!
    Then he'll pick it oop, or it stays where it is
        on't ground.'

The same thing occurred when the Major and Colonel
    Both tried to get Sam to see sense,
But when Old Duke o' Wellington came into view
    Well, the excitement was tense.

Up rode the Duke on a lovely white 'orse,
    To find out the cause of the bother;
He looks at the musket and then at old Sam
    And he talked to Old Sam like a brother.

'Sam, Sam, pick oop tha' musket,'
    The Duke said as quiet as could be,
'Sam, Sam, pick oop tha' musket
    Coom on, lad, just to please me.'

'All right, Duke,' said Old Sam, 'just for thee I'll
    oblige,
  And to show thee I meant no offence.'
So Sam picked it up. 'Gradeley, lad,' said the Duke,
  'Right-o, boys, let battle commence.'

Mad Dogs and Englishmen

Noël Coward

This signature tune was composed without pen, paper or piano
on a nightmare car journey in 1930 from Hanoi to Saigon in
what was then French Indo-China. Coward included it in his
1932 revue, *Words and Music*.

In tropical climes there are certain times of day,
When all the citizens retire
To tear their clothes off and perspire.
It's one of those rules that the greatest fools obey,
Because the sun is much too sultry
And one must avoid its ultry-violet ray . . .
The natives grieve when the white men leave their huts,
Because they're obviously definitely nuts!

Mad dogs and Englishmen
Go out in the midday sun.
The Japanese don't care to,
The Chinese wouldn't dare to,
Hindoos and Argentines sleep firmly from twelve to one,
But Englishmen detest a
Siesta.
In the Philippines there are lovely screens
To protect you from the glare.
In the Malay States there are hats like plates
Which the Britishers won't wear.
At twelve noon
The natives swoon
And no further work is done,
But mad dogs and Englishmen
Go out in the midday sun.

It's such a surprise for the Eastern eyes to see,
That though the English are effete
They're quite impervious to heat.
When the white man rides every native hides in glee,
Because the simple creatures hope he
Will impale his solar topee on a tree . . .
It seems such a shame when the English claim the earth
That they give rise to such hilarity and mirth.

Mad dogs and Englishmen
Go out in the midday sun.
The toughest Burmese bandit
Can never understand it.
In Rangoon the heat of noon
Is just what the natives shun.
They put their Scotch or rye down
And lie down.
In a jungle town
Where the sun beats down
To the rage of man and beast,
The English garb
Of the English sahib
Merely gets a bit more creased.
In Bangkok
At twelve o'clock
They foam at the mouth and run,
But mad dogs and Englishmen
Go out in the midday sun.

Mad dogs and Englishmen
Go out in the midday sun.
The smallest Malay rabbit
Deplores this foolish habit.
In Hong Kong
They strike a gong
And fire off a noonday gun,
To reprimand each inmate
Who's in late.
In the mangrove swamps

Where the python romps
There is peace from twelve to two.
Even caribous
Lie around and snooze,
For there's nothing else to do.
In Bengal
To move at all
Is seldom, if ever done,
But mad dogs and Englishmen
Go out in the midday sun.

She Was One of the Early Birds

T. W. Connor

Song made famous by George Beauchamp in the 1870s. Nothing
is now known of its author.

It was at the pantomime
Sweet Mabel and I did meet.
She was in the ballet (front row)
And I in a five shilling seat;
She was dressed like a dickey bird
Beautiful wings she had on,
Figure divine, wished she were mine;
On her I was totally gone.

She was a dear little dickey bird,
'Chip, Chip, Chip,' she went.
Sweetly she sang to me
Till all my money was spent.
Then she went off song
We parted on fighting terms;
She was one of the early birds
And I was one of the worms.

At the stage-door ev'ry night
I waited with my bouquet
Till my bird had moulted, and then
We'd drive in a hansom away
Oyster suppers and sparkling 'Cham'
Couldn't she go it! What ho!
Fivers I spent; tenners I lent
For to her I couldn't say, 'No'.

She was a dear little dickey bird etc.

Eelskin coats and diamond rings
Knocked holes in my purse alone,
She would have them and in the end
I got hers by pawning my own.
When last I was fairly broke,
'Twixt us a quarrel arose,
Mabel the fair pulled out my hair
And clawed all the skin off my nose.

She was a dear little dickey bird etc.

Full of love and poverty
And armed with a carving knife,
One dark night I knelt in the mud
And asked if she'd be my wife.
Something struck me behind the ear,
Someone said, 'Now go and get
A wife of your own, leave me alone.'
And that was the last time we met.

She was a sweet little dickey bird etc.

Dahn the Plug'ole

Anon

More black humour so heavily Cockney in sound and attitudes that one suspects it may come from Hong-Kong. It is frequently sung at parties.

A muvver was barfin' 'er biby one night,
The youngest of ten and a tiny young mite,
The muvver was pore and the biby was thin,
Only a skelington covered in skin;
The muvver turned rahnd for the soap orf the rack,
She was but a moment, but when she turned back,
The biby was gorn; and in anguish she cried,
'Oh, where is my biby?' – the Angels replied:
'Your biby 'as fell dahn the plug'ole,
Your biby 'as gorn dahn the plug;
The poor little thing was so skinny and thin
E'oughter been barfed in a jug;
Your biby is perfectly 'appy,
'E won't need a barf any more,
Your biby 'as fell dahn the plug'ole,
Not lorst, but gorn before!'

Stately as a Galleon

Joyce Grenfell

Joyce Grenfell at her tenderest and funniest. One misses her own voice and Richard Addinsell's music.

My neighbour, Mrs Fanshaw, is portly-plump
    and gay,
She must be over sixty-seven, if she is a day.
You might have thought her life was dull,
It's one long whirl instead.
I asked her all about it, and this is what she said:

I've joined an Olde Thyme Dance Club, the trouble
    is that there
Are too many ladies over, and no gentlemen to spare.
It seems a shame, it's not the same,
But still it has to be,
Some ladies have to dance together,
One of them is me.

Stately as a galleon, I sail across the floor,
Doing the Military Two-step, as in the days of yore.
I dance with Mrs Tiverton; she's light on her feet
    in spite
Of turning the scale at fourteen stone, and being
    of medium height.
So gay the band,
So giddy the sight,
Full evening dress is a must,
But the zest goes out of a beautiful waltz
When you dance it bust to bust.

So, stately as two galleons, we sail across the floor,
Doing the Valse Valeta as in the days of yore.
The gent is Mrs Tiverton, I am her lady fair,
She bows to me ever so nicely and I curtsey to her
       with care.
So gay the band,
So giddy the sight,
But it's not the same in the end
For a lady is never a gentleman, though
She may be your bosom friend.

So, stately as a galleon, I sail across the floor,
Doing the dear old Lancers, as in the days of yore.
I'm led by Mrs Tiverton, she swings me round and
       round
And though she manoeuvres me wonderfully well
I never get off the ground.
So gay the band,
So giddy the sight,
I try not to get depressed.
And it's done me a power of good to explode,
And get this lot off my chest.

Dear Gwalia

Dylan Thomas

From *Under Milk Wood* come these minimalist verses in praise
of his living spoken by the Rev Eli Jenkins of Llareggub (who
would have been very shocked if you spelled it backwards.)

Dear Gwalia! I know there are
Towns lovelier than ours,
And fairer hills and loftier far,
And groves more full of flowers,

And boskier woods more blithe with spring
And bright with birds' adorning,
And sweeter bards than I to sing
Their praise this beauteous morning.

By Cader Idris, tempest-torn,
Or Moel yr Wyddfa's glory,
Carnedd Llewelyn beauty born,
Plinlimmon old in story,

By mountains where King Arthur dreams,
By Penmaenmawr defiant,
Llaregyb Hill a molehill seems,
A pygmy to a giant.

By Sawdde, Senny, Dovey, Dee,
Edw, Eden, Aled, all,
Taff and Towy broad and free,
Llyfnant with its waterfall,

Claerwen, Cleddau, Dulais, Daw,
Ely, Gwili, Ogwr, Nedd,
Small is our River Dewi, Lord,
A baby on a rushy bed.

By Carreg Cennen, King of time,
Our Heron Head is only
A bit of stone with seaweed spread
Where gulls come to be lonely.

A tiny dingle is Milk Wood
By Golden Grove 'neath Grongar,
But let me choose and oh! I should
Love all my life and longer

To stroll among our trees and stray
In Goosegog Lane, on Donkey Down,
And hear the Dewi sing all day,
And never, never leave the town.

7

In Vacant or in Pensive Mood

Psalm 100

William Kethe

The 'Old Hundredth', the most famous of Kethe's metrical versions of the psalms.

All people that on earth do dwell,
Sing to the Lord with cheerful voice.
Him serve with mirth, his praise forth tell,
Come ye before him and rejoice.

Know that the Lord is God indeed;
Without our aid he did us make:
We are his flock, he doth us feed,
And for his sheep he doth us take.

O enter then his gates with praise,
Aproach with joy his courts unto:
Praise, laud, and bless his name always,
For it is seemly so to do.

For why? the Lord our God is good,
His mercy is for ever sure;
His truth at all times firmly stood,
And shall from age to age endure.

'All the world's a stage'

William Shakespeare

Shakespeare's seven ages of man put in the mouth of that notorious burnt-out case, Jaques in *As You Like It*, and seeming in each age to guy poor worms of humanity. The first line is a version of Petronius's dictum, 'Totus mundus agit histrionem', the motto of the Globe Theatre on Bankside.

All the world's a stage,
And all the men and women merely players:
They have their exits and their entrances;
And one man in his time plays many parts,
His acts being seven ages. At first the infant,
Mewling and puking in the nurse's arms.
And then the whining schoolboy, with his satchel,
And shining morning face, creeping like snail
Unwillingly to school. And then the lover,
Sighing like furnace, with a woeful ballad
Made to his mistress' eyebrow. Then a soldier,
Full of strange oaths, and bearded like the pard,
Jealous in honour, sudden and quick in quarrel,
Seeking the bubble reputation
Even in the cannon's mouth. And then the justice,
In fair round belly with good capon lin'd,
With eyes severe, and a beard of formal cut,
Full of wise saws and modern instances;
And so he plays his part. The sixth age shifts
Into the lean and slipper'd pantaloon,
With spectacles on nose and pouch on side,
His youthful hose well sav'd, a world too wide

For his shrunk shank; and his big manly voice,
Turning again toward childish treble, pipes
And whistles in his sound. Last scene of all,
That ends this strange eventful history,
Is second childishness and mere oblivion,
Sans teeth, sans eyes, sans taste, sans everything.

'The expense of spirit in a waste of shame'

William Shakespeare

Shakespeare in a sex-hating mood but a splendid sermon all the same.

The expense of spirit in a waste of shame
Is lust in action; and till action, lust
Is perjured, murderous, bloody, full of blame,
Savage, extreme, rude, cruel, not to trust,
Enjoy'd no sooner but despised straight,
Past reason hunted, and no sooner had
Past reason hated, as a swallow'd bait
On purpose laid to make the taker mad;
Mad in pursuit and in possession so;
Had, having, and in quest to have, extreme;
A bliss in proof, and proved, a very woe;
Before, a joy proposed; behind, a dream.
  All this the world well knows; yet none knows well
  To shun the heaven that leads men to this hell.

The Bell

John Donne

Donne in his lifetime was more renowned for his sermons than his poems: they had wider audiences and were not so intricate. They have the same elegance and literary contrivance, with a reduction in complexity, for ears rather than eyes. The ending has been often quoted, especially since Ernest Hemingway used it for the title of his 1940 novel of the Spanish Civil War.

Perchance hee for whom this *Bell* tolls, may be so ill, as that he knowes not it tolls for him; And perchance I may thinke my selfe so much better that I am, as that they who are about mee, and see my state, may have caused it to toll for mee, and I know not that. The *Church* is *Catholike, universall,* so are all her *Actions; All* that she does, belongs to *all.* When she *baptizes a child,* that action concernes mee; for that child is thereby connected to that *Head* which is my *Head* too, and engraffed into that *body,* whereof I am a *member.* And when she *buries a Man,* that action concernes me: . . . As therefore the *Bell* that rings to a *Sermon,* calls not upon the *Preacher* onely, but upon the *Congregation* to come; so this *Bell* calls us all: but how much more mee, who am brought so neere the *doore* by this *sicknesse* . . . The *Bell* doth toll for him that *thinkes* it doth; and though it *intermit* againe, yet from that *minute,* that that occasion wrought upon him, hee is united to *God.* Who casts not up his *Eie* to the *Sunne* when it rises? but who takes off his *Eie* from a *Comet* when that breakes out? Who bends not his *eare* to any *bell,* which upon any occasion rings? but who can remove it from that *bell,* which is passing a *peece of himselfe* out of this *world*? No man is an *Iland,* intire of it selfe; every man is a peece of the *Continent,* a part of the *maine;* if a *Clod* bee washed away by the *Sea, Europe* is the lesse, as well as if a *Promontorie* were, as well as if a *Mannor* of thy *friends* or of *thine owne* were; any mans *death* diminishes *me,* because I am involved in *Mankinde;* And therefore never send to know for whom the *bell* tolls; It tolls for *thee.*

O God, Our Help

Isaac Watts

A hymn by the doyen of English hymnologists; it tends to be used in a triumphalist way by the more extreme evangelistic preachers.

O God, our help in ages past,
  Our hope for years to come,
Our shelter from the stormy blast,
  And our eternal home.

Under the shadow of Thy throne
  Thy Saints have dwelt secure;
Sufficient is Thine arm alone,
  And our defence is sure.

Before the hills in order stood,
  Or earth received her frame,
From everlasting Thou art God,
  To endless years the same.

A thousand ages in Thy sight
  Are like an evening gone,
Short as the watch that ends the night
  Before the rising sun.

Time, like an ever-rolling stream,
  Bears all its sons away,
They fly forgotten, as a dream
  Dies at the opening day.

O God, our help in ages past,
  Our hope for years to come,
Be Thou our guard while troubles last,
  And our eternal home.

Elegy Written in a Country Church-Yard

Thomas Gray

One of the greatest and best known of English poems, as rich
a source of quotations as Shakespeare. The relative simplicity
of the thought has tended to obscure the excellence of the poetry.
Fifty years ago it was a common boast of many people that they
could recite it by heart and in 1759, nine years after its
composition, General James Wolfe on the eve of the battle of
Quebec is reported as saying he would prefer to have written
Grey's 'Elegy' than to have taken the city. As if to bear out the
poem's theme he died victorious the next day.

The curfew tolls the knell of parting day,
   The lowing herd wind slowly o'er the lea,
The ploughman homeward plods his weary way,
   And leaves the world to darkness, and to me.

Now fades the glimmering landscape on the sight,
   And all the air a solemn stillness holds,
Save where the beetle wheels his droning flight,
   And drowsy tinklings lull the distant folds:

Save that from yonder ivy-mantled tower
   The moping owl does to the moon complain
Of such as, wandering near her secret bower,
   Molest her ancient solitary reign.

Beneath those rugged elms, that yew-tree's shade,
   Where heaves the turf in many a mouldering heap,
Each in his narrow cell for ever laid,
   The rude Forefathers of the hamlet sleep.

The breezy call of incense-breathing morn,
    The swallow twittering from the straw-built shed,
The cock's shrill clarion, or the echoing horn,
    No more shall rouse them from their lowly bed.

For them no more the blazing hearth shall burn,
    Or busy housewife ply her evening care:
No children run to lisp their sire's return,
    Or climb his knees the envied kiss to share.

Oft did the harvest to their sickle yield,
    Their furrow oft the stubborn glebe has broke;
How jocund did they drive their team afield!
    How bow'd the woods beneath their sturdy stroke!

Let not Ambition mock their useful toil,
    Their homely joys, and destiny obscure;
Nor Grandeur hear with a disdainful smile
    The short and simple annals of the Poor.

The boast of heraldry, the pomp of power,
    And all that beauty, all that wealth e'er gave,
Awaits alike th' inevitable hour:
    The paths of glory lead but to the grave.

Nor you, ye Proud, impute to these the fault
    If Memory o'er their tomb no trophies raise,
Where through the long-drawn aisle and fretted vault
    The pealing anthem swells the note of praise.

Can storied urn or animated bust
    Back to its mansion call the fleeting breath?
Can Honour's voice provoke the silent dust,
    Or Flattery soothe the dull cold ear of Death?

Perhaps in this neglected spot is laid
    Some heart once pregnant with celestial fire;
Hands, that the rod of empire might have sway'd,
    Or waked to ecstasy the living lyre:

But Knowledge to their eyes her ample page
   Rich with the spoils of time, did ne'er unroll;
Chill Penury repress'd their noble rage,
   And froze the genial current of the soul.

Full many a gem of purest ray serene
   The dark unfathom'd caves of ocean bear:
Full may a flower is born to blush unseen,
   And waste its sweetness on the desert air.

Some village-Hampden, with that dauntless breast
   The little tyrant of his fields withstood,
Some mute inglorious Milton here may rest,
   Some Cromwell, guiltless of his country's blood.

Th' applause of list'ning senates to command,
   The threats of pain and ruin to despise,
To scatter plenty o'er a smiling land,
   And read their history in a nation's eyes,

Their lot forebad: nor circumscribed alone
   Their growing virtues, but their crimes confined;
Forbad to wade through slaughter to a throne,
   And shut the gates of mercy on mankind,

The struggling pangs of conscious truth to hide.
   To quench the blushes of ingenuous shame,
Or heap the shrine of Luxury and Pride
   With incense kindled at the Muse's flame.

Far from the madding crowd's ignoble strife,
   Their sober wishes never learn'd to stray;
Along the cool sequester'd vale of life
   They kept the noiseless tenour of their way.

Yet e'en these bones from insult to protect
   Some frail memorial still erected nigh,
With uncouth rhymes and shapeless sculpture deck'd,
   Implores the passing tribute of a sigh.

Their name, their years, spelt by th' unletter'd Muse,
   The place of fame and elegy supply:
And many a holy text around she strews,
   That teach the rustic moralist to die.

For who, to dumb forgetfulness a prey,
   This pleasing anxious being e'er resign'd,
Left the warm precincts of the cheerful day,
   Nor cast one longing lingering look behind?

On some fond breast the parting soul relies,
   Some pious drops the closing eye requires;
E'en from the tomb the voice of Nature cries,
   E'en in our ashes live their wonted fires.

For thee, who, mindful of th' unhonour'd dead,
   Dost in these lines their artless tale relate;
If chance, by lonely contemplation led,
   Some kindred spirit shall inquire thy fate,

Haply some hoary-headed swain may say,
   'Oft have we seen him at the peep of dawn
Brushing with hasty steps the dews away,
   To meet the sun upon the upland lawn;

'There at the foot of yonder nodding beech
   That wreathes its old fantastic roots so high,
His listless length at noontide would he stretch,
   And pore upon the brook that babbles by.

'Hard by yon wood, now smiling as in scorn,
   Muttering his wayward fancies he would rove;
Now drooping, woeful wan, like one forlorn,
   Or crazed with care, or cross'd in hopeless love.

'One morn I miss'd him on the custom'd hill,
   Along the heath, and near his favourite tree;
Another came; nor yet beside the rill,
   Nor up the lawn, nor at the wood was he;

'The next with dirges due in sad array
   Slow through the church-way path we saw him
      borne, –
Approach and read (for thou canst read) the lay
   Graved on the stone beneath yon aged thorn.'

The Epitaph

Here rests his head upon the lap of Earth
   A Youth, to Fortune and to Fame unknown;
Fair Science frown'd not on his humble birth,
   And Melancholy mark'd him for her own.

Large was his bounty, and his soul sincere;
   Heaven did a recompense as largely send:
He gave to Misery all he had, a tear,
   He gain'd from Heaven, 'twas all he wish'd,
      a friend.

No farther seeks his merits to disclose,
   Or draw his frailties from their dread abode,
(There they alike in trembling hope repose,)
   The bosom of his Father and his God.

The Solitude of Alexander Selkirk

William Cowper

Alexander Selkirk on the privateering expedition of the buchaneer, William Dampier, quarrelled with his captain, Thomas Stradling, and on his own request was put ashore on the unhabited island of Juan Fernandez in the South Pacific in 1704. He remained there until he was rescued by Captain Woodes Rogers in 1709. His sojourn formed the basis for Daniel Defoe's *Robinson Crusoe* (1719) and for this poem, written nearly eighty years after the event.

I am monarch of all I survey,
  My right there is none to dispute;
From the centre all round to the sea
  I am lord of the fowl and the brute.
O solitude! where are the charms
  That sages have seen in thy face?
Better dwell in the midst of alarms
  Than reign in this horrible place.

I am out of humanity's reach.
  I must finish my journey alone,
Never hear the sweet music of speech;
  I start at the sound of my own.
The beasts that roam over the plain
  My form with indifference see;
They are so unacquainted with man,
  Their tameness is shocking to me.

Society, friendship, and love
  Divinely bestow'd upon man,
O had I the wings of a dove
  How soon would I taste you again!
My sorrows I then might assuage
  In the ways of religion and truth,

Might learn from the wisdom of age,
    And be cheer'd by the sallies of youth.

Ye winds that have made me your sport,
    Convey to this desolate shore
Some cordial endearing report
    Of a land I shall visit no more:
My friends, do they now and then send
    A wish or a thought after me?
O tell me I yet have a friend,
    Though a friend I am never to see.

How fleet is a glance of the mind!
    Compared with the speed of its flight,
The tempest itself lags behind,
    And the swift-wingéd arrows of light.
When I think of my own native land
    In a moment I seem to be there;
But, alas! recollection at hand
    Soon hurries me back to despair.

But the seafowl is gone to her nest,
    The beast is laid down in his lair;
Even here is a season of rest,
    And I to my cabin repair.
There is mercy in every place,
    And mercy, encouraging thought!
Gives even affliction a grace
    And reconciles man to his lot.

A Man's a Man For a' That

Robert Burns

Burns was no illiterate plowboy but a well-educated and conscious literary artist. His egalitarianism, however, was heartfelt. The poem may not be very original in thought but it was quite revolutionary at the time. It is very soundly written and lively with it and deserves its yearly January recitation.

Is there for honest poverty
　That hings his head, an' a' that?
The coward slave, we pass him by –
　We dare be poor for a' that!
For a' that, an' a' that!
　Our toils obscure, an' a' that,
The rank is but the guinea's stamp,
　The man's the gowd for a' that.

What though on hamely fare we dine,
　Wear hoddin grey an' a' that?
Gie fools their silks, and knaves their wine –
　A man's a man for a' that.
For a' that, an' a' that,
　Their tinsel show, an' a' that,
The honest man, tho' e'er sae poor,
　Is king o' men for a' that.

Ye see yon birkie ca'd 'a lord',
　Wha struts, an' stares, an' a' that?
Tho' hundreds worship at his word,
　He's but a cuif for a' that.
For a' that, an' a' that,
　His ribband, star, an' a' that,
The man o' independent mind,
　He looks an' laughs at a' that.

A prince can mak a belted knight,
   A marquis, duke, an' a' that!
But an honest man's aboon his might –
   Guid faith, he mauna fa' that.
For a' that, an' a' that,
   Their dignities, an' a' that,
The pith o' sense an' pride o' worth
   Are higher rank than a' that.

Then let us pray that come it may
   (As come it will for a' that)
That Sense and Worth o'er a' the earth
   Shall bear the gree an' a' that!
For a' that, an' a' that,
   It's comin yet for a' that,
That man and man the world o'er
   Shall brothers be for a' that.

Auld Lang Syne

Robert Burns

The nearest English equivalent is 'the good old times' and it is a properly sentimental song of youth and friendship. 'Right guid-willie waughts' are unfortunately rather too plentiful when the song is usually sung. It is Burns's most famous and least acknowledged poem.

> Should auld acquaintance be forgot,
>   And never brought to mind?
> Should auld acquaintance be forgot,
>   And auld lang syne?
>
> For auld lang syne, my jo,
>   For auld lang syne,
> We'll tak a cup o' kindness yet
>   For auld lang syne.
>
> And surely you'll be your pint-stowp,
>   And surely I'll be mine,
> And we'll talk a cup o' kindness yet
>   For auld lang syne!
>
>   For auld lang syne, etc.
>
> We twa hae run about the braes,
>   And pu'd the gowans fine,
> But we've wander'd monie a weary fit
>   Sin' auld lang syne.
>
>   For auld lang syne, etc.
>
> We twa hae paidl'd in the burn
>   Frae morning sun til dine,
> But seas between us braid hae roar'd
>   Sin' auld lang syne.

For auld lang syne, etc.

And there's a hand, my trusty fiere,
   And gie's a hand o' thine,
And we'll tak a right guid-willie waught
   For auld lang syne!

   For auld lang syne, etc.

The Daffodils

William Wordsworth

Wordsworth's most quoted poem was the result of a walk by Ullswater on 15 April 1804. The poet admits that the 'two best lines in it (lines 21 and 22) are by Mary' (his wife, Mary Hutchinson) but it was Dorothy the sister who drew the poet's attention to the flowers.

I wandered lonely as a cloud
That floats on high o'er vales and hills
When all at once I saw a crowd,
A host of golden daffodils;
Beside the lake, beneath the trees,
Fluttering and dancing in the breeze.

Continuous as the stars that shine
And twinkle on the milky way,
They stretched in never-ending line
Along the margin of a bay:
Ten thousand saw I at a glance,
Tossing their heads in sprightly dance.

The waves beside them danced; but they
Out-did the sparkling waves in glee.
A poet could not be but gay,
In such a jocund company:
I gazed – and gazed – but little thought
What wealth the show to me had brought:

For oft, when on my couch I lie
In vacant or in pensive mood,
They flash upon that inward eye
Which is the bliss of solitude;
And then my heart with pleasure fills,
And dances with the daffodils.

Lead, Kindly Light

John Henry, Cardinal Newman

The search for truth implicit in this poem, written on a
Mediterranean tour in 1833, shows that Newman was questioning
the basis of his Anglican faith a full decade before he 'poped'.

Lead, kindly Light, amid the encircling gloom,
    Lead thou me on;
The night is dark, and I am far from home,
    Lead thou me on.
Keep thou my feet; I do not ask to see
The distant scene; one step enough for me.

I was not ever thus, nor prayed that thou
    Should'st lead me on;
I loved to choose and see my path; but now
    Lead thou me on.
I loved the garish day, and, spite of fears,
Pride ruled my will: remember not past years.

So long thy power hath blest me, sure it still
    Will lead me on
O'er moor and fen, o'er crag and torrent, till
    The night is gone,
And with the morn those angel faces smile,
Which I have loved long since, and lost awhile.

Nearer, My God

Sarah Flower Adams

A hymn dating from the time when sacred songs were the poor man's poetry and opera too.

Nearer, my God, to Thee;
  Nearer to Thee;
E'en though it be a cross
  That raiseth me,
Still all my song shall be –
Nearer, my God, to Thee!
  Nearer to Thee!

Though, like the wanderer,
  The sun gone down,
Darkness be over me,
  My rest a stone,
Yet in my dreams I'd be
Nearer, my God, to Thee!
  Nearer to Thee!

There let the way appear
  Steps unto heaven;
All that Thou sendest me
  In mercy given:
Angels to beckon me
Nearer, my God, to Thee!
  Nearer to Thee!

Or if on joyful wing,
  Cleaving the sky,
Sun, moon, and stars forgot,
  Upward I fly,
Still all my song shall be –
Nearer, my God, to Thee!
  Nearer to Thee!

Say Not the Struggle Naught Availeth

A.H. Clough

The most famous poem of the nineteenth century equivalent of
the Angry Young Men of the mid-twentieth, who became the
inspiration for the much more respectable 'Scholar Gypsy' by
Matthew Arnold.

Say not the struggle nought availeth,
   The labour and the wounds are vain,
The enemy faints not, nor faileth,
   And as things have been, they remain.

If hopes were dupes, fears may be liars;
   It may be, in yon smoke concealed,
Your comrades chase e'en now the fliers,
   And, but for you, possess the field.

For while the tired waves, vainly breaking,
   Seem here no painful inch to gain,
Far back through creeks and inlets making
   Comes, silent, flooding in, the main,

And not by eastern windows only,
   When daylight comes, comes in the light,
In front the sun climbs slow, how slowly,
   But westward, look, the land is bright.

The Lost Chord

Adelaide Ann Proctor

Sir Arthur Sullivan had tried to set the words of this popular poem in 1872 but failed to find a suitable mode. In 1877 as he nursed his brother Fred through a sudden and terminal illness he came upon them again. This time he found their musical equivalent and composed the setting in one night. It remains one of the world's great songs.

Seated one day at the organ,
    I was weary and ill at ease,
And my fingers wander'd idly
    Over the noisy keys;
I know not what I was playing,
    Or what I was dreaming then,
But I struck one chord of music,
    Like the sound of a great Amen,
    Like the sound of a great Amen.

It flooded the crimson twilight,
    Like the close of an Angel's Psalm,
And it lay on my fever'd spirit,
    With a touch of infinite calm,
It quieted pain and sorrow,
    Like love overcoming strife,
It seem'd the harmonious echo
    From our discordant life,
It link'd all perplexed meanings,
    Into one perfect peace,
And trembled away into silence,
    As if it were loth to cease;
I have sought, but I seek it vainly,
    That one lost chord divine,
Which came from the soul of the organ,
    And enter'd into mine.

It may be that Death's bright Angel,
   Will speak in that chord again;
It may be that only in Heav'n,
   I shall hear that grand Amen.

Onward, Christian Soldiers

Sabine Baring-Gould

The Church Militant on the march.

Onward, Christian soldiers!
  Marching as to war,
With the cross of Jesus
  Going on before.
Christ the royal Master
  Leads against the foe;
Forward into battle,
  See, his banners go:

Onward, Christian soldiers,
  Marching as to war,
With the cross of Jesus
  Going on before.

At the sign of triumph
  Satan's legions flee;
On then, Christian soldiers,
  On to victory!
Hell's foundations quiver
  At the shout of praise;
Brothers, lift your voices,
  Loud your anthems raise:

Like a mighty army
  Moves the Church of God;
Brothers, we are treading
  Where the saints have trod;
We are not divided,
  All one body we,
One in hope and doctrine,
  One in charity:

Crowns and thrones may perish,
  Kingdoms rise and wane,
But the Church of Jesus
  Constant will remain;
Gates of hell can never
  'Gainst that Church prevail;
We have Christ's own promise,
  And that cannot fail:

Onward, then, ye people,
  Join our happy throng,
Blend with ours your voices
  In the triumph song;
Glory, laud, and honour
  Unto Christ the King;
This through countless ages
  Men and angels sing:

Onward, Christian soldiers,
  Marching as to war,
With the cross of Jesus,
  Going on before.

'No worst, there is none'

Gerard Manley Hopkins

From the 'terrible sonnets', the dark night of the soul most
awfully rendered.

No worst, there is none. Pitched past pitch of grief,
More pangs will, schooled at forepangs, wilder wring.
Comforter, where, where is your comforting?
Mary, mother of us, where is your relief?
My cries heave, herds-long; huddle in a main, a chief
Woe, world-sorrow; on an age-old anvil wince and sing –
Then lull, then leave off. Fury had shrieked 'No lingering!
  Let me be fell: force I must be brief'.

  Oh the mind, mind has mountains; cliffs of fall
Frightful, sheer, no-man-fathomed. Hold them cheap
May who ne'er hung there. Nor does long our small
Durance deal with that steep or deep. Here! creep,
Wretch, under a comfort serves in a whirlwind: all
Life death does end and each day dies with sleep.

Invictus

W.E. Henley

The most famous poem of the ultra-patriotic Henley whose lifelong struggle with tuberculosis (it cost him a leg) did not at all diminish his sense of duty nor his zest for life.

Out of the night that covers me,
    Black as the pit from pole to pole,
I thank whatever gods may be
    For my unconquerable soul.

In the fell clutch of circumstance
    I have not winced nor cried aloud.
Under the bludgeonings of chance
    My head is bloody, but unbowed.

Beyond this place of wrath and tears
    Looms but the Horror of the shade,
And yet the menace of the years
    Finds, and shall find, me unafraid.

It matters not how strait the gate,
    How charged with punishments the scroll,
I am the master of my fate:
    I am the captain of my soul.

When Earth's Last Picture is Painted

Rudyard Kipling

The paradise of the artist as seen by one who had been a hack
and had his doubts about the God of Things as They Are.

When Earth's last picture is painted and the tubes are
    twisted and dried,
When the oldest colours have faded, and the youngest
    critic has died,
We shall rest, and, faith, we shall need it – lie down
    for an aeon or two,
Till the Master of All Good Workmen shall put us to
    work anew.

And those that were good shall be happy: they shall sit
    in a golden chair;
They shall splash at a ten-league canvas with brushes
    of comets' hair.
They shall find real saints to draw from – Magdalene,
    Peter, and Paul;
They shall work for an age at a sitting and never be
    tired at all!

And only The Master shall praise us, and only The Master
    shall blame;
And no one shall work for money, and no one shall
    work for fame,
But each for the joy of the working, and each, in his
    separate star,
Shall draw the Thing as he sees It for the God of Things
    as They are!

'They are not long, the weeping and the laughter'

Vitae summa brevis spem nos vetat incohare longam

Ernest Dowson

The quintessential *fin-de-siècle* poet mixing lust, guilt, religion and admonition in a very succinct and charming poem.

They are not long, the weeping and the laughter,
    Love and desire and hate:
I think they have no portion in us after
    We pass the gate.

They are not long, the days of wine and roses:
    Out of a misty dream
Our path emerges for a while, then closes
    Within a dream.

The Donkey

G.K. Chesterton

Chesterton the paradoxist finding glory in unlikely places.

When fishes flew and forests walked
   And figs grew upon thorn,
Some moment when the moon was blood
   Then surely I was born.

With monstrous head and sickening cry
   And ears like errant wings,
The devil's walking parody
   On all four-footed things.

The tattered outlaw of the earth,
   Of ancient crooked will;
Starve, scourge, deride me: I am dumb,
   I keep my secret still.

Fools! For I also had my hour;
   One far fierce hour and sweet:
There was a shout about my ears,
   And palms before my feet.

8

Tales of Land and Sea

Sir Patrick Spens

Anon

This famous early ballad conflates two North Sea tragedies
associated with Alexander III of Scotland (1241 - 1286). His
daughter Margaret married Eric of Norway and many Scots lords
were drowned on the way home from the wedding. Later another
Margaret, Alexander's granddaughter was drowned on her way
to Scotland in 1283.

> The king sits in Dunfermling toune,
>   Drinking the blude-reid wine:
> 'O whar will I get guid sailor,
>   To sail this schip of mine?'
>
> Up and spak an eldern knicht,
>   Sat at the kings richt kne:
> 'Sir Patrick Spens is the best sailor
>   That sails upon the se.'
>
> The king has written a braid letter,
>   And signd it wi his hand,
> And sent it to Sir Patrick Spens,
>   Was walking on the sand.
>
> The first line that Sir Patrick red,
>   A loud lauch lauched he;
> The next line that Sir Patrick red,
>   The teir blinded his ee.
>
> 'O wha is this has don this deid,
>   This ill deid don to me,
> To send me out this time o' the yeir,
>   To sail upon the se!

'Mak haste, mak haste, my mirry men all,
　Our guid schip sails the morne:'
'O say na sae, my master deir,
　For I feir a deadlie storme.

'Late late yestereen I saw the new moone,
　Wi the auld moone in hir arme,
And I feir, I feir, my deir master,
　That we will cum to harme.'

O our Scots nobles were richt laith
　To weet their cork-heild schoone;
Bot lang owre a' the play were playd,
　Thair hats they swam aboone.

O lang, lang may their ladies sit,
　Wi their fans into their hand,
Or eir they se Sir Patrick Spens
　Cum sailing to the land.

O lang, lang may the ladies stand,
　Wi thair gold kems in their hair,
Waiting for thair ain deir lords,
　For they'll se thame na mair.

Haf owre, haf owre to Aberdour,
　It's fiftie fadom deip,
And thair lies guid Sir Patrick Spens,
　Wi the Scots lords at his feit.

The Wife of Usher's Well

Anon

One of the finest and most chilling of the Border ballads with the rich ingredients of greed, guilt and ghosts. Its implicit narrative style assumes intelligent participation on the part of attentive listeners. This version is quite late probably early eighteenth century.

There lived a wife at Usher's Well,
  And a wealthy wife was she;
She had three stout and stalwart sons,
  And sent them oer the sea.

They hadna been a week from her,
  A week but barely ane,
Whan word came to the carlin wife
  That her three sons were gane.

They hadna been a week from her,
  A week but barely three,
Whan word came to the carlin wife
  That her sons she'd never see.

I wish the wind may never cease,
  Nor fashes in the flood,
Till my three sons come hame to me,
  In earthly flesh and blood.

It fell about the Martinmass,
  When nights are lang and mirk,
The carlin wife's three sons came hame,
  And their hats were o the birk.

It neither grew in syke nor ditch,
   Nor yet in ony sheugh;
But at the gates o Paradise,
   That birk grew fair eneugh.

Blow up the fire, my maidens!
   Bring water from the well!
For a' my house shall feast this night,
   Since my three sons are well.

And she has made to them a bed,
   She's made it large and wide,
And she's taen her mantle her about,
   Sat down at the bed-side.

Up then crew the red, red cock,
   And up and crew the gray;
The eldest to the youngest said,
   'Tis time we were away.

The cock he hadna crawd but once,
   And clappd his wings at a',
When the youngest to the eldest said,
   Brother, we must awa.

The cock doth craw, the day doth daw,
   The channerin worm doth chide;
Gin we be mist out o our place,
   A sair pain we maun bide.

Fare ye weel, my mother dear!
   Fareweel to barn and byre!
And fare ye weel, the bonny lass
   That kindles my mother's fire!

Heart of Oak

David Garrick

Often incorrectly called 'Hearts of Oak' it was written in celebration of the Year of Victories, 1759, at Minden, Quiberon and Quebec, against the dastardly French, by the Marquis of Granby, Admiral Lord Hawke and General Wolfe. It was set to music by Dr Boyce and was first sung in public by Mr Champnes at a Christmas entertainment entitled 'Harlequin's Invasion', at Drury Lane.

Come, cheer up, my lads, 'tis to glory we steer,
To add something more to this wonderful year;
To honour we call you, as free men, not slaves,
For who are so free as the sons of the waves?

Chorus
Heart of oak are our ships,
Jolly tars are our men:
We always are ready.
Steady boys, steady,
We'll fight and we'll conquer again and again.

We ne'er see our foes but we wish them to stay;
They never see us but they wish us away:
If they run, why, we follow and run them ashore,
For, if they won't fight us, what can we do more?

We'll still make them fear, and we'll still make them flee,
And drub 'em on shore, as we've drubbed 'em at sea:
Then cheer up, my lads, with one heart let us sing,
Our soldiers, our sailors, our statesmen and king.

Johnnie Cope

Adam Skirving

Sir John Cope was the general in charge of the army mustered against the Young Pretender in the Forty-Five rebellion. His army was routed in a few minutes at Prestonpans on the Forth shore and the Jacobite armies advanced unhindered upon Carlisle. He was of small stature, something of a dandy and no better and no worse than the other non-professional generals of the time.

Hey, Johnnie Cope, are ye wauking yet?
Or are your drums a-beating yet?
If ye were wauking I wad wait
   To gang to the coals i' the morning.

Cope sent a challenge frae Dunbar:
'Charlie, meet me an ye daur,
And I'll learn you the art o' war
   If you'll meet me i' the morning.'

When Charlie looked the letter upon
He drew his sword the scabbard from:
'Come, follow me, my merry merry men,
   And we'll meet Johnnie Cope i' the morning!

'Now Johnnie, be as good's your word;
Come, let us try both fire and sword;
And dinna rin like a frighted bird,
   That's chased frae its nest i' the morning.'

When Johnnie Cope he heard of this,
He thought it wadna be amiss
To hae a horse in readiness
   To flee awa' i' the morning.

Fy now, Johnnie, get up and rin;
The Highland bagpipes mak a din;
It's best to sleep in a hale skin,
   For 'twill be a bluidy morning.

When Johnnie Cope to Dunbar came,
They speered at him, 'Where's a' your men?'
'The deil confound me gin I ken,
   For I left them a' i' the morning.

'Now Johnnie, troth, ye are na blate
To come wi' the news o' your ain defeat,
And leave your men in sic a strait
   Sae early in the morning.

'I' faith,' quo' Johnnie, 'I got a fleg
Wi' their claymores and philabegs;
If I face them again, deil break my legs!
   Sae I wish you a gude morning'.

Lochinvar

Sir Walter Scott

'Lochinvar' is a literary ballad, Scott's sincere flattery of the rougher, stronger folk poetry. It is from his long poem 'Marmion' and recited on the night before the disastrous battle of Flodden (1513). It has given to English an archetypical lover, even though its use is often jocular.

O Young Lochinvar is come out of the west,
Through all the wide Border his steed was the best;
And save his good broadsword he weapons had none,
He rode all unarm'd, and he rode all alone,
So faithful in love, and so dauntless in war,
There never was knight like the young Lochinvar.

He staid not for brake, and he stopp'd not for stone,
He swam the Eske river where ford there was none;
But ere he alighted at Netherby gate,
The bride had consented, the gallant came late:
For a laggard in love, and a dastard in war,
Was to wed the fair Ellen of brave Lochinvar.

So boldly he enter'd the Netherby Hall,
Among bride's-men, and kinsmen, and brothers and all:
Then spoke the bride's father, his hand on his sword,
(For the poor craven bridegroom said never a word),
'O come ye in peace here, or come ye in war,
Or to dance at our bridal, young Lord Lochinvar?'

'I long woo'd your daughter, my suit you denied;
Love swells like the Solway, but ebbs like its tide —
And now I am come, with this lost love of mine,
To lead but one measure, drink one cup of wine.
There are maidens in Scotland, more lovely by far,
That would gladly be bride to the young Lochinvar.'

The bride kiss'd the goblet: the knight took it up,
He quaff'd off the wine, and he threw down the cup.
She look'd down to blush, and she look'd up to sigh,
With a smile on her lips and a tear in her eye.
He took her soft hand, ere her mother could bar,
'Now tread we a measure!' said young Lochinvar.

So stately his form, and so lovely her face,
That never a hall such a galliard did grace;
While her mother did fret, and her father did fume,
And the bridegroom stood dangling his bonnet and plume;
And the bride-maidens whisper'd, ''twere better by far
To have match'd our fair cousin with young Lochinvar.'

One touch to her hand, and one word in her ear,
When they reach'd the hall-door, and the charger stood near;
So light to the croupe the fair lady he swung,
So light to the saddle before her he sprung!
'She is won! we are gone, over bank, bush, and scaur;
They'll have fleet steeds that follow,' quoth young
   Lochinvar.

There was mounting 'mong Graemes of the Netherby clan;
Forsters, Fenwicks, and Musgraves, they rode and they ran:
There was racing and chasing on Cannobie Lee,
But the lost bride of Netherby ne'er did they see.
So daring in love, and so dauntless in war,
Have ye e'er heard of gallant like young Lochinvar?

The Farmer's Boy

Robert Bloomfield

This poem written in 1800 sold 26,000 copies in three years.
It was composed by Bloomfield as he sat at his cobbler's bench
in London and written down afterwards.

The sun had set behind yon hills,
Across the dreary moor,
When weary and lame a boy there came
Up to a farmer's door:
'Can you tell me if any there be
That will give to me employ
To plough and sow, to reap and mow,
And be a farmer's boy
And be a farmer's boy?

'My father's dead, my mother's left
With five children large and small;
And what is worse for mother still
I'm the biggest of them all.
Though little I am I would labour hard
If I could get employ
To plough and sow, to reap and mow
And be a farmer's boy
And be a farmer's boy.

'And if that you won't me employ,
One favour I've to ask:
If you'll shelter me till break of day
From this cold winter's blast,
At break of day I will haste away,
Elsewhere to seek employ
To plough and sow, to reap and mow,
And be a farmer's boy
And be a farmer's boy.'

The farmer's wife cried, 'Try the lad;
Let him no longer seek.'
'Yes, father, do!' the daughter cried,
While the tears ran down her cheek:
'For those who would work, it's hard to want,
And wander for employ;
Don't let him go, but let him stay
To be a farmer's boy!'

The farmer's boy grew up a man,
The good old farmer died
And left the lad the farm he had,
And his daughter for his bride.
Now the lad which was, and the farm now has,
Oft thinks and smiles for joy,
And blesses the day he came that way
To be a farmer's boy.

Ye Mariners of England

Thomas Campbell

A thank-you note by another Scotsman who took Dr Johnson's 'high road that leads to London.' It was written in Hamburg as Campbell observed the effect of the Navy's blockade of continental ports during the Napoleonic Wars.

Ye Mariners of England
　That guard our native seas,
Whose flag has braved, a thousand years,
　The battle and the breeze,
Your glorious standard launch again
　To match another foe:
And sweep through the deep,
　While the stormy winds do blow;
While the battle rages loud and long
　And the stormy winds do blow.

The spirits of your fathers
　Shall start from every wave –
For the deck it was their field of fame,
　And Ocean was their grave.
Where Blake and mighty Nelson fell
　Your manly hearts shall glow,
As ye sweep through the deep,
　While the stormy winds do blow;
While the battle rages loud and long
　And the stormy winds do blow.

Britannia needs no bulwarks,
　No towers along the steep;
Her march is o'er the mountain waves
　Her home is on the deep.

With thunders from her native oak
   She quells the floods below –
As they roar on the shore,
   When the stormy winds do blow;
When the battle rages loud and long,
   And the stormy winds do blow.

The meteor flag of England
   Shall yet terrific burn;
Till danger's troubled night depart
   And the star of peace return.
Then, then, ye ocean warriors!
   Our song and feast shall flow
To the fame of your name,
   When the storm has ceased to blow;
When the fiery fight is heard no more,
   And the storm has ceased to blow.

Casabianca

Felicia Dorothea Hemans

The story of the thirteen-year-old son of Louis de Casabianca who was master of the ship *L'Orient* at the Battle of the Nile (1798). It was popular at the time of its publication, not all that long after the actual event and ever since it has remained a source of parody in a less sensitive age. The use of the word, 'fragments' in the penultimate verse makes one wonder about the sensitivity of the time.

The boy stood on the burning deck
   Whence all but he had fled;
The flame that lit the battle's wreck
   Shone round him o'er the dead.

Yet beautiful and bright he stood,
   As born to rule the storm;
A creature of heroic blood,
   A proud, though childlike form.

The flames roll'd on – he would not go
   Without his father's word;
That father, faint in death below,
   His voice no longer heard.

He call'd aloud – 'Say, father, say
   If yet my task is done!'
He knew not that the chieftain lay
   Unconscious of his son.

'Speak, father!' once again he cried,
   'If I may yet be gone!'
And but the booming shots replied,
   And fast the flames roll'd on.

Upon his brow he felt their breath,
  And in his waving hair,
And looked from that lone post of death,
  In still yet brave despair;

And shouted but once more aloud,
  'My father, must I stay?'
While o'er him fast, through sail and shroud
  The wreathing fires made way.

They wrapt the ship in splendour wild,
  They caught the flag on high,
And stream'd above the gallant child,
  Like banners in the sky.

There came a burst of thunder sound –
  The boy – oh! where was he?
Ask of the winds that far around
  With fragments strewed the sea!

With mast, and helm, and pennon fair,
  That well had borne their part;
But the noblest thing which perished there
  Was that young faithful heart.

Billy Boy

Northumbrian capstan shanty

Anon

Shanties (from the French 'chantez') were work songs to ease the labour and boredom of repetitive tasks. The capstan for those landlubbers like myself is the vertical cylinder round which the anchor-chain is wound with a pole through the top to provide leverage. 'Gairdle cake' is made on a griddle and 'Singin' Hinnies' are honey-cakes'.

Where hev ye been aal the day,
Billy Boy, Billy Boy?
Where hev ye been aal the day, me Billy Boy?
I've been walkin' aal the day
With me charmin' Nancy Grey,
And me Nancy kittl'd me fancy
Oh me charmin' Billy Boy.

Is she fit to be your wife
Billy Boy, Billy Boy?
Is she fit to be yor wife, me Billy Boy?
She's as fit to be me wife
As the fork is to the knife
And me Nancy, &c.

Can she cook a bit o' steak
Billy Boy, Billy Boy?
Can she cook a bit o' steak, me Billy Boy?
She can cook a bit o' steak,
Aye, and myek a gairdle cake
And me Nancy, &c.

Can she myek an Irish stew
Billy Boy, Billy Boy?
Can she myek an Irish Stew, me Billy Boy?
She can myek an Irish Stew
Aye, and 'Singin' Hinnies' too.
And me Nancy, &c.

The Mermaid

Anon

Song of the triumph of fear over experience from one of the most
superstitious groups imaginable. It was easier to blame wrecks
upon sea-creatures, especially those who might fancy jolly tars,
than on poor seamanship.

One Friday morn, when we set sail
And our ship not far from land.
We there did espy a fair pretty maid,
With a comb and a glass in her hand, her hand, her hand,
With a comb and a glass in her hand.

Chorus
While the raging seas did roar
And the stormy winds did blow.
And we jolly sailor boys were up, up aloft
And the land lubbers lying down below, below, below,
And the land lubbers lying down below.

Then up spoke the Captain of our gallant ship,
Who at once our peril did see,
'I have married a wife in fair London town,
And this night she a widow will be.'
            For the raging seas, etc.

And then up spoke the little cabin boy,
And a fair hair'd boy was he,
'I've a father and mother in fair Portsmouth town,
And this night they will weep for me.'
            For the raging seas, etc.

Then three times round went our gallant ship,
And three times round went she;
For the want of a lifeboat they all went down,
As she sank to the bottom of the sea.

        For the raging seas, etc.

What Shall We Do with the Drunken Sailor?

Anon

Another famous sea-shanty showing a concern for temperance that seems more the province of the bo'sun than that of the tar. Scuppers were sluice channels, the taffrail the upper timber of the stern and the yard-arm was part of the mast crossbeam. To be tied to the taffrail when she was yard-arm under would have been a very sobering experience indeed!

What shall we do with the drunken sailor,
What shall we do with the drunken sailor,
What shall we do with the drunken sailor
Early in the morning?

Chorus
Hooray and up she rises,
Hooray and up she rises,
Hooray and up she rises
Early in the morning.

Put him in the long-boat until he's sober,
      Hooray and up she rises, etc.

Pull out the plug and wet him all over,
      Hooray and up she rises, etc.

Put him in the scuppers with a hose-pipe on him,
      Hooray and up she rises, etc.

Heave him by the leg in a running bowlin',
      Hooray and up she rises, etc.

Tie him to the taffrail when she's yard-arm under,
      Hooray and up she rises, etc.

The Arab's Farewell to His Steed

C.E.S. Norton

A farewell we doubt was ever said but it anticipated Ouida and the desert romances. Some quite disturbing fantasies lurked beneath Victorian decorum and this sanitised version of life in North Africa continued to have great appeal.

My beautiful, my beautiful! that standest meekly by,
With thy proudly-arched and glossy neck, and dark and fiery eye!
Fret not to roam the desert now with all thy wingèd speed:
I may not mount on thee again! – thou'rt sold, my Arab steed!

Fret not with that impatient hoof, snuff not the breezy wind;
The farther that thou fliest now, so far am I behind!
The stranger hath thy bridle-rein, thy master hath his gold;
Fleet-limbed and beautiful, farewell; thou'rt sold, my steed,
    thou'rt sold.

Farewell! – Those free untired limbs full many a mile must roam,
To reach the chill and wintry clime that clouds the stranger's
        home;
Some other hand, less kind, must now thy corn and bed prepare;
That silky mane I braided once must be another's care.

The morning sun shall dawn again – but never more with thee
Shall I gallop o'er the desert paths where we were wont to be –
Evening shall darken on the earth: and o'er the sandy plain,
Some other steed, with slower pace, shall bear me home again.

Only in sleep shall I behold that dark eye glancing bright –
Only in sleep shall hear again that step so firm and light;
And when I raise my dreamy arms to check or cheer thy speed,
Then must I startling wake, to feel thou'rt sold! my Arab steed.

Ah, rudely, then, unseen by me, some cruel hand may chide,
Till foam-wreaths lie, like crested waves, along thy panting side,
And the rich blood that in thee swells, in thy indignant pain,
Till careless eyes that on thee gaze may count each starting vein!

Will they ill-use thee; – If I thought – but no, – it cannot be;
Thou art too swift, yet easy curbed, so gentle, yet so free; –
And yet, if haply when thou'rt gone, this lonely heart should
    yearn,
Can the hand that casts thee from it now, command thee to
    return?

'Return!' – alas! my Arab steed! what will thy master do,
When thou that wast his all of joy, hast vanished from his view?
When the dim distance greets mine eyes, and through the
    gathering tears,
Thy bright form for a moment, like the false mirage, appears?

Slow and unmounted will I roam, with wearied foot, alone,
Where with fleet step, and joyous bound, thou oft hast borne
    me on;
And sitting down by the green well, I'll pause and sadly think –
''Twas here he bowed his glossy neck when last I saw him drink.'

When *last* I saw thee drink! – Away! the fevered dream is o'er!
I could not live a day, and know that we should meet no more;
They tempted me, my beautiful! for hunger's power is strong –
They tempted me, my beautiful! but I have loved too long.

Who said, that I had given thee up? Who said that thou wert
    sold?
'Tis false! 'tis false, my Arab steed! I fling them back their gold!
Thus – thus, I leap upon thy back, and scour the distant plains!
Away! who overtakes us now shall claim thee for his pains.

The Charge of the Light Brigade

Alfred, Lord Tennyson

On 26 October 1854 during the Crimean War the Light Cavalry Brigade were ordered to charge the Russian Artillery at Balaclava. 700 men charged 12000 well-prepared Russians with murderous guns and only 195 survived. The poet read the *Times* report and wrote the poem in a sitting. Some friends demurred at the line, 'Some one had blundered' and in deference to the feelings of Lord Lucan it was deleted in the first edition.

Half a league, half a league,
Half a league onward,
All in the valley of Death
   Rode the six hundred.
   'Forward, the Light Brigade!
Charge for the guns!' he said.
Into the valley of Death
   Rode the six hundred.

'Forward, the Light Brigade!'
Was there a man dismayed?
Not though the soldier knew
   Some one had blundered.
Theirs not to make reply,
Theirs not to reason why,
Theirs but to do and die.
Into the valley of Death
   Rode the six hundred.

Cannon to right of them,
Cannon to left of them,
Cannon in front of them
   Volleyed and thundered;
Stormed at with shot and shell,

Boldly they rode and well,
Into the jaws of Death,
Into the mouth of Hell!
  Rode the six hundred.

Flashed all the sabres bare,
Flashed as they turned in air
Sabring the gunners there,
Charging an army, while
  All the world wondered:
Plunged in the battery-smoke
Right through the line they broke;
Cossack and Russian
Reeled from the sabre-stroke
  Shattered and sundered.
Then they rode back, but not,
  Not the six hundred.

Cannon to right of them,
Cannon to left of them,
Cannon behind them
  Volleyed and thundered;
Stormed at with shot and shell,
While horse and hero fell,
They that had fought so well
Came through the jaws of Death,
Back from the mouth of Hell,
All that was left of them,
  Left of six hundred.

When can their glory fade?
O the wild charge they made!
  All the world wondered.
Honour the charge they made!
Honour the Light Brigade,
  Noble six hundred!

The Last Buccaneer

Charles Kingsley

More Victorian sentimentalisation of a career that was anything
but noble and charming.

O England is a pleasant place for them that's rich and high,
But England is a cruel place for such poor folks as I;
And such a port for mariners I ne'er shall see again
As the pleasant Isle of Avès, beside the Spanish main.

There were forty craft in Avès that were both swift and
    stout,
All furnished well with small arms and cannons round
    about;
And a thousand men in Avès made laws so fair and free
To choose the valiant captains and obey them loyally.

Thence we sailed against the Spaniard with his hoards of
    plate and gold,
Which he wrung with cruel tortures from Indian folk of old;
Likewise the merchant captains, with hearts as hard as
    stone,
Who flog men, and keel-haul them, and starve them to
    the bone.

O the palms grew high in Avès, and fruits that shone like
    gold,
And the colibris and parrots they were gorgeous to behold;
And the negro maids to Avès from bondage fast did flee,
To welcome gallant sailors, a-sweeping in from sea.

O sweet it was in Avès to hear the landward breeze,
A-swing with good tobacco in a net between the trees,
With a negro lass to fan you, while you listened to the roar
Of the breakers on the reef outside, that never touched the
shore.

But Scripture saith, an ending to all fine things must be;
So the King's ships sailed on Avès, and quite put down
were we.
All day we fought like bulldogs, but they burst the booms
at night;
And I fled in a piragua, sore wounded, from the fight.

Nine days I floated starving, and a negro lass beside,
Till, for all I tried to cheer her, the poor young thing she
died;
But as I lay a-gasping, a Bristol sail came by,
And brought me home to England here, to beg until I die.

And now I'm old and going – I'm sure I can't tell where;
One comfort is, this world's so hard, I can't be worse off
there:
If I might but be a sea-dove, I'd fly across the main,
To the pleasant Isle of Avès, to look at it once again.

Drake's Drum

Sir Henry Newbolt

A poem about the need for readiness of a sovereign island race
to repel invaders by sea. It was a jolly fine concert piece always
but it had a particularly heady effect in 1940 in the weeks after
Dunkirk when great Armadas might have come again.

Drake, he's in his hammock and a thousand mile away,
   (Captain, art thou sleeping there below?)
Slung atween the round shot in Nombre Dios Bay,
   And dreaming all the time of Plymouth Hoe.
Yonder looms the island, yonder lie the ships,
   With sailor lads a dancing heel an' toe,
And the shore-lights flashing, and the night-tide dashing.
   He sees it all so plainly as he saw it long ago.

Drake he was a Devon man, and ruled the Devon seas,
   (Captain, art thou sleeping there below?)
Roving tho' his death fell, he went with heart at ease,
   And dreaming all the time of Plymouth Hoe.
'Take my drum to England, hang it by the shore,
   Strike it when your powder's running low;
If the Dons sight Devon, I'll quit the port of Heaven,
   And drum them up the Channel as we drumm'd them
     long ago.'

Drake he's in his hammock till the great Armadas come,
   (Captain, art thou sleeping there below?)
Slung atween the round shot, listening for the drum,
   And dreaming all the time of Plymouth Hoe.
Call him on the deep sea, call him up the Sound,
   Call him when ye sail to meet the foe;
Where the old trade's plying and the old flag flying,
   They shall find him ware and waking, as they found him
     long ago!

The Trumpeter

John Francis Barron

Famous parlour piece recorded by Peter Dawson. The second verse's last line was at times regarded as too strong and was, as occasion required, softened.

Trumpeter, what are you sounding now?
(Is it the call I'm seeking?)
'You'll know the call,' said the Trumpeter tall.
'When my trumpet goes a-speakin'.
I'm rousin' 'em up, I'm wakin' 'em up,
The tents are a-stir in the valley,
And there's no more sleep, with the sun's first peep,
For I'm soundin' the old "Reveille"!
Rise up!' said the Trumpeter tall.

Trumpeter, what are you sounding now?
(Is it the call I'm seeking?)
'Can't mistake the call,' said the Trumpeter tall.
'When my trumpet goes a-speakin'.
I'm urgin' 'em on, they're scamperin' on,
There's a drummin' of hoofs like thunder.
There's a mad'nin' shout as the sabres flash out,
For I'm soundin' the "Charge" – no wonder!
And it's *Hell*!' said the Trumpeter tall.

Trumpeter, what are you sounding now?
(Is it the call I'm seeking?)
'Lucky for you if you hear it at all.
For my trumpet's but faintly speakin'.
I'm callin' 'em home! Come home! Come home!
Tread light o'er the dead in the valley,
Who are lyin' around face down to the ground.
And they can't hear me sound the ''Rally''.
But they'll hear it again in a grand refrain,
When Gabriel sounds the last ''Rally''.'

The Green Eye of the Yellow God

J. Milton Hayes

One of the most famous monologues ever and one of the most parodied. It was written and performed by Mickey Hayes until he was prevented by Bransby Williams who claimed he owned the rights. Little is known about the author, except that he wrote many such monologues.

There's a one-eyed yellow idol to the north of Khatmandu,
There's a little marble cross below the town;
There's a broken-hearted woman tends the grave of Mad Carew,
And the Yellow God forever gazes down.

He was known as 'Mad Carew' by the subs at Khatmandu,
He was hotter than they felt inclined to tell;
But for all his foolish pranks, he was worshipped in the ranks,
And the Colonel's daughter smiled on him as well.

He had loved her all along, with a passion of the strong,
The fact that she loved him was plain to all.
She was nearly twenty-one and arrangements had begun
To celebrate her birthday with a ball.

He wrote to ask what present she would like from Mad Carew;
They met next day as he dismissed a squad;
And jestingly she told him then that nothing else would do
But the green eye of the little Yellow God.

On the night before the dance, Mad Carew seemed in a trance,
And they chaffed him as they puffed at their cigars;
But for once he failed to smile, and he sat alone awhile,
Then went out into the night beneath the stars.

He returned before the dawn, with his shirt and tunic torn,
And a gash across his temple dripping red;
He was patched up right away, and he slept through all the day,
And the Colonel's daughter watched beside his bed.

He woke at last and asked if they could send his tunic through;
She brought it, and he thanked her with a nod;
He bade her search the pocket saying, 'That's from Mad Carew,'
And she found the little green eye of the god.

She upbraided poor Carew in the way that women do,
Though both her eyes were strangely hot and wet;
But she wouldn't take the stone and Mad Carew was left alone
With the jewel that he'd chanced his life to get.

When the ball was at its height, on that still and tropic night,
She thought of him and hastened to his room;
As she crossed the barrack square she could hear the dreamy air
Of a waltz tune softly stealing thro' the gloom.

His door was open wide, with silver moonlight shining through;
The place was wet and slipp'ry where she trod;
An ugly knife lay buried in the heart of Mad Carew,
'Twas the 'Vengeance of the Little Yellow God.'

There's a one-eyed yellow idol to the north of Khatmandu,
There's a little marble cross below the town;
There's a broken-hearted woman tends the grave of Mad Carew,
And the Yellow God forever gazes down.

9

Sunset and Evening Star

A Lyke-Wake Dirge

Anon

The progress of the soul whether to Heaven through Purgatory
or to the other place is seen here as a journey through the barest
part of North Yorkshire. Nowadays it is possible to do the Lyke-
Wake Walk without necessarily coming to judgement.

This ae nighte, this ae nighte,
  Every nighte and alle,
Fire, and sleet, and candle-lighte;
  And Christe receive thye saule.

When thou from hence away art paste,
  Every nighte and alle,
To Whinny-muir thou comest at laste;
  And Christe receive thye saule.

If ever thou gavest hosen and shoon,
  Every nighte and alle,
Sit thee down and put them on;
  And Christe receive thye saule.

If hosen and shoon thou ne'er gavest nane,
  Every nighte and alle,
The whinnes shall pinch thee to the bare bane;
  And Christe receive thye saule.

From Whinny-muir when thou mayst passe,
  Every nighte and alle,
To Brig o'Dread thou comest at laste;
  And Christe receive thye saule.

From Brig o'Dread when thou mayst passe,
  Every nighte and alle,
To purgatory fire thou comest at laste;
  And Christe receive thye saule.

If ever thou gavest meate or drinke,
  Every nighte and alle,
The fire sall never make thee shrinke;
  And Christe receive thye saule.

If meate or drinke thou gavest nane,
  Every nighte and alle,
The fire will burn thee to the bare bane;
  And Christe receive thye saule.

This ae nighte, this ae nighte,
  Every nighte and alle,
Fire, and sleet, and candle-lighte;
  And Christe receive thye saule.

'That time of year thou may'st in me behold'

William Shakespeare

Sonnet 73 and the dying fall must be seen as metaphorical since Shakespeare was in his early thirties when he wrote it and had twenty more years of life in him. The image of 'bare ruin'd choirs' is a reference to the monastery chapels despoiled by Henry VIII's dissolution.

That time of year thou may'st in me behold
   When yellow leaves, or none, or few, do hang
Upon those boughs which shake against the cold,
   Bare ruin'd choirs, where late the sweet birds sang.
In me thou see'st the twilight of such day
   As after sunset fadeth in the west,
Which by and by black night doth take away,
   Death's second self, that seals up all in rest.

In me thou see'st the glowing of such fire,
   That on the ashes of his youth doth lie
As the death-bed whereon it must expire,
   Consumed with that which it was nourish'd by:
 – This thou perceiv'st, which makes thy love more strong.
To love that well which thou must leave ere long.

'Fear no more the heat o' the sun'

William Shakespeare

This most beautiful of dirges is from Shakespeare's great ragbag of a play, *Cymbeline*. It is sung by Guiderius and Arviragus, the king's sons, who think that they are called Polydore and Cadwal, when they find what they take to be the dead body of their new friend, Fidele, who is not a boy but their sister, Imogen, and who is not really dead.

Fear no more the heat o' the sun
   Nor the furious winter's rages;
Thou thy worldly task hast done,
   Home art gone and ta'en thy wages:
Golden lads and girls all must,
As chimney-sweepers, come to dust.

Fear no more the frown o' the great,
   Thou art past the tyrant's stroke;
Care no more to clothe and eat;
   To thee the reed is as the oak:
The sceptre, learning, physic, must
All follow this, and come to dust.

Fear no more the lightning-flash
   Nor the all-dreaded thunder-stone;
Fear nor slander, censure rash;
   Thou hast finish'd joy and moan:
All lovers young, all lovers must
Consign to thee, and come to dust.

'Adieu, farewell earth's bliss'

Thomas Nashe

Another relinquishing of life which if not actually happy is certainly contentful. Strangely it comes from a comedy called *Summer's Last Will and Testament*, written a year before Nashe's own death. The death anticipated seems to have been that of the plague and this has caused some editors to suggest that the magic third line of the third verse should read, 'Brightness falls from the *hair*', which just shows what strange fellows editors are.

Adieu, farewell earth's bliss,
This world uncertain is;
Fond are life's lustful joys,
Death proves them all but toys,
None from his darts can fly.
I am sick, I must die.
　　　　Lord have mercy on us!

Rich men, trust not in wealth,
Gold cannot buy you health;
Physic himself must fade,
All things to end are made.
The plague fell swift goes by;
I am sick, I must die.
　　　　Lord have mercy on us!

Beauty is but a flower
Which wrinkles will devour;
Brightness falls from the air,
Queens have died young and fair,
Dust hath closed Helen's eye.
I am sick, I must die.
　　　　Lord have mercy on us!

Strength stoops unto the grave,
Worms feed on Hector brave,
Swords may not fight with fate.
Earth still holds ope her gate;
Come! come! the bells do cry.
I am sick, I must die.
　　　　　Lord have mercy on us!

Wit with his wantonness
Tasteth death's bitterness;
Hell's executioner
Hath no ears for to hear
What vain art can reply.
I am sick, I must die.
　　　　　Lord have mercy on us!

Haste, therefore, each degree,
To welcome destiny.
Heaven is our heritage,
Earth but a player's stage;
Mount we unto the sky;
I am sick, I must die.
　　　　　Lord have mercy on us!

'How many miles to Babylon?'

Anon

A rhyme for a children's game yet really suggesting the journey of life. The German version gives the distance as 'Jedoch, ein Leben lang' (a lifetime!).

How many miles to Babylon?
Threescore miles and ten.
Can I get there by candle-light?
Yes, and back again.
If your heels are nimble and light,
You may get there by candle-light.

Mr Valiant-for-Truth Crosses the River

John Bunyan

The death of Mr Valiant-for-Truth, one of the happier moments of Bunyan's great allegory, whose strong simple style did so much to establish later English prose.

After this, it was noised abroad that Mr. *Valiant-for-truth* was taken with a Summons, by the same *Post* as the other, and had this for a Token that the Summons was true, *That his Pitcher was broken at the Fountain*. When he understood it, he called for his Friends, and told them of it. Then said he, I am going to my Fathers, and though with great difficulty I am got hither, yet now I do not repent me of all the Trouble I have been at to arrive where I am. *My Sword*, I give to him that shall succeed me in my Pilgrimage, and my *Courage* and *Skill*, to him that can get it. My *Marks* and *Scars* I carry with me, to be a Witness for me, that I have fought his Battles who now will be my Rewarder. When the Day that he must go hence, was come, many accompanied him to the River side, into which, as he went, he said, *Death, where is Thy Sting?* And as he went down deeper, he said, *Grave, where is thy Victory?* So he passed over, and the Trumpets sounded for him on the other side.

The Flowers of the Forest

Jean Elliot

A poem like Scott's 'Marmion' commemorating the battle of
Flodden Field, Northumberland, where on 9 September 1513,
James IV and the flower of the Scots nobility were killed by the
English under the Earl of Surrey. It remains one of the black
spots in the nation's memory.

I've heard the lilting at our yowe-milking,
   Lasses a-lilting before the dawn o' day;
But now they are moaning on ilka green loaning;
   'The Flowers of the Forest are a' wede away.'

At buchts, in the morning, nae blythe lads are scorning;
   The lasses are lonely, and dowie, and wae;
Nae daffin', nae gabbin', but sighing and sabbing:
   Ilk ane lifts her leglen, and hies her away.

In hairst, at the shearing, nae youths now are jeering,
   The bandsters are lyart, and runkled and grey;
At fair or at preaching, nae wooing, nae fleeching:
   The Flowers of the Forest are a' wede away.

At e'en, in the gloaming, nae swankies are roaming
   'Bout stacks wi' the lasses at bogle to play,
But ilk ane sits drearie, lamenting her dearie:
   The Flowers of the Forest are a' wede away.

Dule and wae for the order sent our lads to the Border;
   The English, for ance, by guile wan the day:
The Flowers of the Forest, that foucht aye the foremost,
   The prime o' our land are cauld in the clay.

Proud Maisie

Sir Walter Scott

A deliberate attempt on Scott's part to replicate the rough magic and condensed narrative style of the older ballad. It appears in his novel, *The Heart of Midlothian*. He succeeds rather well – only the 'grey-headed' sexton betrays modern artifice.

Proud Maisie is in the wood,
  Walking so early;
Sweet Robin sits on the bush,
  Singing so rarely.

'Tell me, thou bonny bird,
  When shall I marry me?'
'When six braw gentlemen
  Kirkward shall carry ye.'

'Who makes the bridal bed,
  Birdie, say truly?'
'The grey-headed sexton
  That delves the grave duly.

'The glow-worm o'er grave and stone
  Shall light thee steady.
The owl from the steeple sing,
  'Welcome, proud lady.' '

The Land o' the Leal

Carolina Oliphant

The word 'leal' means 'loyal' or 'true' and the poem describes
the paradise of those of little expectations.

I'm wearin' awa', John,
Like snaw-wreaths in thaw, John;
I'm wearin' awa'
  To the land o' the leal.
There's nae sorrow there, John;
There's neither cauld nor care, John;
The day is aye fair
  In the land o' the leal.

Our bonnie bairn's there, John;
She was baith gude and fair, John;
And oh! we grudged her sair
  To the land o' the leal.
But sorrow's sel' wears past, John,
And joy that's a-comin' fast, John –
The joy that's aye to last
  In the land o' the leal.

Sae dear's that joy was bought, John,
Sae free the battle fought, John,
That sinfu' man e'er brought
  To the land o' the leal.
Oh, dry your glist'ning ee, John!
My saul langs to be free, John;
And angels beckon me
  To the land o' the leal.

To, haud ye leal and true, John!
Your day it's wearin' thro', John;
And I'll welcome you
   To the land o' the leal.
Now fare ye weel, my ain John,
This warld's cares are vain, John;
We'll meet, and we'll be fain
   In the land o' the leal.

We'll Go No More a-Roving

Lord Byron

The relinquishing here might seem to belong to an earlier age-group, a kind of farewell to adventure and a-wooing instead of slippers and the telly. Yet for Byron the end of roving late into the night might have been a kind of death had fate not been a better scriptwriter.

> So, we'll go no more a-roving
>   So late into the night,
> Though the heart be still as loving,
>   And the moon be still as bright.
>
> For the sword outwears its sheath,
>   And the soul wears out the breast,
> And the heart must pause to breathe,
>   And love itself have rest.
>
> Though the night was made for loving,
>   And the day returns too soon,
> Yet we'll go no more a-roving
>   By the light of the moon.

Abide With Me

Henry Francis Lyte

One of the finest English hymns and certainly the most pleasantly melancholy. The third line in the second stanza is so hopeless it is almost optimistic.

Abide with me! fast falls the eventide;
The darkness deepens; Lord, with me abide!
When other helpers fail, and comforts flee,
Help of the helpless, O abide with me!

Swift to its close ebbs out life's little day;
Earth's joys grow dim, its glories pass away;
Change and decay in all around I see:
O Thou Who changest not, abide with me!

I need Thy presence every passing hour;
What but Thy grace can foil the tempter's power?
Who like Thyself my guide and stay can be?
Through cloud and sunshine, O abide with me!

I fear no foe, with Thee at hand to bless;
Ills have no weight, and tears no bitterness:
Where is death's sting? where grave, thy victory?
I triumph still, if Thou abide with me!

Sunset and Evening Star

Alfred, Lord Tennyson

Tennyson's own funeral song, written at the end of a long and
apparently satisfactory life.

Sunset and evening star,
   And one clear call for me!
And may there be no moaning of the bar,
   When I put out to sea,

But such a tide as moving seems asleep,
   Too full for sound and foam,
When that which drew from out the boundless deep
   Turns again home.

Twilight and evening bell,
   And after that the dark!
And may there be no sadness of farewell,
   When I embark;

For tho' from out our bourne of Time and Place
   The flood may bear me far,
I hope to see my Pilot face to face
   When I have crost the bar.

Tears, Idle Tears

Alfred, Lord Tennyson

Another song from Tennyson's strange long poem called 'The Princess'. It was the sort of effusion that made his Victorian readers very happy with him and he with them.

'Tears, idle tears, I know not what they mean,
Tears from the depth of some divine despair
Rise in the heart, and gather to the eyes,
In looking on the happy Autumn fields,
And thinking of the days that are no more.

'Fresh as the first beam glittering on a sail,
That brings our friends up from the underworld,
Sad as the last which reddens over one
That sinks with all we love below the verge;
So sad, so fresh, the days that are no more.

'Ah, sad and strange as in dark summer dawns
The earliest pipe of half-awakened birds
To dying ears, when unto dying eyes
The casement slowly grows a glimmering square;
So sad, so strange, the days that are no more.

'Dear as remember'd kisses after death,
And sweet as those by hopeless fancy feign'd
On lips that are for others; deep as love,
Deep as first love, and wild with all regret;
O Death in Life, the days that are no more.'

The Darkling Thrush

Thomas Hardy

Written on 31 December 1900 as a valedictory ode to the first
year of the twentieth century, when Hardy was sixty and regretful
of his own incapacity to feel blessed hope. The apparently affected
epithet 'darkling' was first used as long ago as 1450.

I leant upon a coppice gate
  When Frost was spectre-gray,
And Winter's dregs made desolate
  The weakening eye of day.
The tangled bine-stems scored the sky
  Like strings of broken lyres,
And all mankind that haunted nigh
  Had sought their household fires.

The land's sharp features seemed to be
  The Century's corpse outleant,
His crypt the cloudy canopy,
  The wind his death-lament.
The ancient pulse of germ and birth
  Was shrunken hard and dry,
And every spirit upon earth
  Seemed fervourless as I.

At once a voice arose among
  The bleak twigs overhead
In a full-hearted evensong
  Of joy illimited;
An aged thrush, frail, gaunt, and small,
  In blast-beruffled plume,
Had chosen thus to fling his soul
  Upon the growing gloom.

So little cause for carolings
   Of such ecstatic sound
Was written on terrestrial things
   Afar or nigh around,
That I could think there trembled through
   His happy goodnight air
Some blessed Hope, whereof he knew
   And I was unaware.

Love's Old Sweet Song

J. Clifton Bingham

One of the great 'drowsers', its lyrics were written by **Bingham** in 1882 and offered for setting. The composers' race was won by James Lynam Molloy, who wrote 'The Kerry Dance' and 'Bantry Bay', by using the electric telegraph, then a novelty.

Once in the dear dead days beyond recall,
    When on the world the mists began to fall,
Out of the dreams that rose in happy throng,
    Low to our hearts Love sang an old sweet song;
And in the dusk where fell the firelight gleam,
    Softly it wove itself into our dream.

Chorus:
Just a song at twilight, when the lights are low,
    And the flick'ring shadows softly come and go,
Tho' the heart be weary, sad the day and long,
    Still to us at twilight comes Love's old song,
    Comes Love's old sweet song.

Even today we hear Love's song of yore,
    Deep in our hearts it dwells for evermore,
Footsteps may falter, weary grows the way,
    Still we can hear it at the close of day;
Still to the end when life's dim shadows fall,
    Love will be found the sweetest song of all.

Biographical Index

Sarah Flower Adams was born in Great Harlow, Essex, in 1805. She wrote poems for the *Monthly Repository*, which her husband edited, and several hymns, the most famous of which is 'Nearer My God To Thee'. She died in 1848.

Sabine Baring-Gould was born in Exeter in 1834 and educated at Clare College, Cambridge. He was ordained in 1865 and became rector of Lew Trenchard, Devon, in 1881. He wrote much about Devonshire in fiction and also collected folklore. His hymn 'Onward Christian Soldiers' has secured his fame. He died in 1924.

William Barnes was born at Rush Hay in Dorsetshire in 1801. He became a teacher and later pastor of Whitcombe. He wrote many poems in his native Dorset dialect which later greatly influenced Hardy. He died at Winterborne Carne in 1886, having been rector there for twenty-five years.

John Francis Barron was born in London in 1870. He wrote a number of very popular late Victorian and Edwardian ballads, mostly of a military nature. Little else is now known of him.

(Joseph) Hilaire (Pierre) Belloc was born at St Cloud, Paris, in 1870 and educated at Balliol College, Oxford. He became an active and effective apologist for Roman Catholicism. His travel books are still readable but his lasting fame rests on his comic verse. He died in 1953.

A(rthur) C(hristopher) Benson was born in Wellington College in 1862 where his father (later Archbishop of Canterbury) was headmaster. He went to Cambridge like his brothers, Robert Hugh (who became a Roman Catholic and wrote several religious novels) and Edward Frederic (the author of the *Lucia* books). All three were known by their initials. A C became a housemaster at Eton and resigned to become a fellow of Magdalen College, Oxford and afterwards its Master. He edited the correspondence of Queen Victoria and wrote several biographies. He died in 1925.

E(dmund) C(lerihew) Bentley was born in 1875 and was a schoolfellow of Chesterton at St Paul's School. He was called to the bar in 1902 but did not practice, choosing to earn his money by journalism. He invented the 'Clerihew', an epigrammatic verse-form of uneven rhythm. He is also known as the author of *Trent's Last Case* (1911), one of the few detective stories that people know by name. He died in 1956.

John Betjeman was born in London in 1906 and educated at Marlborough and Magdalen College, Oxford. He decided not to work in the family business of furniture making, preferring literature. He became an authority on Victorian architecture, especially that of churches and railway stations, and on English topography. It is as a poet he will be remembered, his verse touching a vein of nostalgia and celebration of things British and Irish. (He was Cultural Attaché to the British Embassy in Dublin during the Second World War.) His poetry had the widest popular appeal of any poet since Kipling, a popularity that has caused the excellence of his craft to be frequently overlooked. He died in 1984 and is buried in Cornwall, his adopted home.

J Clifton Bingham was born in 1859 and died in 1913. He was a professional lyricist, remembered now mainly as the author of the words of 'Love's Old Sweet Song'.

William Blake, the artist, poet and visionary, was born in London in 1757. He was an engraver by trade and his poems with their illustrative designs were etched on copper plate. His mystical books show a powerful if troubled mind and his shorter pieces are still popular. He died in 1827.

Robert Bloomfield was born in Suffolk in 1766 and worked as an agricultural worker and shoemaker. He gained some fame with his poem, 'The Farmer's Boy', and his patron, the Duke of Grafton, obtained him a post in the Seal Office but he found the work dull and became a bookseller. His business failed and he tried to earn a living by making and selling wind-harps. He died in poverty in 1823.

Sir Harold Boulton, born in 1859, was a popular balladeer, author of 'Glorious Devon' and 'The Skye Boat Song' which many think is a folk-song. He died in 1935.

Rupert (Chawner) Brooke was born in 1887 at Rugby School, where his father was a housemaster, and educated there and at King's College, Cambridge. Afterwards he settled at the Old Vicarage, Granchester. His charm, good looks, anticipatory patriotic poems and early death made him the type of the Flower of English Youth sacrificed in World War I. He was neither as naïve nor as sentimental as his adulators made out. He died of septicaemia on a hospital ship in the Aegean in 1915.

Robert Browning was born in London in 1812, the son of a bank clerk. He married Elizabeth Barrett, then a much more popular poet, in 1846 and they lived in Italy until her death in 1861. Thereafter he lived a personally untroubled life until his death in 1889. His poetry is vigorous and at times over-compressed but his dramatic monologues, a form he perfected, show him as one of the most impressive of the Victorian poets.

Alfred Bunn, known gibingly as 'The Poet Bunn', was born in 1796. He had a backstage career as stage-manager at Drury Lane, as manager of the Patent Theatre, Birmingham, and later as manager of Drury Lane, which he debased considerably. He wrote the libretto for Balfe's opera, *The Bohemian Girl*, but is chiefly remembered as a pander for his wife and for his literary feuds. These were fought bitterly, particularly the one with *Punch* in which he lampooned Mark Lemon and Douglas Jerrold. Towards the end of his life he became a Roman Catholic and died at Boulogne in 1860, not uncharacteristically, of apoplexy.

John Bunyan was born near Bedford in 1628, the son of a tinsmith, a trade he followed after a brief education. He fought on the Parliamentary side in the Civil War and in 1646 married a poor woman whose only dowry was a pair of devotional books, *The Plain Man's Pathway to Heaven* and *The Practice of Piety*. He struggled with religious doubt for ten years and then, on his wife's death, he became an itinerant preacher. At the Restoration he was imprisoned for preaching without licence and spent the next dozen years in prison. His first substantial work was *Grace Abounding* (1666), a spiritual autobiography and when in 1675 he was again imprisoned he wrote his great book *The Pilgrim's Progress*. This work had a remarkable effect upon the English language and literary style. He died in 1688 from a chill caught while on a journey of spiritual mercy.

Robert Burns was born in 1759 in Alloway, near Ayr, the son of a farmer who, together with the local schoolteacher, gave him an excellent education. Far from being an 'illiterate ploughboy genius' he continued his education throughout his short, bibulous and intermittently wild life. He was a skilled ploughman but all his agricultural ventures failed and it was as an exciseman that he had his most settled period of life. *His Poems Chiefly In The Scottish Dialect* (1786) brought him fame. He settled down to marriage with Jean Armour, a lady from a troubled period of his past. He died in 1796. His poems, especially the love pieces, are among the finest written in English and his title of the Scots national bard will not lightly or advisedly be disproved.

Thomas Campbell was born in Glasgow in 1777 and educated at the university there. He abandoned law studies for verse and wrote many long narrative poems, including the poetic romance, *Gertrude of Wyoming*. He lived in England from the age of twenty-six and gained fame from his war-lyrics, 'Ye Mariners of England', 'Hohenlinden' and 'The Battle of the Baltic'. He died in 1844 in Boulogne, where he had gone to improve his health.

Henry Carey was born in 1687 and achieved fame as the writer of plays, musical shows and burlesques. His most famous song is 'Sally in Our Alley' and he is credited with a version of 'God Save the King'. His attack on the fulsome poetry of Ambrose Phillips gave a new word, 'namby-pamby', to the language. He wrote *Chrononhotonthologos* (1734) which he described in characteristically mocking terms as 'The Most Tragical Tragedy that ever was Tragedized by any Company of Tragedians'. He died in 1743.

Lewis Carroll was the name used by Charles Lutwidge Dodgson for his fantasy writings. He was born in Cheshire in 1832 and educated at Rugby and Oxford. He took a double first in Classics and Mathematics and for thirty years, from 1851 to 1881, was lecturer and fellow of Christ Church. He published several books on geometry and mathematical logic – forerunner of the so-called 'modern' mathematics. He was friendly with Dean Liddell and the famous *Alice* books were written to amuse the Dean's younger daughter, Alice. His shyness with adults and ease with young girls (and his practice of taking nude photographs of them) have led psychologists to vulgar speculation about his sex-drive. His own scrupulous Christian practice would have eschewed such considerations. In fact his 'childrens' books are much more popular with adults. He died in 1898 without having taken full orders.

G(ilbert) K(eith) Chesterton was born in London in 1874, the son of an estate agent. He was educated at St Paul's School and later at the Slade School of Art. He became a journalist and earned a world reputation with essays in which he exploited a paradoxical view of life. His verse, short stories and novels were informed by odd humour, a firm belief in Christianity and a celebration of a Merrie England whose pre-Reformation virtues he persistently celebrated. He was a fine, if occasionally inaccurate critic, and when he became a Roman Catholic in 1922, the priest who garnered him for that faith, Fr O'Connor, became the model for his most famous creation, 'Father Brown', the theologian detective. His books on St Francis of Assisi and St Thomas Aquinas are marvels of compressed insight. He died in 1936.

Albert Chevalier, the famous exponent of sentimental 'coster' songs, was born in 1861 and started his career as an opera-singer and lyricist. He was persuaded with great difficulty to perform his songs on the Halls and he became extremely popular with such pieces as 'Knocked 'em in the Old Kent Road' and the perennial favourite, 'My Old Dutch'. The latter expression he himself coined because of his wife's supposed resemblance to 'an old Dutch clock'. He died in 1923.

Sir Winston (Leonard Spencer) Churchill was born in 1874 in Blenheim Palace, Woodstock, (the home of his kinsman, the Duke of Marlborough) eldest son of Lord Randolph Churchill and Jenny Jerome. He was educated at Harrow and Sandhurst and served at Omdurman. He was a war correspondent during the Boer War and was elected to Parliament in 1900 as a Conservative. He joined the Liberals in 1903 and held several offices until in 1911 he became First Lord of the Admiralty. He was made the scapegoat for the Dardanelles disaster but was recalled from the army in France to become Minister of Munitions. After the First World War he did his best to keep the Forces modern and to develop air power but the Thirties saw him as a voice in the wilderness urging resistance to Mussolini and Hitler When in 1940 Chamberlain was forced to resign he became the leader of the Coalition Government and the crystallisation of the national spirit of resistance. After the war he fostered NATO, led the movement which became the EEC and coined the phrase 'The Iron Curtain', a warning against another kind of Hitlerism. He was awarded the OM in 1946, the KG in 1953 and the Nobel Prize and the CL in 1961. Even had his career not made his name famous he would have been regarded as one of the leading writers of modern times. He died in 1965.

Colley Cibber was born in Bloomsbury, the son of a Danish sculptor, in 1671. He served in the army and then at the age of twenty made his first appearance as an actor on the stage at Drury Lane. He was one of the eighteenth century 'improvers' of Shakespeare. His version of *Richard III* contains some famous Cibberian, non-Shakespearean lines: 'Off with his head! So much for Buckingham!' and 'Richard's himself again!' which Olivier retained for his otherwise impeccably Shakespearean film. He was a fine actor, and a prolific playwright but an indifferent poet and when he accepted the post of Poet Laureate in 1730 he became the chief target of Pope's *Dunciad*. His autobiography, *An Apology for the Life of Mr Colley Cibber* (1740), is one of the best books of theatrical reminiscence in English. He died in 1757.

Arthur Hugh Clough was born in Liverpool in 1819 but was taken to Charleston, South Carolina, where he was four. He was sent back to England for education and while at Rugby became friendly with the headmaster's son, Matthew Arnold. He became a fellow of Oriel College, Oxford and was much influenced by Newman. Religious difficulties caused him to resign and seek a non-sectarian post. He became an Inspector for the Examinations Office in 1854 and died in Florence in 1861 while on education business.

Samuel Taylor Coleridge was born in 1772 at Ottery St Mary in Devonshire where his father was vicar, educated at Christ's Hospital, where he met Charles Lamb, and began his university studies at Jesus College, Cambridge. He had various careers as editor, Unitarian Minister, translator, critic and poet. He suffered continually from neuralgia and the opium he took to relieve the pain made him an addict. He spent the last twenty-five years of his life in the homes of various devoted friends, including the Wordsworths at Grasmere and the Wedgewoods. His work as a commentator on Shakespeare is as famous as his poems 'Christabel' and 'The Rime of the Ancient Mariner'. He died in his sleep in the summer of 1834, in Lamb's words, 'an archangel, a little damaged'.

William Johnson Cory was born in Torrington, Devonshire and educated at Eton and King's College, Cambridge. He was an assistant master at his old school for twenty-six years. In 1872 he inherited an estate, assumed the name Cory and settled in Hampstead. His best known poem is 'Heraclitus' and his 'Eton Boating Song' was published in the school magazine in 1863.

Noël Coward was born Noel Pierce (the diaeresis was assumed later) at Teddington on Thames in 1899 and early in life became a boy actor. After brief, invalided-out war service he became a playwright, revue composer, songwriter and novelist while continuing to appear on stage. His wit and acute showbusiness flair caused him in later years to be known as 'the Master'. His sophistication and wit went hand-in-hand with a remarkable sentimentality and an old-fashioned patriotism. His comedies, *Private Lives* (1930) and *Blithe Spirit* (1941) are comic classics. His songs mix wit and mush equally. He died in 1973.

William Cowper was born in 1731 and his three score and nine years are a story of a gentle personality beset with periodic bouts of insanity who wrote some memorable poetry. Born in Great Berkhampstead in Hertfordshire, the son of the rector, he spent the happiest period of his life in the house of his friends, Morley and Mary Unwin in Huntingdonshire. On Morley's death Cowper and the widow moved to Olney in Buckinghamshire where they lived decorously until her death. The insanity which he considered an impediment to their marriage beset him for the remainder of his life. He died in 1800.

Thomas Dekker was born about 1572, probably in London, since the city is specifically celebrated in his pamphlets and plays. This lack of knowledge about his career is characteristic of the time. Much more is known about Shakespeare than about his contemporaries. His play, *The Shoemaker's Holiday*, is still presented. He was a sharp and effective pamphleteer, an art form in which the Elizabethans delighted and in which their writers excelled. *The Gull's Hornbook* (1609) is a satirical manual for the Jacobean gallant. He suffered from recurring poverty but his writings show a sunny nature and a concern for the urban poor. He died in 1632.

Charles Dibdin, the writer of over a thousand sea-songs, was born appropriately enough in Southampton in 1745. The songs were written in admiration of his brother, Thomas, who was a sea captain, and it was said of them that they brought more men into the navy than the press-gang. Typical of his style are the lines: 'But the standing toast that pleased the most / Was "The wind that blows, the ship that goes, And the lass that loves a sailor." ' He also wrote for the stage and was a friend of Garrick and Mrs Siddons. He died in 1814.

John Donne was born in London in 1572, the son of a wealthy ironmonger. He was brought up a Roman Catholic but after study at Oxford, Cambridge and the Inns of Court his Catholicism lapsed and he took Anglican Orders in 1615. He became Dean of St Paul's in 1621. He wrote many different kinds of poetry, all of it noted for the intellectual complexity of its imagery. He was noted as a preacher and his sermons were more famous than his poems. He died in 1631, having had the morbid foresight to have an artist sketch him in his shroud so that the commissioned ornamental sculpture would have a model.

Ernest (Christopher) Dowson was born in Kent in 1867 and spent much of his youth and later life in France. He left his Oxford college, Queen's, to work at his father's dry dock. The 'Cynara' of his famous poem was the daughter of an Italian restaurant owner who afterwards married a waiter. Like many of his fellow 'Decadent' writers, he had tuberculosis aggravated by drink and was a Catholic. He died in 1900.

Sir Francis (Hastings) Doyle was born in Nunappleton, Yorkshire, in 1810. He was educated at Eton and Oxford, called to the Bar in 1837 and appointed Commissioner of Customs in 1869. He had a non-participant love-affair with the army, for though his father was a general and many of his connections officers he never became a soldier himself. He was elected Professor of Poetry at Oxford in 1867 and died in 1888.

T(homas) S(tearns) Eliot was born in St Louis, Missouri in 1888 and educated at Harvard, the Sorbonne and Merton College, Oxford. He taught school, worked in a bank and became a regular reviewer for the *Times Literary Supplement*. His poetry, begun when he was still at Harvard, caused quite a stir when *Prufock and Other Observations* appeared in 1917. *The Waste Land*, published in 1922, infuriated many conservative critics but it made Eliot famous. Later work shows more clearly the evidence of his Anglicanism, especially *Ash Wednesday* (1930) and *Four Quartets* (1943). He achieved a wider popularity with his verse-plays, notably *Murder in the Cathedral* (1935) and *The Cocktail Party* (1949). His book for children, *Old Possum's Book of Practical Cats* (1939) formed the basis of the musical *Cats*. He died in 1965.

Queen Elizabeth I was born at Greenwich in 1533, the daughter of Anne Boleyn, Henry VIII's second wife, and she lived for many years under the cloud of her mother's adultery and early death, her Protestantism while her Catholic sister, Mary, reigned, and, after she ascended the throne, the constant threat of a counter-reformation from Spain or France through such agents as Mary, Queen of Scots. Her police state organised by such ministers as Walsingham was remarkably efficient and kept her safely on the throne for forty-five years. She lived in a period of great literary activity which she in some measure encouraged and she was herself a notable Greek scholar. She died in 1603.

Jean Elliot was born in Teviotdale in 1727, the daughter of the Lord Justice Clerk of Scotland. She wrote 'The Flowers of the Forest' anonymously and published it as an old ballad. Burns was certain it was contemporary and said so. She died in 1805, apparently without having written anything else.

Henry Fielding was born in Glastonbury in 1707, educated at Eton where he was a contemporary of Charles James Fox and the Elder Pitt and graduated to being a London hack for the theatre. This work was stopped when as a result of his own political satire the Stage Licensing Act was passed in 1737. He took up the law again and he and his brother John ('the blind Beak') established The Bow Street Runners to curb the lawlessness of the city. His fiction writing began with *Joseph Andrews* (1742) a burlesque of Samuel Richardson's *Pamela* and it reached its height with *The History of Tom Jones, a Foundling* (1749). This effectively established the novel as a form. He died in Lisbon in 1753 where he had gone to recover his health.

Edward Fitzgerald was born in Suffolk in 1809 and educated at Bury St Edmunds Grammar School and Trinity College, Cambridge, where he was a close friend of Thackeray. He later cultivated the friendship of Tennyson. His marriage to a Miss Barton barely lasted a year. He learned Persian and in 1859 produced anonymously a version of the quatrains of Omar the Tentmaker. The homosexual elements of the poem seem to have eluded him but it is now agreed that he manage to catch the mood well. He was a notably entertaining letter-writer. He died in 1883 after living most of his secluded life in Suffolk.

James Elroy Flecker was born in Lewisham in 1884 and educated at Oxford and Cambridge where he studied Oriental languages as a preparation for the Consular Service. In 1910 he was posted to Constantinople and there married a Greek girl, Hella Skiardessi. From 1911 to March 1913 he was Vice-Consul at Beirut. Then his health broke and he died in a sanatorium at Davos in 1915. His poetry, heavily steeped in the Middle East, was published in *The Old Ships* and in *The Golden Journey to Samarkand* (1913). His verse play *Hassan* with choreography by Fokine and music by Delius was produced in 1922.

Lena Guilbert Ford is remembered mainly for her share in writing the words of Ivor Novello's most famous song, *Keep The Home Fires Burning*. She was killed in an air-raid in London in 1918.

David Garrick, one of England's greatest actors, was born in Herefordshire in 1717 but lived as a boy in Lichfield where he had the great Dr Johnson as teacher. When Johnson's school failed they walked together to London. Garrick, in spite of his small size and the inappropriateness of the contemporary dress used, was a remarkable Hamlet and a powerful Lear. He was more respectful to Shakespeare than earlier 'improvers' and was responsible for the famous washed-out *Jubilee* at Stratford in 1769. He wrote several plays including the regularly revived *The Clandestine Marriage* (1766) which he contrived with George Colman. He died in 1779 and Johnson observed, 'His death eclipsed the gaiety of nations'.

Edward Gibbon was born at Putney in 1737 and educated privately. He left Oxford after fifteen months, having become a Roman Catholic. He toured Europe with a Calvinist clergyman, a client of his father, who succeeded in having him renounce his conversion. He travelled widely and would have married the lady who afterwards became the mother of Madame de Staël but again his father interfered. In his own words, he 'sighed like a lover but obeyed like a son'. It was on a visit to Italy in 1764 that he had the grand conception of writing a history of the end of the empire. The mammoth work was completed in 1787. He lived quietly at Lausanne until 1793 when at the height of the terror he returned to England and died there the next year.

Sir W(illiam) S(chwenk) Gilbert was born in London in 1836 and at the age of two was kidnapped in Italy by brigands and ransomed for £25. The effect on his work was incalculable. He was called to the bar in 1863 but preferred to earn a living by writing. During the sixties he established a reputation as a writer of comic verse with the *Bab Ballads* which combined skilful rhyme with black humour. He wrote some fanciful plays but his fame rests upon the comic operas he wrote with Sir Arthur Sullivan whom he met in 1870. Their first success was the short 'cantata', *Trial By Jury* and the rest of the Savoy Operas followed, presented mostly at the Savoy Theatre in the Strand, built for them by Richard D'Oyly Carte. Their relationship was something stormy, hardly surprising when one considers the difference of their temperaments. Gilbert died in 1907 of a heart attack after saving a guest from drowning.

Oliver Goldsmith was born in Lissoy, County Westmeath, the son of Charles Goldsmith, the local curate, in 1728. He began his education at Trinity College, Dublin, and after a politic interruption, graduated in 1749. He continued his university career at Edinburgh and Leyden. When he returned to England in 1756 he claimed to have acquired a medical qualification in Padua. In 1761 he became a member of Johnson's Literary Club, appropriately enough since he earned much more by his pen than by physic. He is the author of three English classics in three different genres, *The Deserted Village, The Vicar of Wakefield* and *She Stoops To Conquer*. He is also well known as an essayist. He was penniless for most of his life, because of a relentlessly generous nature and an unfortunate addiction to gambling. His friends, Edmund Burke, Sir Joshua Reynolds and Samuel Johnson were greatly affected by his early death of fever in 1774.

Harry (Jocelyn Clive) Graham was born in London in 1874 and educated at Eton and Sandhurst. He served in the Coldstream Guards in the Boer War and rejoined the Army in 1914 and served in France. He was an early exponent of black humour in such publications as *Ruthless Rhymes* (1899). He wrote many humorous pieces and contributed to such West-End hits as *The Maid of the Mountains*. He died in 1936.

John Woodcock Graves, born in 1795, is famous as the man who wrote the hunting song 'John Peel'. Peel was a real character and

Graves' *Memoirs* tell how the song came to be written one day when the snow prevented hunting. They sat by the fire and Graves composed the lyrics to a tune that was being sung by Graves's mother. He died in 1886.

Thomas Gray was born in London in 1716, the son of a mentally-unbalanced financier. After one distressing attack, his mother left her husband taking him with her. She used money earned from a millinery business to send her son to Eton and thence to Peterhouse, Cambridge. He became a friend of Horace Walpole, the son of England's first Prime Minister. In his thirties he wrote his famous *Odes*, of which one, 'On a Distant Prospect of Eton College' contains the famous line about the folly of wisdom. His great 'Elegy Written in a Country Churchyard' was completed in 1750. He died in 1771 and was buried in Stoke Poges, in Buckinghamshire, the churchyard of the poem. He had a sprightly sense of humour as his 'Elegy on the Death of a Favourite Cat' and his many sunny letters indicate.

Joyce Grenfell was born Joyce Irene Phipps in 1910 and married Reggie Grenfell in 1929. She began doing sketches to entertain friends and soon became a diseuse and actress of great ability and popularity. Her sketches and songs are very English and gently humorous. She died in 1979, having made a further career as a television personality.

Thomas Hardy was born in Dorset, the Wessex of his novels, in 1840. He trained as an architect but began writing in his thirties a series of novels which increased in excellence until with *Tess of the D'Urbervilles* (1891) and *Jude the Obscure* (1895) his pessimistic view of humanity and unacceptable frankness caused a public outcry and he gave up fiction in disgust. He turned again to poetry and wrote a verse epic on the Napoleonic Wars, *The Dynasts*, (completed in 1908). He was awarded the OM in 1910 and died in 1928.

Christopher (Vernon) Hassall was born in London in 1912 and educated at Wadham College, Oxford. He became an actor and writer with a novel, *Devil's Dyke* (1937) and a biography of *Eddie Marsh* (1959). He was commissioned in the Education Corps during the War. He was famous as the librettist of many of Ivor Novello's shows and wrote many modern versions of foreign opera libretti in English. He died 1963.

Robert Stephen Hawker was born in Devon in 1803 and educated at Cheltenham and Oxford where he won the Newdigate Prize for poetry. At the age of nineteen he married a widow of forty. He became vicar of Morwenstow on the north Cornwall coast, just south of the Devon border, a community dedicated to smuggling and wrecking. He exercised what influence he could and was extremely popular with all his parishioners. He wrote some excellent poetry including the appropriately Arthurian *The Quest of the Sangraal* (1836). He became a Roman Catholic shortly before his death in 1875.

J Milton Hayes is famous as the author of the most famous and the most parodied of all music-hall monologues, 'The Green Eye of the Yellow God'. He wrote many others, reflecting the unthinking Imperialist assumptions of his late Victorian and Edwardian audiences. Research reveals little of his personal life except that he was from the North and was known to his friends as 'Micky'.

Felicia Dorothea Hemans was born in 1793, the daughter of George Browne, a Liverpool merchant and brought up in Wales. She married an Irish officer in 1812 and six years and five sons later he abandoned her. She wrote many poems which drew the praise of Shelley and Keats. Wordsworth and Byron at different times commended her work. She died in Ireland in 1835 of the 'decline', regarded as the greatest woman poet of her time.

W(illiam) E(rnest) Henley was born in 1849, the son of a Gloucester bookseller. He lost a foot through tuberculosis and had to spend much time in hospital to save the other one. He had a career in literature and journalism, was a friend of Kipling and Robert Louis Stevenson and wrote much patriotic and imperialistic verse, especially for the young. He died in 1903.

Robert Herrick was born in 1591 the son of a goldsmith. He went to Cambridge, took orders and was given the living of Dean Prior, a parish in Devonshire in 1629. This he lost at the end of the Civil War but had it restored shortly after the Restoration. He wrote religious poetry but seems to have been more at home in the profane style. His poems of love and countryside are classics. He died in 1674

Stanley Holloway was born in East London in 1890 and became star of early films and musical comedy. After war service in France he returned to the theatre but now was as famous for his monologues and comic songs as for his work in other media. Of extreme versatility (he played the Clown in Olivier's film of *Hamlet*) he continued to appear in films, make many records and finally achieved world reputation as Eliza Doolittle's father in *My Fair Lady*. His comic songs and monologues, performed in a variety of authentic accents, are imperishable. He died in 1983.

'Laurence Hope' was the pen-name of Adela Florence Nicolson who was born in Stoke Bishop, Gloucestershire in 1865, the daughter of an Indian Army colonel, Arthur Cory. She joined her parents in Bengal and married Colonel Malcolm Nicolson who was Queen Victoria's aide-de-camp from 1891 to 1894. She published a volume of near-erotic poetry, *The Garden of Kharma*. She committed suicide by poisoning two months after her husband's death in Madras in 1904.

Gerard Manley Hopkins was born in Stratford, Essex (now part of London) in 1844, the son of the consul for Hawaii. He was educated at Highgate School and Balliol College, Oxford, where he met Robert Bridges. He became a Roman Catholic in 1866 and was ordained as a Jesuit in 1877. He worked in various English cities and taught for some time at Stonyhurst College. In 1884 was appointed Professor of Classics at the Catholic University of Ireland which had been founded by his mentor, Cardinal Henry Newman. His delicate nature made him unsuitable for the work, especially in the setting and marking of examination papers. He died in 1889 and was buried in Dublin, a 'modern' poet before his time. His work was first published only in 1918, and subsequently his poetic technique was extremely influential.

A(lfred) E(dward) Housman was born in 1859 in Worcestershire in sight of the 'blue remembered hills' of Shropshire to which he gave poetic fame. An academic career which finally flourished was initially thwarted by a poor degree but after ten years at the Patent Office he became Professor of Latin at University College, London in 1892 and was appointed to the equivalent post in Cambridge in 1911. He was the best textual scholar of his age and a sharp critic. His fame rests on *The Shropshire Lad* and other sequences reflecting his solitariness and repressed homosexuality. He died in 1936.

James Henry) Leigh Hunt was born in 1784 in Southgate, Middlesex and after education at Christ's Hospital became a journalist. He and his brother were imprisoned for two years in 1813 for among other things calling the Prince Regent, 'A fat Adonis of fifty'. He was a friend of Byron, the first publisher of Shelley and Keats and an essayist of great charm. His wife was something of a domestic disaster and his children ran wild, especially in other people's houses. In general he was gentle and superficial but was an effective populariser of art and poetry. He outlived his great contemporaries by many years, dying in 1859.

Samuel Johnson, whom Smollett called 'the Great Cham of Literature', was born in Lichfield, Staffordshire, in 1709 and educated locally. Poverty cut short a university career at Pembroke College, Oxford, and stalked his early life. He moved to London in 1737 and earned his living as a hack. The publication of his great *Dictionary of the English Language* in 1755 made him famous and he became the friend of Sir Joshua Reynolds and Oliver Goldsmith. A civil list pension of £300 was granted in 1762, he met James Boswell, his equally famous biographer, in 1763 and in 1764 became a semi-permanent guest at the house of the brewer, Henry Thrale, where for twenty years Mrs Thrale recreated his battered psyche. He died in 1784.

Ben Jonson was born in Westminster in 1572 and educated at Westminster School. His widowed mother married a bricklayer and for a while he was apprenticed to the trade. He ran away, fought the Spanish in the Low Countries, returned and took to the stage as actor and dramatist. He was imprisoned in 1594 with Thomas Nashe for their satirical (and now lost) play, *The Isle of Dogs*. In 1598 he killed a fellow-actor, Gabriel Spencer, in a duel and about the same time became a Roman Catholic. He remained in that faith for twelve years. His most famous plays are *Volpone* (1606), *The Alchemist* (1610) and *Bartholomew Fair* (1614). With the coming of James I, Jonson joined with Inigo Jones, the designer, to devise masques which became the entertainment of the Court. He died in 1637. He had a quarrelsome temperament, a turbulent life but his plays and his critical writings about the theatre are still powerful.

John Keats was born in London in 1795 and began medical studies at Guy's Hospital. In 1817 he published his first volume of *Poems* which included the famous sonnet, 'On First Looking into Chapman's Homer'. He was already affected by the tuberculosis which ended his life and an inconclusive love affair with Fanny Brawne, a Hampstead neighbour, may have aggravated the condition. Over the next year he wrote the poems for which he is now famous. In 1820 his condition had worsened and as a qualified surgeon he knew that his one slight hope was a warmer climate. He left for Italy in the autumn of that year and died in February, 1821 at the age of twenty-five. He was not (*pace* Shelley) 'one whose name was writ in water' but a strong, vigorous passionate young man who with better health could have taken the strictures of the *Edinburgh Review* in his stride.

William Kethe was born in Scotland, became a Presbyterian minister and fled to Frankfurt to escape the Marian persecutions in 1554. He was at Geneva between then and 1558 and it was here that he wrote the metrical versions of the Psalms for which he is now remembered. He died about 1608.

Charles Kingsley was born a vicar's son near Dartmoor in 1819. He was intended for a career in law but an early tendency towards the Cloth was evidenced when he began writing sermons at the age of four. After education at King's College, London and Magdalene College, Cambridge, he took orders and in 1846 became Rector of Eversley, Hampshire. His claim to literary fame rests on some very well-known poems and a novel, *Westward Ho!* which grafted Victorian values onto the England of Elizabeth I. He was mildly anti-Catholic but in a public controversy with Newman was no match for the apologist. He was vigorously involved in social reform but his attitudes were gradualist rather than revolutionary and he was very opposed to the Chartists. He was a man of strong passions, a 'muscular Christian', whose febrile temperament led to a comparatively early death in 1875.

Hugh Kingsmill (Lunn) was born in London in 1889, the son of Sir Arnold Lunn, the religious leader and travel agent. He rejected early his family's puritanism and was a kind of happy stoic for the rest of his life. He won a scholarship to Harrow and at eighteen an exhibition to New College, Oxford. He, like the playwright, Enid Bagnold, worked as editorial assistant to the infamous Frank Harris (1856-1931). In 1914 he enlisted in a regiment of cyclists and proceeded thence to the RNVR. He was captured on the Western Front (incredibly) and was led off quoting Heine to his literate captor. He remained a prisoner-of-war until 1918. After the war he worked for a while in the family travel company but eventually became a full-time writer, spending a period as Literary Editor of *Punch*, and generally as biographer and witty essayist. He died in 1949.

(Joseph) Rudyard Kipling was born in Bombay in 1865, the son of a sculpture teacher who afterwards became Curator of the Museum of Lahore. His early life in England was very unhappy but later he enjoyed his schooldays in Devon. He became a journalist in India and soon was producing much verse and many short stories. He married an American girl in 1892 and lived for four years in Vermont where the *Jungle Books* were written. He returned to England in 1896 in time for a fully imperialistic appreciation of the Boer War. His verse made him the laureate of the Empire at its greatest and it is of finer quality that his detractors will admit. Whatever about walking with kings he certainly had the common touch, and his poems about India, serving soldiers and Britain's imperial responsibilities are as reluctantly irresistible as the ancient mariner. His prose has a Biblical strength and his stories for children, *Just So, Rewards and Fairies* and *Stalky & Co.* show a genuine knowledge of the child. He was awarded the Nobel Prize for literature in 1907 but refused the OM three times. He died in 1936.

Charles Lamb one of England's finest essayists, was born in London in 1775, the son of a lawyer's clerk. He was a Blue Boy and it was at Christ's Hospital that he met his lifelong friend, Coleridge. From 1792 to 1825 he worked for the East India Company when he retired on a pension of £450. The Lamb family had a history of mental illness: he himself had an attack in 1795, and in 1796 his sister Mary, ten years his senior (the 'Bridget' of the essays) in a fit of madness killed their mother with a table-knife. Lamb devoted the rest of his life to looking after her, did not marry and became addicted to drink. He took the name *Elia* (borrowed from a fellow clerk in India House) for the essays upon which his lasting fame rests. He died in Edmonton in 1834; Mary survived till 1847.

Edward Lear was born in London in 1812, the son of a stockbroker. A victim of asthma and epilepsy, he was forced to earn his own living by drawing and illustrating when his father was imprisoned for debt. The Earl of Derby employed him to illustrate an inventory of his private menagerie at Knowsley Hall. The nonsense poems for which he is famous were first written for Derby's grandchildren but they are in fact unnerving psychological documents. A regular traveller, he died at San Remo in 1888.

Richard Leveridge was born in London around 1670 and early won fame as a song-writer and composer. He was responsible for a typically 'improved' *Macbeth* with songs, dances and interludes for which he wrote the music, arranged the dances and played the (singing) part of Hecate. He had a notably fine bass voice and he appeared frequently in operas and oratorios at the Theatre Royal, Drury Lane. In 1730, at the age of sixty, he bet all comers £100 (a considerable sum in those days) that no one in England could hit a lower note than he. There were no takers. He died in 1758.

George Leybourne was born Joe Saunders in 1842. His first job was as a mechanic but he soon began appearing in London music-halls, earning eventually the colossal sum of £120 a week. He was the original 'lion comique' and his songs, especially 'Champagne Charlie' were sung as by a mid-Victorian dandy with Dundreary whiskers, monocle, cigar and fur-collared coat. He sang about the delights of high living and practised what he preached so effectively that he died poor at the age of forty-two in 1884.

Richard Lovelace was born in Woolwich in 1618 and educated at Charterhouse and Gloucester Hall, Oxford. He was a noted royalist, imprisoned well before the start of the Civil War for criticism of Parliament. He was unable to fight for the king because of his bail but all his money was spent in Charles's cause. He died poor in 1658, two years before the Restoration.

Henry Francis Lyte was born near Kelso in 1793 of an old Somerset family. He graduated from Trinity College, Dublin, took orders and became vicar of Lower Brixham, Devonshire. He published *Poems, Chiefly Religious* in 1833 but he is especially remembered for his hymns, notably 'Abide With Me'. He died in 1847.

Thomas Babington (1st Baron) Macaulay was born in Leicestershire in 1800, the son of the philanthropist, Zachary Macaulay. He had a brilliant university career at Trinity College, Cambridge, of which he became a fellow in 1824. He read law but never practised and made a living as a regular contributor to the *Edinburgh Review*. He became an MP in 1830 and later was a member of the board of the Supreme Council of India whose education system he anglicised and whose laws he codified. He wrote essays of characteristically rhetorical swing and obscure learning and some popular poetry. He is chiefly remembered as a Whig historian, especially of the Glorious Revolution that saw the end of the Stuart dynasty. He died in 1859 and was buried in Westminster Abbey.

Christopher Marlowe, the literary firebrand, was born in Kent in 1564, a few months before his greater contemporary, Shakespeare. He was the son of a shoemaker who was sufficiently prosperous to send his son to Corpus Christi College, Cambridge. Between 1587 and 1593 he had produced seven tragedies including *Dr Faustus, Tamburlaine* and *The Jew of Malta*. He seems to have been one of Walsingham's spies, may have been a Catholic and was accused of atheism and blasphemy. He was at an inn in Deptford on 1 June 1593 with three other police spies and he was slain by a dagger thrust above the eye at the hand of Ingram Frizier. His dramatic and poetic ability was second only to that of Shakespeare and at his death his achievement was considered the greater.

Eric Maschwitz was born in Birmingham in 1901 and educated at Repton and Gonville and Caius, Cambridge. He joined the BBC in 1920 and was later editor of *Radio Times*. He married the revue star, Hermione Gingold, in 1926 but the marriage was later dissolved. His career in broadcasting lasted till 1961 when he was Head of Light Entertainment. He wrote the libretti for many West End shows including *Zip Goes a Million, Balalaika* and *Love From Judy*. He was also a song writer of note with such 'standards' as 'Room 504', 'These Foolish Things' and 'A Nightingale Sang in Berkeley Square.' He was awarded the OBE in 1936 and died in 1969.

John Masefield was born in Herefordshire in 1878 and educated at King's School, Warwick, and the training ship, *Conway*. He went to sea as an apprentice at age fifteen and rounded the Horn on his first voyage. He left the sea after illness in Chile and supported himself by odd jobs in New York. He returned to England in 1897 and began a career of journalism and editorship. He served in the Red Cross in the First World War and wrote several books about his experiences. Two novels followed in the Twenties, *Sard Harker* (1924) and *ODTAA* (1926) which is an acronym for 'One damn thing after another'. H became Poet Laureate in 1930 and was awarded the OM in 1935. He died in 1967, chiefly remembered for his sea poems.

Leonard McNally was born in Dublin in 1752 and called to the English Bar in 1783. He married Miss I'Anson the daughter of William I'Anson of Hill House, Richmond, Yorkshire, the 'lass' of his song. He was a United Irishman and defended Napper Tandy and Wolfe Tone and other leaders of the '98 Rebellion. It was only after his death that it was discovered that he was an informer and government agent. He died in 1820.

W(illiam) J(ulius) Mickle was born in 1735, the son of the minister of Langholm, Dumfriesshire. He failed as a brewer and afterwards became an editor for the Clarendon Press. His translation of the *Lusiad* of Camoens, Portugal's national epic, brought him fame and money and his poem *Cumnor Hall* suggested the theme of the novel *Kenilworth* to Scott. He died in 1788.

Thomas Nashe was born in Lowestoft in 1567, the son of a preacher, and educated at St John's College, Cambridge. He became famous as a sharp and witty pamphleteer and as the author of *The Unfortunate Traveller, or the Life of Jacke Wilton* (1594), a picaresque narrative which played its part in the establishment of the English novel. He was the author with Ben Jonson of the satirical play, *The Isle of Dogs* (1597) and imprisoned with him in the Fleet for sedition. He died in 1601 not long after writing his famous threnody, 'Adieu, farewell, earth's bliss'.

Sir Henry Newbolt, known as a weaker Kipling, has come in for his share of satire because of the confident murderous patriotism of some of his poems. He was a kind of laureate of the public school (especially of his own school, Clifton) and such conceits as 'jammed gatlings' and 'playing up and playing the game' now seem spurious. Yet in his day he was thought to be little worse and much safer than Kipling. He was a vicar's son, born in Staffordshire in 1862 and educated at Clifton and Corpus Christi College, Cambridge. He was called to the Bar in 1887 and wrote poetry in his leisure time. He was knighted in 1915 and made a CH in 1922. He was chief of Telecommunications during the First World War and an official Naval historian. He died in 1938.

John Henry Newman was born in London in 1801 and educated at Trinity College, Oxford. He became a fellow of Oriel College in 1822 and took Anglican orders two years later. One of the jewels of his Church, his work in the Tractarian Movement caused him to reexamine his own beliefs and he 'poped' in 1845. He returned to England in 1847 and founded the Oratory in Birmingham and that in Brompton Road, London in 1850. From 1854 to 1858 he was Rector of the Dublin Catholic University. His relations with the Irish hierarchy were uneasy but out of the preparation for his Irish venture came his work, *The Idea of a University* (1852). A slighting remark made by Charles Kingsley caused him to write *Apologia pro Vita Sua* (1864). His devotional poem, *The Dream of Gerontius*, describing the soul's journey from Judgement to Purgatory, was set as an oratorio by Elgar in 1900. He was made Cardinal in 1879 and died in 1890.

C(aroline) E(lizabeth) S(arah) Norton, born in 1808, was the granddaughter of Richard Brinsley Sheridan, the Irish-dramatist. Her marriage to the Hon George Norton was notably unhappy and after separation he sued her for her earnings from her writing. The results of this prolonged litigation made her espouse the cause of Women's Rights and her pamphlets helped to get the Married Woman's Property Act passed. She also led the fight for better factory conditions. She married Sir William Stirling-Maxwell in 1877 but died a few months later.

Ivor Novello was born David Davies in Cardiff in 1893, son of Dame Clara Novello Davies, a well-known teacher of music. He was educated at Magdalen College School where he was a chorister. He served with the RNAS during the First World War and wrote one of its great songs, 'Keep the Home Fires Burning'. Of remarkable good looks, including a matchless profile, he quickly became a matinee idol in films and on stage. He is famous for a series of gorgeous musical comedies, *Glamorous Night* (1935), *Careless Rapture* (1936), *The Dancing Years* (1939), *Perchance to Dream* (1945) and *King's Rhapsody* (1949), which endeared him and his music to playgoers of the time. The songs still have the capacity to recover the period.

Alfred Noyes was born in Wolverhampton in 1880 and educated at Exeter College, Oxford. Apart from a period as Professor of English Literature at Princeton from 1914 to 1923 he lived entirely by his verse. He became a Roman Catholic in 1921 and became a fervent apologist. He was also a defender of the memory of Roger Casement. He died in 1958.

Carolina Oliphant, Baroness Nairne was of the house of Gask in Perthshire where she was born in 1776. She married her cousin who became the 5th Lord of Nairne. Of Jacobite stock she is famous for many Scottish songs including the purely sentimental (and apolitical) 'Charlie is My Darling'. She died in 1845.

Thomas Oliphant was born in Strathearn, Perthshire, in 1799 and flourished as librettist and composer. His English versions of *Fidelio*, and *Lohengrin* were popular and his rendering into singable English of Welsh songs, particularly those of Talhaiarn, have made them available beyond the Severn. He died in 1873.

Adelaide Anne Proctor was born in 1825, the daughter of Bryan Waller Proctor who as Barry Cornwall wrote much popular poetry. She contributed verse to *Household Words*, Dickens's periodical. She became a Roman Catholic in 1851 about the time she wrote 'A Lost Chord'. She died of tuberculosis in 1864.

Walter (Horatio) Pater, the prose stylist and apostle of aestheticism, was born in London in 1839. After education at Canterbury and Queen's College, Oxford, he became a fellow of Brasenose where he spent most of his life. He published several books of art history, especially of the Renaissance. His greatest work was *Marius the Epicurean* (1885) and though ostensibly set in the Rome of Marcus Aurelius (121 - 180) it is really a self-portrait. While Wilde and the more vigorous elements of the Aesthetic Movement carried his critical method and principles to extremes, Pater maintained a restrained and philosophical approach. He died in 1894.

Christina Rossetti was born in London in 1830, the younger sister of Dante Gabriel, one of the founders of the Pre-Raphaelite Brotherhood. She was a fervent Anglican, three quarters Italian and bilingual, and though of great physical intensity she refused marriage twice. She stayed at home looking after her mother who did not die till 1886, living the life of a lay religious. She died in 1894 and is considered one of the greatest of English woman poets.

Sir Walter Scott was born in Edinburgh in 1771 and graduated from the university there to become an advocate. He was lame from childhood and rejection by his first love left a sore and lasting affliction. He had leisure as Clerk of Sessions at Edinburgh to roam his beloved

Border country and his collection of ballads, *Minstrelsy of the Scottish Border* (1803) was one of the great spurs in the Romantic Movement in poetry. His own poetry resembled and sometimes imitated the folk verse but his international fame came with a series of historical novels – a *genre* he may be fairly said to have invented. His first, *Waverley* (1814), was followed by two dozen more including the famous *Ivanhoe* (1819) and *Quentin Durward* (1823). The last five years of his life were spent in a desperate attempt to earn enough money from writing to pay off the debt incurred by a publishing firm of which he was a partner. He died in 1832 and with the sale of his copywrights the debt was cleared. Scott's prodigious literary skill and output, his great humanity and his influence upon many successors including Dumas and Hugo ranks him in greatness beside Shakespeare.

William Shakespeare, the greatest of English writers, was born in Stratford-on-Avon in April 1564. He was the son of one of the leading citizens of the town, John Shakespeare, who had married minor gentry in the person of Mary Arden. Uniquely among the poets and playwrights of the time there is plenty of documentary biographical evidence about most of his life. In 1582 he married Anne Hathaway of Shottery, a woman eight years his senior, and they had three children one of whom, Hamnet, died in boyhood. There follows a lacuna of ten years that has given rise to much speculation, some of it silly. By 1592 he was established in London as actor and playwright and over the next twenty years wrote at least thirty-four plays, including comedies, tragedies, histories and unclassifiable ones that Coleridge called romances. As poet and dramatist his use of language and creation of character has made him a world figure. His talent is so sympathetic to the condition of ordinary men that all factions can find catch-cries in his work but as Matthew Arnold says in apostrophe, 'Others abide our question, thou art free'. He died on 23 April 1616.

William Sharp was born in Paisley in 1855, educated at Glasgow University and was a known poet in his twenties. When he was thirty-five he began a series of romantic, neo-Celtic romances published under the name Fiona Macleod, a pseudonym he resolutely refused to acknowledge. He had some influence upon Yeats and other figures in the Celtic Twilight. He died in 1905.

Percy Bysshe Shelley was born in Sussex in 1792 and educated at Eton and University College, Oxford. He was sent down for publishing a pamphlet called *The Necessity of Atheism* in 1811 and was forbidden to return home by his father who was squire of Field Place. He married sixteen-year-old Harriet Westbrook the same year. They lived in poverty for a while until both fathers relented and made them an allowance of £400 each. In 1814 he eloped with Mary Wollstonecraft and married her in 1816 when Harriet committed suicide by drowning. They moved to Italy and formed a coterie of poets which included Byron and Keats. In 1821 they moved to Lerici on the Bay of Spezia and he died there sailing the next year. He remains the type of the pure poet like his Skylark, unaffected by earthly decay or even appetite. He was buried in Rome near the grave of his younger friend, Keats.

Adam Skirving was born in Haddington in 1719 and educated at Preston Kirk. He was a literary Jacobite and was one of the spectators of the Battle of Prestonpans (1746) which provided the theme of one of his most famous songs. He died in 1803 and most of his work is lost.

Talhaiarn was the druidical name of John Jones, an architect who was born at Llanfairtalhaiarn in Clwyd in 1810. He was a colleague of Sir Joseph Paxton who built the Crystal Palace for the Great Exhibition of 1850 but his permanent fame rests on Welsh verse written to old Cymric airs which have attained the level of national songs. A combination of gout and cancer led him to end his own life in 1869.

Alfred Tennyson was born in Somersby, Lincolnshire, in 1809, the son of the rector. He attended Trinity College, Cambridge where his close friend was Arthur Hallam. Hallam's death in 1833 had a profound effect and in 1850 he published *In Memoriam*, regarded as his finest work, in his friend's memory. He became Poet Laureate that year on the death of Wordsworth and married Emily Smallwood. He published many volumes of poetry and some extremely popular patriotic verse. He was essentially the Victorian poet and his reputation suffered as Victorianism became execrated between the World Wars. He was, however, an extremely gifted poet, a writer of some unforgettable lyrics. He was made a peer in 1884 and when he died in 1892 his pall-bearers to Poet's Corner, Westminster Abbey, were representative of church, government, universities and the aristocracy.

Dylan Thomas was born in Swansea in 1914 and was famous as a poet by the time he was twenty. He was a journalist and worked for the BBC during the war but his true career seemed to be that of wild man and loveable boy and his excessive drinking contributed to his early death in 1953. His poetry-writing he always took seriously and it is likely to survive. He is popularly known as the author of the radio play, *Under Milk Wood* (broadcast 1954).

(Philip) Edward Thomas was born in London in 1878 and educated at St Paul's School and Lincoln College, Oxford. He married while still an undergraduate and he and his wife, Helen, lived in near poverty while he tried to earn a living by books about the countryside and hack journalism. He wrote no poetry till 1912 but his work is clear and carefully wrought. On the outbreak of war he enlisted as a private and had received a field commission by the time he was killed at Arras in 1917.

James Thomson was born in Roxburghshire in 1700, the son of a Border minister. He studied for the ministry at Edinburgh University but on being told that his sermons were too flowery gave up divinity and came to London. His poem *The Seasons* (completed 1730) rejected the Augustan, formal approach to nature and anticipated the Romantics. He wrote several plays for the London stage but his only successes were patriotic pageants for which he wrote such songs as 'Rule, Britannia!' He lived an easy-going, tolerant life and died of a chill in 1748.

A(laric) A(lexander) Watts was born in London in 1797, first taught school and then had a long and not very successful career as a journalist. His compendium of worthies, *Men of the Time*, was notable in that the editor received three times the space of Tennyson. He died in 1864.

Isaac Watts was born in 1674 in Southampton, the son of a clothier who was also a nonconformist preacher. He became an Independent minister at Stoke Newington but was forced through ill-health to resign and he spent the last thirty-six years of his life at the house of his friend Sir Thomas Abney. He wrote several works of theology but he i remembered now for his hymns, notably, 'O God, Our Help in Ages Past' and *Moral Songs for Children* (1715) which were parodied by Lewis Carroll in the *Alice* books. He died in 1748.

Fred(eric) E(dward) Weatherly was born in Somerset in 1848, one of thirteen children of a doctor. He was educated at Hereford Cathedral School and Brasenose College, Oxford where his tutor was Walter Pater. He worked as an Oxford crammer for twenty years and then in 1887 he was called to the Bar and became an expert on copyright. He appeared in many criminal cases, mainly for the defence. His interests were otherwise in song lyrics. He composed the first English versions of *Cav* and *Pag* and the famous line, 'On with the motley, the paint and the powder' is his. He was the author of 1500 songs including 'Danny Boy' and 'Roses of Picardy'. He seems to have been of genial, unegotistical temperament. He died in 1929.

William Wordsworth, one of the best known of English poets, was born in Cumberland in 1770, the son of a lawyer who died when he was thirteen. He was educated at St John's College, Cambridge. He had an affair with Annette Vallon, the daughter of a Blois surgeon and he became briefly an ardent republican ('Bliss it was that dawn to be alive.') Annette bore his child Caroline whom he acknowledged at the christening but marriage was too fraught with difficulties. The excesses of the 'Terror' destroyed his revolutionary ardour and he lived ever after with recurring guilt and confusion. He settled in Dorset with his sister, Dorothy, and later at Alfoxden, Somerset, where he became friendly with Coleridge. The *Lyrical Ballads* (1798) gave the world 'Tintern Abbey', 'The Rime of the Ancient Mariner' and the statement that the language and content of poetry need not be stylised or elaborate. The following year he and Dorothy settled at Grasmere in the Lake District. He married his cousin, Mary Hutchinson, in 1802 and settled down to a comfortable living on a sinecure as Distributor of Stamps. Dorothy never recovered from a breakdown in 1829. William became Poet Laureate in 1843 and died in 1850.

Index of Titles

Abide with Me   322
Absent-Minded Beggar, The   49
'Adieu, farewell earth's bliss'   313
Adlestrop   182
After Dunkirk   54
Against Idleness and Mischief   73
Against Quarrelling and Fighting   74
Alice, Where Art Thou?   101
'All the world's a stage'   242
All Through the Night   106
Arab's Farewell to his Steed, The   295
Armada, The   31
Auld Lang Syne   256
Austrian Army, An   202

Battle of Britain, The   56
Bell, The   245
Billy Boy   290
Blind Boy, The   72
Bredon Hill   110
British Grenadiers, The   23

Ca' the Yowes to the Knowes   97
Caller Herrin'   163
Casabianca   288
Champagne Charlie   213
Charge of the Light Brigade, The   297
Clerihews   223
Come, Lasses and Lads   70

Daffodils, The   258
Dahn the Plug'ole   233
Darkling Thrush, The   325
Dashing Away with the Smoothing Iron   103
Dear Gwalia   236
Derby Ram, The   152
Donkey, The   271
Drake's Drum   301
Drink to me only'   87

Early One Morning	94
Elegy on the Death of a Mad Dog	198
Elegy Written in a Country Churchyard	247
England, My England	44
Englishman, The	42
'expense of spirit in a waste of shame, The'	244
Fairy Chorus, The	137
Farmer's Boy, The	284
Father William	207
'Fear no more the heat of the sun'	312
Fine Old Englishman, The	150
Flowers of the Forest, The	317
Girl I Left Behind Me, The	95
Glorious Devon	173
Glory of the Garden, The	178
Goblin Market, *From*	78
Golden Slumbers	68
Green Eye of the Yellow God, The	304
Heart of Oak	279
Henry King	218
Home-Thoughts from Abroad	169
Homes of England, The	29
'How many miles to Babylon'	315
Hunting Song	159
I Leave My Heart in an English Garden	191
I Saw a Peacock with a Fiery Tail	121
In Youth Is Pleasure	67
Invictus	268
'It was a lover and his lass'	86
Jenny Kiss'd Me	100
Jerusalem	165
John Peel	166
Johnnie Cope	280
Kashimiri Song	114
Keep the Home Fires Burning	59

Knocked 'em in the Old Kent Road   176
Kubla Khan   126

Ladies, The   216
Lamb, The   75
Land of Hope and Glory   46
Land of My Fathers, The   39
Land of the Leal, The   319
Lass of Richmond Hill, The   98
Last Buccaneer, The   299
Lead, Kindly Light   256
Leisure
Letter to the Right Honourable, the Earl of Chesterfield   196
Lincolnshire Poacher, The   155
Linden Lea   167
Lochinvar   282
London Bells   146
Lost Chord, The   263
Love's Old Sweet Song   327
Lovliest of Trees   175
Lyke-Wake Dirge, A   309

Mad Dogs and Englishmen   228
Madrigal, A   64
Man on the Flying Trapeze, The   214
Mandalay   51
Man's a Man for a' That, A   254
Matilda   219
Mermaid, The   292
Miller of Dee, The   156
Modern Major-General, The   209
Monna Lisa   136
Mr Valiant-for-truth Crosses the River   316
My Old Dutch   112

Nearer, My God   260
Nightingale Sang in Berkeley Square, A   187
'No worst, there is none'   267
Non Sum Qualis Eram   115
Nursery Rhymes   65

O Caledonia!   28
O God, our Help   246
Ode to a Nightingale   130
Old Brigade, The   43
Old Father Thames   183
Old Sam   225
Old Ships, The   140
On First Looking into Chapman's Homer   129
On his Life-Work   122
On Ilkley Moor Baht 'at   184
Onward, Christian Soldiers   265
Owl and the Pussy-Cat, The   205
Ozymandias   128

Passionate Shepherd to His Love, The   83
Patriot, The   40
Pied Beauty   170
Polly Perkins   104
Pot-Pourri from a Surrey Garden   189
Private of the Buffs, The   37
Proud Maisie   318
Psalm 100   241

Reaper, The   124
Red, Red Rose, A   90
Ring a-Ring o' Roses   63
Roast Beef of Old England, The   158
Rolling English Road, The   180
Rubàiyàt of Omar Khayyam, The   133
Ruined Maid, The   212
Rule Britannia   24
Ruthless Rhymes   221

Sally in Our Alley   91
Say Not the Struggle Naught Availeth   262
Scots, Wha Hae   26
'Shall I compare thee?'   85
She Was One of the Early Birds   23
She Was Poor but She Was Honest   20
Sir Patrick Spens   27

Soldier, The   58
Solitude of Alexander Selkirk, The   252
Song of the Western Men, The   35
Splendour Falls, The   135
Spring   149
Stately as a Galleon   234
Subaltern's Love-Song, A   117
Sumer is Icumen in   145
Sunset and Evening Star   323
Sussex by the Sea   185

Tears, Idle Tears   324
'That time of year thou may'st in me behold'   311
There's Nae Luck aboot the Hoose   161
There Was a Naughty Boy   76
'They are not long, the weeping and the laughter'   270
Thora   108
Tit-Willow   211
To a Louse   200
To Althea from Prison   88
To the Virgins, to Make Much of Time   69
Trumpeter, The   302
Twa Corbies, The   195
Two Poems (After A.E. Housman)   224
Tyger, The   123

Up from Somerset   171

Vitaï Lampada   47

We'll Gather Lilacs   116
We'll Go No More a-Roving   321
What Shall We Do with the Drunken Sailor?   294
When Earth's Last Picture is Painted   269
'When I am dead'   107
'When I set out for Lyonesse'   138
When I Was a King in Babylon   109
When I Was One-and-Twenty   80
When 'omer smote 'is bloomin' lyre'   139
Wife of Usher's Well, The   227
Winter   148

Ye Mariners of England 286
Young and Old